IN THE BIG CITY

DOUG INGOLD

Wolfenden

IN THE BIG CITY

Copyright ©: 1996 by Douglas A. Ingold

Printed in the USA

ISBN: 0-9642521-2-0
Library of Congress No. 95-061980

Published by

WOLFENDEN

U.S.A.
P.O. Box 789
Miranda, Ca 95553-0789
Tel:(707)923-2455 Fax: (707)923-2455

This novel is a work of fiction. Names, characters, places and incidents are either the product of the author's imagination or are used fictitiously. Any resemblance to actual events or locales or persons, living or dead, is entirely coincidental.

Cover and layout design
Robert Stedman Pte. Ltd., Singapore

For Nina

With special thanks to Kay Kidde and Ray Duff

Great cities are not like towns, only larger. They differ from towns and suburbs in basic ways, and one of these is that cities are, by definition, full of strangers

—*Jane Jacobs*

The first rule is to keep an untroubled spirit.

—*Marcus Aurelius*

1

It was late afternoon before we got everything loaded and well after dark when we finally arrived in the big city. Kim was asleep in the back seat, curled up among the boxes next to the philodendron. Anne, too, was dozing. Jim Fletzer, an old friend from the Randy days, followed our squareback in his primered pickup, its right headlight askew like a glass eye.

It occurred to me as I glanced in the rearview mirror that Jim Fletzer was imagining himself driving into a nightmare. He had last visited Chicago as an uninvited guest during the 1968 Democratic National Convention and had caught a nightstick across the shoulder. That had been eleven years ago and he hadn't been back since. The injury still bothered him whenever the weather changed, or so he claimed, and every twinge reminded him of the city where it happened. Randy used to tease him about it. You're a lucky guy, he'd say. You not only got the glory, you got an internal barometer compliments of the Chicago P.D.

As for myself I was excited. This was going to be my new home and I had the window down to catch the flavor of the place. It must have showered shortly before we arrived because the paved surfaces were wet and reflecting light. The city gleamed with secrets, it seemed to me. It rumbled, it smelled of chemicals left loose to drift above the sleeping millions.

A curious thing happened as we came up the Dan Ryan

from the south. Something seemed to brush against the side of my face. The sensation was different from the wind swirling through the open window. It was more like a breath, a warm and beery breath.

This is what I knew about Chicago that Friday night in June.

— Mrs. O'Leary's cow, Al Capone, John Dillinger.

— Crowd sounds broadcast from Wrigley Field when as kids my brother and I had played catch in the shade on a hot summer day in our small town, the radio blaring from the porch.

— The voice of Franklin McCormick reading poetry late at night after the house was dark and the family asleep and the radio soft at the edge of the bed.

— A story told in southern Illinois about some gentlemen who traveled to Shawneetown, a new and bustling spot on the banks of the Ohio River, to get a loan. They were starting a new city, they said, at an outpost called Fort Dearborn where the Chicago River flowed into Lake Michigan.

The good fathers of Shawneetown turned them down. Not a good risk.

— Television pictures coming from the Convention where Jim thought he was at the beginning of a revolution.

— The first paragraph of Saul Bellow's novel *The Adventures of Augie March* . . . "Chicago, that somber city"—Studs Lonegan. Willard Motley's novels. Carl Sandburg's poem about the big shoulders.

— The cold in the winter when Anne and I made our Christmas visits to Nora, Anne's mother; filthy snow heaped along side streets. Our June wedding in her back yard.

In short, next to nothing.

We parked on the street in front of Nora's house. I

carried Kim in, her cheeks full and flushed, her hair tangled and moist with humidity. Nora was nervous in her housecoat, bringing sodas. She had expected us earlier and had a full meal waiting in the warm oven. The table was set with good china, a plaid pastel tablecloth with matching napkins slid into holders.

Since everything we owned was either in the back of our station wagon or in the bed of Jim's pickup, I decided to spend the night in the cab of the truck. Jim followed me out. He unlocked the door of the cab and then stood in the middle of the street.

"Listen," he said.

"What?"

"No, really. Just listen. The roar."

I noticed it then. The undertone of the City's life—a streaming current of sound.

"The City," I said. "Just millions of people living their lives."

"Pig City, that's what it is. This place is brutal. I was here, remember?"

"That was years ago."

Jim put his hands in his pockets and turned in a slow full circle.

"It's not you, man. This place. I don't think this is you. Linen tablecloths? Napkin holders for Christ sake."

"It wasn't linen, Jim. Just a nice tablecloth."

"You're Carbondale funk, man. You're gritty in the street funk." He shook his head slowly as if faced with bad tea leaves.

I was tired and didn't want to hear it. "There's no problem, Jimbo. Anne grew up here. I'm ready for a change. It'll be a piece a cake. A few years from now I'll own this city."

Jim was not convinced. I caught him actually glancing

over his shoulder as if he half expected a horde of cops to suddenly descend upon us with clubs. Then he said:

"Careful what you buy, man. You might end up owning more than you can pay for."

As I settled myself bone-weary on the seat of the pickup, I thought about Anne back in the house arranging everyone for the night. She's the kind of person who organizes these things. Jim, she had decided, should sleep in her old room. The best bed was in there and he had done us a favor by hauling our furniture all the way to Chicago. She had packed a small foam pad with a plastic cover for Kim and had relegated herself to the couch. All this had been arranged beforehand with Nora: the number of pillows and sheets, a housecoat she could borrow for the night. She had packed small overnight bags for us and Kim. Kim's blanket was available, her favorite bear.

Anne was probably in the bathroom now wearing her mother's robe and washing her face with the special soap she used every night. Tired as I was I got a little horny thinking of her leaning over the lavatory and scrubbing her face before the mirror.

We had met five years before in a university town deep in southern Illinois. Carbondale has a railroad, a Union general to brag about, a southern past it would rather forget. It was April when we met, well into spring. In southern Illinois spring has a luxury and a length not found farther north. On campus and in the neighborhoods that Friday afternoon there were dogwoods, lilacs blooming in door yards, tulip trees covered with shameless flowers. Along Illinois Avenue where I had my leather shop, the doors of the bars stood open and music poured out, raucous and loud, a different tune coming from each bar. Cars passed up and down loaded with fraternity boys yelling at one another. The sidewalks were crowded with students, each with his or her private anticipation. A day rich with expectation, with hormones and fresh pollen.

She entered the shop alone and began to browse among the merchandise while I pretended to work at my bench. Five-five, I guessed, dark-haired, small boned, blue-eyed. She was wearing a baggy blue T-shirt, white shorts, and licking a strawberry ice cream cone. The end of an easel protruded from her knapsack. I watched slyly as her hands slid over embossing I had done, as her fingers traced the lip of a handbag that I had shaped and then stained.

She was just another customer, one of thousands who had stood on the other side of the display case with its row of macho buckles, its somewhat dusty collection of feather and bead. And yet I found myself glancing repeatedly toward the street, awaiting the golden god who any minute now would surely come to claim her, midriff exposed, flipping a Frisbee. He never showed and she bought a pair of sandals for her father.

Anne. Anne Dycheck. A sophomore, an art major from Chicago.

"City girl." I must have frowned. I had a thing about cities.

"Born and raised. And you?"

"Winnok"

"Winnok?"

"It's near Peoria."

"I've never been there."

"You wouldn't likely remember if you had."

"Have. . . ."

"One time," I said. "Graduation trip. The stockyards, Museum of Science and Industry."

"Ah, the mine shaft, the pickled fetuses in bottles."

"And the muscles on the black man. Remember him? Bringing his sledge hammer down on the head of cow after cow?"

She made a face over the dwindling cone. "I've never been to the stockyards."

"Really? I thought that was compulsory. The way out of junior high leads through the stockyards."

"Not at St. Teresa's."

"At the end of the tour they fed us hamburgers, a lesson in the real price of meat."

She had begun to fondle the belts hanging by the door. "And that led you into hides?"

I had to laugh. "You going back there?"

"Chicago?" She looked alarmed. "No, well, after I graduate I suppose. Is that bad?"

She had paused at the door, her mouth slightly parted. She was ready to walk away and I realized that I had been holding my breath.

"I'd like to see you again."

She smiled, a warm smile, a delightful smile.

"That might be nice," she said.

I know this sounds ridiculously mushy, but that's the way it was. We locked onto each other that spring like magnetized scottie dogs, and the energy released by the fusion formed a sort of shrine which in later, flatter, years we would attempt to revisit with certain foods, or songs, or recollections.

In the beginning there was what seemed at the time a small incongruity. She considered herself an artist and yet she constructed her world with thought rather than vision. Her assignments were to see, but she always preferred to argue. Her teachers sent her in search of found objects and she returned with philosophies.

I was living that spring in a little shack within a few yards of the Illinois Central Railroad. You would wake in the middle of the night in a cold sweat, bed shaking, the approaching freight roaring down on you like an angry god who'd just found your hiding place. That shack would germinate in Anne a latent fear that a traveling man hid in the recesses of my personality. Years later she would remember parties where Randy had stood with one boot on a rail and sung songs of the road while strumming his twelve-string. Or how sometimes in the evening she and I would walk along the tracks, smelling creosote and diesel, and watch how the lines of rubbed steel seemed to draw and hold the last light. Once she even dredged from her memory a dog-eared paperbound Kerouac that on her first visit she had found resting on the back of the toilet and which she assumed I took as a sort of personal text, when in fact I had bought it well worn at a yard sale and never finished.

Her voice was husky and lower pitched then you might expect given her size and the delicacy of her features. And she was comfortable with the familiar earthy swear words, but for one raised in the big city she could seem surprisingly naive. I was forever explaining jokes to her, defining the lingo of the bars and streets where I spent much of my time. After one unfortunate experience with marijuana she never touched it again. Nor would she skinny-dip if anyone other than myself were present. Randy, my business partner and the man who had introduced me to my craft, Randy, the peddler of weed and other mind benders, Randy my friend and with disturbing quickness her enemy, Randy said that spring, "In her heart of hearts your woman's a Republican."

The following autumn I returned to school part time. Three days a week we lunched in the Union on mushroom soup and crackers, and the surprising little things she would pull from her backpack always safely sealed in tight plastic containers.

One day she confessed, "The nuns always rewarded the *exactness* of my drawing."

She had decided to minor in philosophy and we were taking a logic course together. Now she was forever explaining things to me.

"And my father has something to do with it," she added.

"Your choice of art as a major." Frank, Anne's father, was an executive with a car rental company, but as a young man he had studied sculpture at the Art Institute.

"It's the life he never lived."

A few days later she signed up for the Law School Admissions Test. Her announcement strangely troubled me. I had fallen in love with an artist.

"You're a good artist. I like your work."

"It's just for fun," she said. "To see how I do."

We graduated together and that summer were married in Frank and Nora's back yard on Chicago's north side. My friend Randy couldn't attend the ceremony. On a stormy night the previous April he had left town just ahead of the posse.

Anne's scores on the LSAT placed her in the top two percent nationally. She could have attended a more prestigious law school but I had my leather shop so we stayed in Carbondale.

I still thought of her as shy and I had doubts about her becoming a lawyer. I remember how at the dean's reception the first week of law school, she sat quietly against the wall while I went and got her punch. That first semester a Professor Rector seemed to save the hardest cases for the women students. Then he would demolish their briefs. "Dictum!" he would shout. "Dictum! What's the holding?" It was astonishing the way the challenge terrified and captured my wife. She did nothing but study—except in November of that year, as if stealthily ordering a policy of insurance, she discovered that she was pregnant. But that fall and spring she got A's from the notorious Professor Rector and the following summer as we sat on the couch timing her contractions she was reading a biography of Supreme Court Justice Oliver Wendell Holmes, Jr.

One afternoon in February in the middle of her last year of law school, we sneaked free for an afternoon. It was one of those audacious winter days in southern Illinois when warm air comes up out of the Gulf, tracks the Mississippi and settles over the Ozarks. Mid-seventies, the few clouds puffy and well defined. Ten degrees cooler but not unlike the day we met. We bought a bottle of sauterne, a loaf of French bread and two jars of pickled herring packed in sour cream. We drove to the lake at Thompson Point. The year we met Anne had lived in Kellogg Hall, a dorm near the lake. We were returning to our beginnings, but we had come to discuss the future.

She had been offered a position with each of the three places where she had interviewed: the Attorney General's Office in Springfield, a mid-size firm outside St. Louis that specialized in representing large shippers on the major waterways, and a big La Salle Street firm. Nora still lived in the same Chicago neighborhood where Anne had grown up. Frank had left her a few months after Anne and I married and she was alone. My parents had been killed in an accident shortly before I met Anne and I had little family left other than Anne and now Kim our daughter.

The Chicago firm was large, diverse, and had a first class reputation. The starting salary was excellent. Kim would have a chance to know her grandmother. I set the bottle of sauterne in the water to hold its chill. Fish on bread, ripples on the surface of the lake.

"I was thinking of our first date," she said.

"Jethro Tull."

"Right. And remember afterward? You had been invited to a party and we went to the street but must have gotten the wrong house."

"That's Carbondale. Pick any house on a Saturday night and there's likely a party going on."

"We had brought a pizza."

"Sausage and green pepper."

"Of course," Anne said. "And we shared the pizza with the people there and they had some jugs of wine and a few joints. And we drank and talked about the concert, and finally you asked . . ."

"'Where's John?'"

". . . the guy who had invited you to the party."

"John Rolfe, I think it was. A friend of Randy's. I didn't know him too well. He's not around anymore."

"Anyway, nobody knew John. Or had even heard of him. And you and I realized that we didn't know anybody there and nobody knew us. So, we left."

"The pizza was gone anyway."

"I was embarrassed," Anne said. "But you said there was no reason to be embarrassed, because . . . ."

"Because, I said, none of those people knew each other any better than they knew us."

"You said it was a 'Lost People's Party.'"

"Yep. A party for people who were lost."

"It made me afraid when you said that. So I asked, 'Well, we were there. Does that mean we're lost?' And you said, 'No, that's why the lost people were so happy to see us. Because together we aren't lost.'"

"It might have been the pizza."

"'Together we're not lost.' I have never forgotten that. You said that our coming to their party was like a gift to the lost people."

"It really might have been the pizza, Anne, not us at all."

"Don't spoil it. That's when I knew I loved you. When you explained that our being together was a gift to the lost people."

After we left the party that first night Anne Dycheck had stood beneath a street light and slowly twirled around, hands out, twirling effortlessly and slowly in the light of the lamp. I felt myself in the presence of a marvel, a mystery coiled in a sort of heavy syrup that seemed to lubricate everything around her.

I forked up some herring and fed it to my wife. Five years had now passed, one marriage, one child, two graduations and soon a third.

As if trimming herself for speed, Anne's hair had grown progressively shorter until now her neck and the lower halves of her ears were exposed to the sun. She seemed more solid, ready for what lay ahead. I thought of our modest rental on Sycamore, soon to be vacated with its garden in the back yard, its slanting kitchen floor that sent each dropped object scurrying beneath the refrigerator. I had been ten years in Carbondale, comfortable to a fault.

Time for an affirmation. I refilled our glasses and offered a toast.

"To Chicago."

She smiled. "To us," she said. "Together."

I sat up in the cab of Jim's pickup and looked toward Nora's house. It was dark. Settling back down I thought about my dad. Whenever he had used the word "home," you had to decide whether he was talking about the house in which we lived or the farm where he had grown up. "I'm going out home," he would say. Or, "On the home place we always. . . ."

He had two homes, my dad. It was a luxury given him by the times and the proximity of things. For me it was different.

"You have moved," I said to myself as the engine ticked to cool. "This is our new home. We're going to make it here."

2

The apartment Nora had found for us was on the north side one flight up in a six-flat, away from the Lake and not far from the house where Anne had grown up. We knew from calls and letters that Nora had begun her search early in March. She studied the papers and made the rounds in the evenings after she got off work and on weekends. When she came down for Anne's graduation she brought pictures.

It had been a lot of work and she had done a good job. We were lucky she found a place that was clean and affordable in a neighborhood that was relatively quiet and safe. Inflation and interest rates were like puppies chasing each other around in the land of double digits, and landlords, grown weary of economic fluctuations and the vagaries of renters, had begun to convert their holdings into condominiums, which we had neither the cash nor the credit to buy.

Still and all, I hated the apartment.

You might have found some charm in the building had you set it apart and studied its pattern of brick and cement ornamentation. But squeezed into a block filled with structures of similar age and style, it struck me as stolid. As dark and dreary. I sensed a thickness of brick. An idea too long repeated.

The locked front door had a buzzer system. You got the impression in the dusty burgundy lobby with its fake marble bench and usual bank of mailboxes, that everyone who had ever passed through had been thinking about someplace else. There seemed to be no other tenants in the building. Just stairs worn to the fiber backing of the carpet; mail appearing and disappearing, muffled sounds in the hallway, doors rubbing over carpet, locks clicking into place. The eggshell paint had aged in layers. Where, I wondered, was the earth, some small stirring of life along a branch?

We moved in the following day and that evening after Jim Fletzer left, Anne, Kim, and I ate dinner in an air-conditioned Italian restaurant with Nora and Charlie her boy friend. It was a neighborhood place a couple of blocks from Nora's house. The day had been hot, humid, and we were beat from the move. I had been drinking beer most of the afternoon. In my experience that's what you did when you moved.

I started talking about the apartment. I pointed out that the windows had been painted shut. That the back yard was tiny and covered with trash. My point was not the apartment so much as the attitude these conditions reflected. The previous tenants, I suggested, had ignored nature or feared it.

When I paused, Nora turned to Anne and said: "I wish I could have found a place more to Jason's liking."

I heard something in my mother-in-law's tone of voice that put me on edge. The remark, it occurred to me, was a dagger disguised as an apology.

For a moment nobody said anything and I found myself looking at Anne's black hair which was still wet from the quick shower she had taken at the apartment. With her ears exposed, the hair slick against her skull, she looked younger, smaller. A daughter. My own daughter had discovered you could eat spaghetti by slurping it up one strand at a time.

Nora continued: "I should have given more thought to the fact that Jason enjoys gardening and other out-of-door things."

She did not look at me. She gripped her gin and tonic. She firmed herself at the table. This was the woman we had just moved to get closer to.

"Well, there is a back yard," Anne said laconically, wiping Kim's face with a napkin. "It's not *that* small." She glanced at me. The glance suggested that maybe I should crawl under the table and weep. I remembered then how Nora had found the apartment for us. How she had spent the day on her hands and knees washing out the closets.

"Nora, I. . . ."

Nora turned in her seat. She moved her eyes straight past me until she was facing Charlie. "I just thought that with Anne starting out and Jason not really having a job— you know, not a store or anything like he had in Carbondale—and the prices of rent being what they are, that a house would not be a good idea even if I could have found one."

"Nora, I just want. . . ."

Charlie nodded. Charlie was in full agreement. "Finding a decent house to rent is next to impossible," he said. "I looked all over the city after Fern and I broke up. By the way, Bud, what is it you did down there anyway?"

"I'm a leather worker," I said. "Nora, I didn't. . . ."

"A leather worker," Charlie said slowly. I had met the man for the first time that afternoon. He had fought with Migs over Korea. He found the idea that I was a leather worker kind of funny. "Is that sort of like an autoworker, you know, assembly line kind of thing?"

"I had my own shop. I make things from leather."

"Shoes?"

"Sandals, not shoes. Caps, purses, vests, belts."

"Billfolds?"

"I can do billfolds, Charlie. You need a billfold?"

"Don't believe I do. I was just asking, you know. You make that cap?"

"The cap, yes."

"The cap is Jason's trademark," Anne said, coming to my rescue. "Southern Illinois is full of Jason Winter's leather caps."

"I just didn't think a house was a realistic idea," Nora went on. She had turned back to Anne.

"Nora. . . ." I think I was pleading at that point.

"Bud," Charlie interrupted, "you and me should shoot a game of pool." He got up and started toward the bar side of the restaurant. "You coming?"

Charlie knew his way around the table. When he lined up a shot, his broad forehead crinkled and his fiery right eyebrow cocked.

"You were stepping in your own shit back there, Bud." He knocked in the nine ball. "You make Nora nervous as it is."

Charlie continued knocking stripes into pockets. He made most every ball by banking it. He was the best bank shot I ever saw.

"Show a little gratitude, for Chris sakes. You start in about this nature thing. That just makes it worse. Nora hates nature. She spots a bug in her house and she sprays a whole can of that poison shit just to get rid of it."

The words flowed out smooth and even as Charlie slid around the table dropping stripes. A well-lubed mechanism, Charlie was. He moved and poised and shot. He rubbed me in my own abrasive.

When he had finished, Nora and Anne were ready to leave.

On the way to the apartment I told Anne, "Charlie says I make your mom nervous."

"She was just pissed at what you said."

"I wasn't criticizing her. I don't think she likes me."

"That's silly. Of course she likes you. You're her only son-in-law."

It occurred to me the following Monday that I had not given a lot of thought to exactly what I would do when we got to Chicago. We had decided to keep Kim at home for a while, give her a chance to adjust before shipping her off to child care, but beyond that, my plans were indefinite. Anne's schedule by contrast was full: She left for the Loop a little before eight. The bar review course met in the morning. Then in the afternoon she worked at the firm and at night she studied.

I found the building superintendent in an apartment on the ground floor beside the laundry room. This guy had rings on sixty percent of his fingers, a large stomach and a black cowboy hat. He was practicing on an electric bass guitar. I had been wondering where the low deep thumping sound was coming from.

He said of our President, "What'da expect from a man who grows fucking peanuts? Got a first name like some kid in the third grade who picks his nose. What we need is that Reagan guy. He'll balance the goddamn budget and kick out the welfare bums."

The deal I made with the building superintendent was that I would paint the apartment and he would provide the materials. The deal I made with my daughter was that she would paint with water.

Five minutes into the project Kim began to insist on the real stuff. It was hot. The Cubs were in New York playing the Mets and I had the radio on.

I finally spread drop cloths everywhere and dressed her in a T-shirt formerly owned by her mother, snugging the neck with a safety pin.

"You paint this corner," I explained. "You stay in this corner and paint."

A two-year old's conception of how you paint a wall differs from an adult's. The idea of a smooth even layer of paint is not part of the two-year old's conception. The two-year old wants to get as much paint out of the can and onto the wall as possible, thus wiping the brush against the rim of the can to remove excess paint before applying the brush to the wall is counter productive. She listened carefully as I explained this technique but immediately rejected it.

A two-year old wants to paint as high as she can reach. "Not above your head!"

She turned toward me baffled by the suggestion. The handle of the brush was still gripped firmly in her left hand, but now the right squeezed down on the bristles. White paint oozed out from between her fingers. A thick glob drooled from her hairline on its way toward her eyes.

At night I did the trim while Anne studied at the dining room table. The painting took most of the first week.

With Anne's first paycheck we bought a color TV. It fit wonderfully in the freshly painted living room. That evening we settled in to watch the news. Halfway through, the screen filled with a dismal staircase in a housing project. It was a dirty, cold and loveless place, its walls scarred with obscene, belligerent markings. A tourist had been dragged there after being pulled from her car when her husband stopped to read a road map. She was raped by three men while her husband stood outside screaming for help.

"Welcome Wagon," I tried to joke, "Chicago style."

Anne didn't laugh, and she was right. There was nothing funny about it.

"Where did this happen?" I asked.

"Not here," Anne said. "Not close to here."

3

In the evolution of the Winter family from farm to city, my dad played the role of the amphibian. He came back from World War II with an itch and rather than return to farm work—which had been the work of every member of the family as far back as anyone could remember—he took a job maintaining heavy equipment for Caterpiller at their proving grounds outside Peoria. A short time later he married the woman who would become my mother and they rented a house in Winnok, a small town about five miles from my grandparents' farm. My brother and I grew up town kids.

But if dad thought he'd moved, he fooled himself. Most Saturdays, and during the summer, often in the evenings as well, he worked out on the farm. It was a family tradition: every able hand helped when needed. But he was also expressing, it seems to me, a kind of longing. He went to the farm in search of a clarity that was missing from his life in town and his work as an employee. He seemed steadiest mending a fence or cultivating a field of corn.

As a boy I spent a lot of time on the farm. I remember gathering eggs and feeding chickens and bringing quarts warm milk into my grandmother. Later I learned to drive tractors and the old pickup we used around the place. I milked cows and castrated pigs and built hog houses. As a teenager I hired out to bale hay and detassel corn. Farms wrapped around our little town like a protective shield. A long way from Chicago.

In the boxes stacked around the apartment that I now began to put away, I found a photograph of the family farm taken from the air. It had been shot in late afternoon on a clear day well into summer. The shadows were long and precise, the white buildings, the ordered fields a rich green. My great-grandparents had owned much of the surrounding land, but divisions among heirs had left this one 300 acre homestead, now in the hands of my aunt and uncle, my cousin and his wife.

I found my parents' clock with its bell shape, its glass face that opened on hinges, the key for winding. This I placed above the mantle of the fake fireplace in the living room. In another box I came upon some old sketch pads of Anne's. Charcoal, line drawings, a couple of pastels. Kim and I sat down on the couch and poked through them. There were several of my hands working with leather, portraits I had been persuaded to poise for, my mustache and hair longer and bushier. An early self portrait done before a mirror, showing a rough likeness of the long haired woman who had walked into my leather shop but diminished by the stiffness of inexperience. Many she had done after we met and these came immersed in context. That fireplace at Giant City, the day we had walked a section of the Trail of Tears; this log half-submerged in water, sketched on a warm autumn day at Devil's Kitchen. Later that afternoon Anne had almost stepped on a copperhead sunning against a rock. Here was the teapot in the apartment she had shared with Paula. How often we had made heated love there!

I was surprised at how strongly these artifacts attracted me. I wanted to touch them, smell their musty surfaces.

Kim and I went out and bought some cheap frames and pre-cut mats and when Anne came home we had the farm photograph and seven of our favorite drawings hung around the house, an innovation that surprised, pleased and embarrassed her. That night after she had put away the bar review outline, I pulled out the photo album from our wedding, another of the things I had found in the bottom of a box. We sat in bed and went through it. My brother had been best man. My aunt and uncle, smiling and uncomfortable. Anne's father was there. That was only a few months before he left for Kansas City with his secretary. He was running around pouring champagne, leering it now seemed at all the young women. There was a shot of Nora embracing me.

"That's the only time we've ever touched each other, I think."

"Mom's not real physical with anybody."

I studied the photograph. "I think she's grimacing."

Anne jabbed me in the ribs and flipped the album shut. I was hoping the memories would turn her on, but instead she turned over.

"I'm exhausted," she said.

When I had the living quarters in general order I turned to the summer kitchen behind the dining room. It seemed to me the most pleasant space in the apartment. You entered through French doors and before you were three windows looking out over the back yard. A dreary view, but I preferred it to the wall of the adjacent building, which is what you saw out of the bathroom, the kitchen and Kim's little bedroom.

I set up my work table and lamp. Organized the chest, stationed the old treadle sewing machine in a convenient corner, drilled some holes in the walls, inserted dowel rods and hung shoulder bags and belts around. The leather released from confinement gave off its wonderful array of familiar smells.

I had no clear purpose in mind with the leather. I certainly did not want customers coming to the apartment. I decided to build up the inventory as time permitted. Anne and I had talked about a trip to Wisconsin after the bar exam. My family had gone there most every summer when I was a child, and the time, and distance, and the death of my parents had lent to those vacations a luminosity that might not have been there when they happened. I began to formulate how we could combine a vacation with a business trip. There had to be a number of stores appealing to tourists. A few might want to supplement their inventory with leather products.

I tried to work during the day but it was difficult. Strips of rawhide might fascinate Kim on one day and not another. Patches of leather with their sizes, colors and textures held her attention for a few minutes and were thrown aside. It was hit or miss, and inherently frustrating. I came to realize that my relationship to leather had a meditative element. A slow rhythm had developed around the work, a sustaining pattern behind the efficiency. In Kim's presence all this was lost.

Mostly I avoided leather work until her naps, though often by nap time, I, too, was exhausted. In Carbondale we had had a sitter and I had worked at my shop nearly full time. Anne and I split our free time with Kim as close to evenly as we could, but I had never before cared for her alone over regular extended periods. The days began to drag. They felt amorphous, dense with a fog that weighed and resisted. Almost against my will I came to organize our days toward her naps: strenuous fun exercise in the mornings, a walk, a trip to the beach, the park, then try to keep her awake on the drive home, a meal, and finally we would lie down and I would read to her. Many things could go wrong: a quiet morning caused by rain or interruption and she would not want to nap; if she fell asleep in the car she could not be moved without waking; or I, too, might fall asleep only to wake frustrated and clammy a few minutes before she. I could have worked in the evenings after she was in bed, but I found that after doing the dishes, I had enthusiasm for little more than the tube, supplemented more and more frequently with a fat joint.

During our first six weeks on this flat lake shore with the prairie stretching out suburb upon suburb, the bar exam loomed above us like some craggy, mist-covered Annapurna. Whatever direction we turned, it faced us. There was no escaping, no going around, no thought of the other side. She had chosen to become a lawyer and she had worked for three years to prepare herself, but lawyers were people who had passed the exam. Everybody else was just a former student, a chef without a kitchen.

As the exam grew closer Anne stopped working in the afternoons. Now she attended class in the morning, studied at the office during the afternoon and at home at night. Then near the end she just studied morning, noon and night. Nothing in her behavior suggested that there existed a reachable point where her preparation would be complete. It was simply a matter of stamina and a shrinking amount of time and using it all as fully as she could. It was Professor Rector all over again, and the commitment, it seemed to me, physically narrowed her. Her skin drew tighter across her cheeks, her lips thinned and pressed together. In the evenings she tried to be cheerful—to relate some incident she had observed at the office, or pass along a joke one of the review course instructors had told, or express an interest in Kim's day or my own—but this was passing and strained. She took comfort in being home with us but her mind wanted to return to its primary focus.

"I'm worried about you," I confessed one morning as I watched her dress. "You've lost weight, the tan you had this spring has faded. Maybe you should take a breather."

"I'm all right," she insisted. "I'm just glad you're here to give Kim the attention she needs. I'm giving this all I've got. I don't intend to go through it more than once."

One Sunday afternoon I did convince her to accompany Kim and me to the beach. The process was more complicated than a camping expedition: blankets, towels, diapers, food, drink, sunscreen, shovel and bucket, swimsuits, bar review outlines, the Sunday paper. We staked out our square of sand, coated ourselves and settled down, she with her study, I with the paper, Kim hardy and flushed burrowing with the shovel.

Soon I noticed my wife flinching. A blaring radio, a child running past the blanket, an errant beachball. In my mind I began to apologize for everything you do at a beach. "Why does he have to stand there and yell like that?" I would ask myself. "Does she have to cackle every time he says something?" I wanted a sandy law library for Anne and a beach for the rest of us.

"Maybe we could find a less crowded spot," I said finally.

"It's all right," she said, closing the book. "Give me the funnies."

Game, but no contest. Before, she couldn't keep her mind on what she was doing. Now she couldn't keep her mind off what she wanted to do.

"Maybe if we went back to the park," she suggested a few minutes later. "Some shade might be nice. And it will be less crowded."

"Not yet, Mommy! Not yet!"

Anne sighed, sat back down. "She's right. We just got here."

I felt responsible. "No, you're right. The park would be better. We can have fun in the park."

We burdened ourselves and sloshed off through the hot sand. Now she felt like she shouldn't be studying and I felt she should. It was my fault she couldn't. Kim was less independent in the park. Thing about a beach is that kids can't injure it. A park is a different environment. Besides, Kim was weighted with a residue of disappointment. She wanted our attention now. I needed to have Anne study but I didn't want to entertain Kim; I had been doing that all week. We ended up on Wells eating ice cream at an outside table, each of us off key and strangely weary.

One evening we went shopping with Nora. Anne needed a new wardrobe commensurate with her new responsibilities. We left for Nora's house as soon as Anne got home from work. The idea was to get to the mall as soon as possible, catch some fast food and do the shopping before Kim grew tired and cranky.

When we arrived, Nora was in the bedroom getting dressed. After a while she came out, wearing slacks and a blouse. In her left hand was another blouse on a hanger, in her right a third. She stopped in front of the couch where we were sitting, posed a moment, then held the left-hand blouse in front of her, took it away and replaced it with the right.

"What do you think?" She was speaking to her daughter.

"The mauve," Anne said.

Nora groaned and returned to her bedroom. I looked down at my grungy feet and battered sandals, struck by what seemed to me an astonishing revelation.

"Your mother *dresses* to go shopping?" I whispered.

"Well. . . ." Anne was caught off guard. There had been this big deal about getting started.

"It's not like she wasn't dressed, right? She is a loan officer at the bank. She must have been dressed when she got home."

"This isn't like it is in Carbondale," Anne tried to explain. "People do dress here."

"To go shopping? A special outfit to go shopping?"

"Out," she said, flustered and starting to get annoyed. "Shopping, yes. Anywhere out."

"I see. Well, you could have chosen the one she was wearing."

Anne laughed. "You're just hungry," she said by way of explanation. Which to my mind is like saying you're just choking.

At the mall Kim and I tagged along, entertaining ourselves with food and drink, with the bits of nature and art they build into those places to give the impression you are somewhere other than in a warehouse at the bottom of the commercial food chain. Anne and Nora were consummate shoppers. The way they rubbed fabric between their fingers and spoke with lips close to ears convinced you of that. And the process delighted them. Anne had allocated a set amount of money. The purchases were necessary, and to good purpose. "Investments," Anne explained to me. Buying good fabric was an investment. "A statement." What you wore in the workplace made a statement about who you were.

All of which was true, and being a buyer of leather, I could understand. Still it was the delight they took in the process that intrigued me. Something in their eyes reminded me of lust, or dogs on a scent. "Let's see what they have at Fields!"

It had never seemed to me that Anne and her mother were particularly close. They weren't physical. They didn't chat excitedly the way women friends sometimes do. They seemed to treat each other with a caring caution, as if their psychic interface was somewhat sensitive or bruised. But the shopping provided a subject, a conspiracy of purpose that permitted them to enjoy one another. Our decision to move closer to Nora, I came to realize, presented both an opportunity and a burden.

Over the days I tried to be nice to my mother-in-law, polite, reasonably attentive. Nora was guarded toward me, but not hostile. When we talked it was about Anne or Kim, and then only the necessaries. On the telephone she would say, "Hello, Jason, is Anne there?" If not, she might add, "Have her call at her convenience. I know how busy she is."

In my darker moments I imagined Nora as a person at an estate sale who had to buy a box of junk in order to get the two figurines that she wanted. I was the left overs.

In my memory the three days of the bar exam take on the quality of a variegated nightmare. The night before the exam started I heard a voice in a dream. I had already begun having a lot of dreams by then. Sometimes all that remained when I woke was a booming voice. In one of them I recall my dad shouting, "I died, son." It was as though he were passing by on his way out and had time only to yell a quick report. Since he and Mom had been dead for five years I considered this an odd sort of post pre-cognitive experience.

The voice I heard the night before the bar exam was not my father's, but it was shouting. In that dream I was in an auditorium watching a magician. "Wake up!" the magician shouted. Then he disappeared behind a swirl of his white silk scarf, leaving on stage a table, a top hat and a rather confused rabbit. The trick was inside another trick. The rabbit was supposed to have disappeared but instead it was the magician. From off stage the magician laughed. It was a mischievous, perhaps a cruel laugh that echoed in the empty fading auditorium.

The dream slid into physical reality because when I did wake my daughter was crying. I looked at the clock. It was four in the morning. Anne had insisted on leaving the shade up so she wouldn't oversleep in case the alarm failed. The glow from the street lamp lay in a swatch on the floor. I stepped through the light, opened the door and followed the corridor to Kim's room. In the dim light my fingers touched clammy pajamas and a body that was too warm. For a few moments as her arms and legs clung to me, the crying subsided. Then like an old engine it sputtered back to life and her hand began to grope the air without direction. I pulled her blanket from the crib. Her fingers clasped its tattered edge and her thumb slipped into her mouth.

I carried her to the bathroom, opened the medicine cabinet with a free hand and removed the rectal thermometer. In the dim glow of the night-light, I paused, undecided. A car passed down the road. Someone on the floor above us was moving around. My daughter slurped her thumb.

"Anne, she's burning up."

I laid Kim down beside her and switched on a light.

My wife rose up out of troubled sleep and flipped over with a jerking almost spastic motion.

"My God!" Her face seemed crushed by the intensity of the light. She buried it again beneath her pale arms.

"She has a fever."

"Oh my God!" Anne reached out and touched Kim's

neck. "I cannot believe this. Of all the nights in all my life. God, I cannot believe it."

I unscrewed the plastic cap and removed the thermometer.

"Well, get the Vaseline," she grumbled. "We can't just stick it in there."

Kim was lying on her stomach across a pillow when I returned. Her cheeks were flushed but her expression appeared almost serene. Anne had removed Kim's pajamas and diaper and was stroking the damp hairs back from her forehead. She coated the tip of the thermometer and inserted it slowly.

"My, God," she said again, looking at the clock, "it's after four. I have to get up in less than two hours. Of all the nights for this to happen!"

"Do you think it's ready?"

"I want to make sure," she said, staring up at the ceiling.

We waited. Anne's lips moved as she silently counted off the seconds. It was like a prayer. I felt awful for waking her. She withdrew the thermometer and held it toward the light.

"Dammit, I can never find it." And then, "Oh, shit, 101.5. Of all the times to get it. Now her ears will become infected again and she'll be sick for the next two weeks. You can forget your trip to Wisconsin."

My wife had doom on the brain. She was like a clerk in a stock room during an earthquake looking around at everything poised to fall in on her. She sat up and glared at me.

"Did you do this? Did you take her someplace where she got this?"

I felt the muscles in my neck bulge and tighten. I clamped down, contained it. It wasn't her fault, I told myself. The damn exam has her crazed. And it had been selfish of me, timid, cowardly, grossly unfair, to have waked her.

"I'll take her now."

I gave Kim some painkiller, carried her back to her dim room and changed her pajamas. Then we went to the living room, where out the window, by the light of the street lamp, I could see rain falling. The rain was steady but there was no sign of wind or lightening. Anne would be driving down to the Loop in the morning. She needed the car because she was typing the exam and she was taking two typewriters in case one of them broke. One was ours and the other belonged to Nora. They stood now in their cases in the corridor by the outside door. Both of the typewriters were electric and the previous night at dinner Anne told about a bar exam where the power had gone out. She had become bloated with bar exam horror stories.

Kim and I rocked until her thumb fell from her mouth and she dropped her blanket. After putting her back in bed, I banged my head on the mobile hanging from the ceiling light in her bedroom and then in the corridor I jammed a toe into one of the typewriters and nearly fell on my face.

4

It was a car accident that had killed my parents. I thought I had buried them, first literally, then figuratively, but after our move to Chicago I started thinking about them again. I thought about August, the month they were killed. There is a lull, it seemed to me, peculiar to August, a pause that settles on the hemisphere. Summer lingers but the excitement is over. Weeds begin to creep into gardens; kids grow bored. Fish settle low in the water and lose their appetites. Insect populations explode, algae spreads. And the mind drifts, waiting for the jolt of a cold morning, a changed leaf.

There had been a party at a small well-stocked lake; two teenage boys in a hand-painted blue pickup rushing to get there, a gravel road with a dogleg. The humidity and the grasshoppedy heat. The gravel road splitting corn fields in the late afternoon. My parents driving home from a day of fishing, their minds defused over time and place. The sun low and bright.

I would think of the corn, tall and tasseled out, thick of leaf and ear, and so green on nitrogen that it appeared white in the sun and black beneath its own shadow. The level monotony of the fields, the seldomness of curves, the illusion that everything will go on as it has, when it won't, and didn't. That's what stuck in the mind.

When the radio came on that first morning of the bar exam it said: "More than seven acres of new and used cars and trucks."

The day's first salvo from the land of buy and sell.

Anne sat up and announced: "My God, it's raining. What if the power was off?" She had become as predictable as a metronome.

The radio confirmed the time. "5:59."

This seemed to satisfy her not at all. "I'm going to get soaked," she moaned. "Who knows where I'll have to park. If she wasn't so sick you could drive me." She stood, still staring at the window. "Maybe it wouldn't hurt her to go out. What do you think?" She fled the room before I had a chance to answer.

A moment later she stuck her head in. "She's sleeping. Feels warm but not like last night. Would you make me a cup of coffee? I put the water on."

The bathroom door closed and the shower started. In the kitchen I made two cups of instant coffee. One I placed on the back of the toilet, the other I took to the bedroom. I paced. I felt like someone at a disaster who doesn't know first aid.

"Toast or something?" I asked when she emerged from the shower. "Long day out there."

Anne closed her eyes tightly and shuddered. "Please don't mention food, okay? And I would really appreciate your not eating anything until I've left."

"It's that bad?"

"You wouldn't believe." She turned on the hair dryer. From the movement of her mouth I could tell she was chewing on the inside of her lower lip. During the week of her first law school exams her mouth became so sore she had to go to the health service. "Is it still raining?" she asked again, a moment later. I went to the window and looked down into the street.

"A drizzle, that's all."

A man in a Volvo was trying to get out of a parking space. Only inches separated his car from the ones in front and behind. He banged angrily, first forward and then back, the power steering hissing. The air seemed to vibrate around his banging car. His eager frustration spread out along the street, permeated walls. It bittered coffee, burned toast, nudged the susceptible toward a mid-morning headache.

"I'm going to look like a damn porter," Anne muttered. "Two typewriters and an umbrella. Maybe I'll balance the end of the umbrella on the tip of my nose." She was grim, no levity intended.

She took down a blouse and the hanger fell with a clatter to the floor. She reached down, tried to pick it up and then dropped it again.

"Shit." She gave the hanger a kick. "I'm a fucking mess."

She began to grope for her cigarettes. Her mind was torqued too tightly—preparation had spilled over into panic. On the other side of the sealed window I imagined smells of sodden gutter litter, of drowned worms stretched on the sidewalk.

I picked up the hanger and set it on the bed. I came up behind her and placed my hands on her shoulders. Taut, they tightened more at my touch.

"Breathe," I said. She took a shallow breath. "Deeper." I began to button the blouse while at the same time trying to avoid contact with the fabric that stuck to the rough skin of my fingers.

"Jesus Christ, am I going to make this?"

"Breathe deeper."

She lit a cigarette. "Know what I did? You're not going to believe this. I stole some of Mom's downers."

"That's funny," I lied. It was not funny at all.

"Well, I knew she wouldn't give me any. I'm not even supposed to know she's taking it. Right?"

"You wouldn't have known if I hadn't been snooping around in her medicine cabinet." I squatted down in a catcher's crouch to confront the bottom buttons.

"I took three. One for each day. I wasn't planning on really. . . ."

"A second chute." I said.

"I think maybe I'm going to. . . ."

"Don't." I had a picture of her slumped over her whirring typewriter, a limp rag at the bar. I straightened up and began to massage the muscles at the base of her neck. "You're going to get there."

"You can say that, but I'm not there! And it's raining and I've got two typewriters and Kim wakes up in the middle of the night sick and . . . shit." She had set her lighter too close to the edge of the vanity and it fell off onto the floor. "And," she continued now more slowly, bending over to pick it up, "the day is not starting out all that well, as you can see." A short tight laugh seemed to pop out of her like a surprised belch. Tears glistened at the edges of her eyes. "And furthermore my horoscope probably says to stay away from tall buildings."

"Or maybe don't trust mechanical devices?"

"Or whatever you do don't make career decisions." She stifled a cascading giggle. "I am so close to hysteria, you would not believe. I can't even pick up a goddamn hanger or hold a lighter. How am I going to think, let alone type?"

"You'll be okay. I'll drive you."

"And Kim, what about Kim?"

"We'll bundle her up and put her in the car seat."

"But what if she's not awake?"

"Anne, we'll wake her."

She let out an explosion of smoke-filled air. "Okay-that's-good-we-have-plenty-of-time-we'll-be-okay." Not a pause, not a breath. Her eyes skipped around the room for a moment as though she were disoriented. She blinked. "Get the car!" Then she rushed toward the bathroom. The coffee was coming through.

I got the car around to the front of the building where Anne waited in the foyer. She carried Kim out and strapped her in the safety seat. The kid was sucking her thumb, her eyes large and passive.

"I'm being a bitch."

"You're all right. It's a terrible day."

"I'll make it up, promise." She put her hand on my knee and then jerked it off. "Wait." From her handbag she removed a small notebook and quickly flipped through a few pages until she found the right list. "Typewriters." She looked in the back and made a check. "Admission pass . . . pens . . . ribbons . . . money."

The woman was, if anything, organized. She is one of those people who if they do something that's not on a list they write it down anyway just so they can check it off.

"Which way?" It was her town, I merely followed directions.

By the time I double parked on Erie Street the rain had stopped, at least momentarily. A group of people were milling around in front of a building across the street. They were smoking, pacing in random silent circles.

"Hun?" She stood waiting. "Are you going to get them out?"

"Yeah." I removed the two typewriters from the back of the wagon and set them on the pavement.

Anne swung the strap of her bag across her shoulder and hooked the umbrella loop on her wrist. She leaned into the back seat and kissed Kim. Then she stood for a moment looking at me.

Her face just then was the face of a little girl and I had the sudden sense that the whole thing was a mistake: this move to Chicago, this idea of becoming a lawyer. It had a forced feel about it, a too-fast-for-conditions kind of dread. I glanced again at the pacing men across the street. They were aggressive, hard; their determination was exposed like bedrock.

"Well," she said, "this is it, I guess. I can leave these overnight so I'll take the El home."

"You don't have to go over there, Anne," I suddenly blurted out. "There's a thousand other things we could do."

She looked at me surprised. "But I want to go."

Of course she did. She had gone through three years of hell to reach this day. What was I thinking about?

"You'll shine," I stammered.

"I just hope I don't piss my pants."

I kissed her then. She was wonderful and brave. "Do you have everything?"

"I think so." She gripped the handles of the typewriter cases and straightened up. "I want to get these set up so I can hit the john and have a cigarette before it starts."

"All right."

I watched while behind me horns honked. Small and thin, the two typewriters suspended from her arms like burdens of penance, my wife crossed the street and passed through the crowd. Some guy, a black and a human being on this inhuman morning, opened the door for her and she disappeared inside.

The honking was getting serious now. I scuffed the sole of my sandal against the pavement. I had been a fool. Her day of agony, and the only thing I could offer her was doubt.

There was a snake on the wall outside the convenience store where I stopped to buy a newspaper and two quarts of orange juice. It was shaped like a cobra and painted in garish yellows, greens and browns. It had a diameter of a yard or more and extended for more than seventy writhing feet from one end of the wall to the other. Its head was erect, penile in shape, the flaps of skin extended. Its eyes were red and black; large tear-shaped dollops of white venom dripped from its fangs. A magnificent snake. A portrait done in rage.

By eight o'clock Kim and I had returned to the apartment. In the kitchen I put on enough water for three servings of oatmeal, sprinkled in some salt and measured out the designated amount of dry cereal. The juice was made from concentrate, no sugar, no preservatives added. It was made by a company that was a division of another company that was a subsidiary of a third. Kim said she did not want any juice but I poured a glass for each of us anyway and coaxed her up into the high chair. Wrong glass; she wanted the other glass and refused to touch the one I had chosen. Smears of snot had dried and crusted on her cheeks and around her nostrils. She looked puffy, miserable and deserving of whatever glass she wanted. I found the blue glass, the one with the built-in straw and the picture of the rabbit on the side, and transferred the juice.

I always insist on regular oatmeal. They tell you five minutes cooking time with frequent stirrings but don't believe it. Half that time is plenty. For thicker oatmeal, the box suggested, use less water, for thinner oatmeal use more water. On the other hand, for a creamier texture, one should combine the water, salt and oats and then bring to a boil. I knew this information by heart but standing at the stove I found himself absently reading it again. When the toast came up I located the jar of homemade strawberry jam in the door of the refrigerator. It was half empty so I went to the pantry and examined the top shelf. Only one jar remained of the double batch I made in late May just before we moved. I had picked the berries in a field behind a huge U PICK sign, and made the jam in a warm kitchen on a Sunday morning while Anne read aloud from the newspaper and Kim licked the utensils until her cheeks and bare chest glistened a strawberry red.

According to Kim the orange juice didn't taste right.

"It might taste better," I suggested, "if you drink some more." The phone rang.

"Nora, can I call you back? We're in the middle of breakfast."

Kim would not eat any oatmeal, not even when I offered to spread raisins on top and throw in some honey. She would not drink her orange juice either.

"Toast, Daddy. Toast and Daddy's jam."

The kid knew the way to her father's heart. I spread some jam across half a piece of toast and handed it to her. My bowl of oatmeal was so full I could only pour in a little milk at a time. Rather than eat the toast, Kim smeared the jam around with her finger.

"At least drink your juice and eat some of the toast."

I ate, and I glanced at the paper, and I coaxed my daughter without success. The day before in the City of Chicago, a nine year old boy playing in the street threw a baseball that struck a passing car. The motorist jumped out and shot the boy with a pistol. This happened in broad daylight while Kim and I were visiting the big cats in Lincoln Park.

By the time I finished my oatmeal and toast, Kim had torn her slice into a number of tiny well-fingered pieces.

I begged her to eat just one piece. She started to cry.

"Okay, then drink your juice."

"Little bit, Daddy?"

"As much as you can." Doctors could not say to what extent the boy's spine had been damaged but he was in serious condition. Police were looking for the motorist.

Her toast was so mutilated that I could not bring himself to eat it. I cleared the table, scraping the oatmeal and bits of toast into the garbage. In the South China Sea thousands of people in small boats were fleeing turmoil, madness and rage. I felt their large empty eyes watching me waste this food. It was 8:30.

"It's time, Kim." I set her down and followed her into the living room, carrying her orange juice.

The TV suggested: Warm family feelings . . . fear of death . . . fear of being left . . . guilt of abandoning your family . . . Life Insurance. I changed the channel.

Mr. Rogers was coming through the door in bold color singing his song. I had just settled in the rocker with Kim on my lap when Nora phoned again.

"Anne called and. . . . "

"Isn't she taking the exam?" I experienced a moment of panic. She had flipped out. She was wandering the city carrying two typewriters, her umbrella balanced on her nose.

"Before the exam, Jason. She said she had forgotten to give you the name of Kim's doctor. I called earlier but you weren't home yet."

I copied down the name and number Nora methodically provided and the trolley car rolled off to the Land of Make Believe.

"I just gave her a painkiller. Maybe she'll be better off resting than going to the doctor."

"Well, Anne said to definitely call him. And she said

to be sure and tell him about her ears." Nora paused and I could hear her take a drag from her cigarette. "What is the problem with her ears, Jason?"

Nora's voice intrigued me. The dominant tone was school-marm, but beneath that I thought I heard a shyness, a reticence. She didn't know yet how to address me. Was I a man, or a wayward child her daughter had dragged home for instruction?

"Well," I said, playing the dutiful child, "when she has a cold, fluid gets in her ears somehow. In the canals. Infection develops in there and it takes her longer to get over it than a normal cold. She usually ends up on antibiotics."

Nora considered this. "I wonder if it's the same thing Charlie's grandson had. They did an operation on his ears."

"An operation? Well, this couldn't be the same thng. An operation wouldn't help this. This is just an infection in the inner ear."

"It sounds like what Braden had. They placed little pieces of plastic tubing in his ears so they would drain. It seemed to solve the problem."

I was astounded. "They put gutters in the kid's ears? That's ridiculous."

"Tubes, Jason. Tiny plastic tubes."

I decided to change the subject.

"So, how is Charlie, anyway?"

Nora's voice dropped suddenly and thickened. "It's not good."

"Well, is he all right?"

"It's a long story. I told Anne."

"I see."

I found the vaporizer in the hall closet still packed in a box. I filled the bowl with water and plugged it in. Mr. Rogers was pulling off his slippers and putting on his shoes. He was about to say goodbye for another day. Kim sat up and we waved goodbye to Mr. Rogers while I washed her face with a warm cloth.

Big Bird followed in a dancing mood, but the bird's enthusiasm did not infect Kim. My daughter looked puffy, pale. Still, things were moving along. The painkiller was taking hold and she appeaared more solid, as if her consciousness were again willing to accept her body. The vaporizer was hissing a storm of cool mist. Kim had finished her orange juice. I dreaded the idea of leaving the apartment again and going to the doctor's office.

Sesame Street ended and Kim wanted to play with her toys. I brought out the large colored box filled with blocks. It was a good sign, I thought, that she should want to play. I set her up and then went to the medicine cabinet. If we had some of the decongestant left from the last time I would give her a dose and see how she did before calling the doctor. I was looking through our stash of old medicine when an agonized whine sent me running back to the living room. The structure she was building had collapsed around her. The cold had perverted the physics of her world. It warped the angles, tipped the balance, distorted the responses. Nothing worked. The carpet was a rough sea; her fingers were thick and independent. The blocks tilted, tumbled and slid. Her breath rasped at her throat and could not breach the phlegm in her nose. She kicked the blocks. Her face reddened, and she began to cry.

I went to the phone and dialed the number. The doctor was a friend of Dr. Brown, Kim's doctor in Carbondale. Dr. Brown was a good guy. Maybe the doctor would just phone in a prescription. A female voice answered. It said something long and unintelligible. Then I was offered three minutes of easy listening.

"Thank you for waiting." The voice was very nasal

and not thankful at all.

"Yes. My name is Jason Winter and my family and I recently moved. . . ."

"Do you have a sick child, Mr. Winter?"

"Yes, and Dr. Brown down in Carbondale recommended. . . ."

"Have you been to see us before?"

"No, like I said we only recently. . . ."

"Does your child have a fever?"

"Yes, I believe so, though not too bad. I was thinking that perhaps the doctor could call in a prescription. This thing happens. . . ."

"This office does not telephone in prescriptions without the benefit of an examination. Bring your child in at 1:30 and we will try to work you into his schedule." The voice was replaced by a dial tone.

I went flat when I heard that dial tone. It took the last of the gas right out of me.

On the mantel of the fake fireplace hidden behind my parents' old clock I kept a cigar box. I took the box down, placed it on the coffee table and removed the contents. I rolled a fat two-paper joint, which I stuck in the band of my leather cap. I put the contents back in the box and the box back behind the clock. Through the window I could see that the rain had stopped. The sun was breaking through. It was broad daylight.

I changed the tube to a commercial channel and sat down on the couch. From here I could see down the hallway through the dining room to the sun porch where my work waited. I had planned to cut out the leather for a vest this morning and begin the stitching. It was a new design and I was anxious to see how it came together. But unless Kim took an extended nap, there would be no leather work. The cold had stolen her security and she needed my attention to fill the void.

Discarded blocks lay scattered around the room. Kim was demanding another toy, one that worked. I persuaded her to lie down on the couch with her head in my lap. I stroked her warm forehead and a tall slinky woman came on the screen. She was standing on a slowly rotating platform stroking a microwave oven with long sensual fingers. I lit the joint and held the smoke as long as I could before releasing it. A game show. It was better than nothing.

When Anne returned home late that afternoon, the living room was covered with toys that had failed to bring solace to Kimberly. On the coffee table were bits of toast and graham cracker that she had said she was hungry for and then refused to eat. On the carpet near the couch was a wet spot where she had spilled half a glass of orange juice. I was watching a re-run of Sergeant Bilko when I heard the buzzer. I released the downstairs lock and groped my way to the landing.

There was something surprisingly vivid and three dimensional about my wife as she climbed the stairs. The sensation I experienced must have been related to one that women have shared for centuries when they first see their man returning from a war or a long journey at sea. Memories, however strong, are suddenly put to shame.

The afternoon had turned warm. She was carrying her coat and umbrella. She climbed the stairs slowly.

"Well?" I asked, reaching to take her things.

She shrugged. "Well, that's one day." Certain muscles in her face had thickened as they did when she was tired, subtly altering the contours.

"So, how do you feel about it?" I was trying to sound

cheerful.

Anne sniffed the air and then looked around the living room. She walked over to the couch where Kim was sleeping and placed the back of her hand against the child's forehead. She dropped into the rocker.

"I don't know. I wrote a lot. I really don't want to talk about it, I guess. I don't even want to think about it. If I start thinking about it I might realize I blew a question. That would depress the hell out of me, and depression is not an emotion I can afford at the moment." She lit a cigarette and sighed. "Well, the questions made sense, if you know what I mean. I felt I understood what they wanted. I just don't want to find out I blew one."

"The typewriter worked all right?"

"Yeah, the typewriter was fine."

"No power failure?"

Anne smiled. "No power failure. I didn't faint. I wasn't run down by a herd of elephants. You drove superbly and got me there on time. I'm still alive." She looked over at Kim. "What did the doctor have to say?"

"They wouldn't let me talk with the doctor. You want a beer?"

"No. I'd probably pass out and I have to study tonight. So what did you do, take her in?"

"No." I didn't want to talk about the doctor.

"She feels warm to me. Have you taken her temperature?"

"She may feel warm," I admitted. "But she's all right. I couldn't get her in unless we were willing to wait around and I thought it was better if she stayed home and rested."

This news annoyed her. She looked around the room again. The place did look miserable and I began to gather up the bits of food.

"Have you been smoking?" she asked.

"I had a hit," I muttered, looking away.

"A hit?" She glanced at the ash tray on the coffee table where, good lawyer that she was, the evidence suggested otherwise.

"A couple of joints, okay? There was nothing to do here. And what could he have told me? That she has a cold? We already know she has a cold. That she needs fluids and rest?"

The phone rang. Saved by the bell. I rushed to pick it up. It was Nora; she wanted to talk to Anne.

"What happened to Charlie?" I asked, palm over the speaker.

"Went back to his wife," Anne said, rolling her eyes.

She and her mother talked and I cleaned and watched the local news. There had been a five car crack-up on the Dan Ryan, an armed robbery on the west side, a fire on the near south side that looked like arson. The rain was over and the next day would be humid. The Cubs lost, the Sox had a day off. A baby seal was born at the Brookfield Zoo. Nothing about the boy who had been shot by the motorist.

"Get this," I said when Anne got off the phone. "Yesterday, a little kid threw a baseball that hit a car, okay? The driver got out and shot him."

"Crazy," Anne said. "You know, I think I will have a beer. Then we can call out for something. What do you say? Poor Mom. Is she miserable."

"I was hoping there would be something about it on the news. I'd like to know how the kid's doing and whether they caught the guy." I switched the TV to another newscast. Then I got the beers and ordered a sausage pizza with green peppers. More about the accident on the Dan Ryan, and, according to this channel, the fire was definitely arson. A guy with curly hair analyzed the

Chicago condominium craze. As he talked, the knot of his tie seemed to grow larger and larger at his throat.

"I thought Charlie was divorced," I said during a commercial.

"Jason," Anne interjected suddenly, coming from left field. "I can't handle this!" She stood up and put her hands against the sides of her head. "I can't handle Kim sick, you stoned and Mom miserable. Not now. Not now."

"Okay, I'm sorry. I fucked up."

"It's just too heavy. I can't deal with it."

"I understand. It's okay. I'll take her in tomorrow. We'll go to the doctor."

"And the dope?" She was rubbing her temples.

"A one time thing. Look, I was bored bananas, okay? It's a drag. It's raining, Kim's sick, you're out there going through hell."

The buzzer rang, the pizza kid. Another welcome interruption. When I got back Anne was on the phone again, this time talking to Bill Trowbridge. Bill Trowbridge had joined the firm the same day as Anne. They shared a cubicle on the nineteenth floor of a skyscraper on La Salle Street with Marty Flanagan, another new associate. They were just names to me, voices on the phone.

"Bill," she was saying, "I just don't want to talk about the exam. Not till it's over."

"Bill thinks he blew a contracts question," she said when she hung up. "I think he did too, though I didn't tell him that. I think he read it wrong. Christ! I don't even want to think about it."

"Let's have some pizza." I had chosen sausage and green pepper as a form of communion, a commemoration of that first date long ago, the Lost People's Party and all that. I tore open the box and worked past the steaming cardboard stink to the real stuff. "Hey, it looks great!"

"Bill had just gotten off the phone after talking to Marty. Marty thinks he blew about half of them. Poor Marty, he's been so shook the last couple of weeks he couldn't study. Just couldn't bring himself to concentrate."

She went back to her seat and I got napkins and plates and handed her a slice of pizza.

"I keep wondering about that boy. Why don't they say something about him?"

"The reason they're not saying anything is probably because he's all right. Why are you so preoccupied about that?"

"It's the way he's being abandoned." I sat down on the floor beside the rocker and found the article in the newspaper. "Jimmie Rodriguez, that's his name. Nine years of age, that's seven years older than Kim. Think about it. Shot through the stomach, this kid. The bullet grazed his spinal column. 'Doctors are uncertain at this time just how much damage has been done.'"

"It's just the city," Anne said vaguely, her mind at a distance. "Crazy things happen."

I began to gently stroke her lovely calf. The skin felt wonderfully smooth and I could smell, just faintly, the warm scent of her flesh.

"I can't eat this," she said, dangling the slice of pizza over the edge of the chair. "I haven't been hungry for a week."

"It's Warhol's fifteen minutes of fame," I said. "Only in this place the fame is generated by agony. Suffer enough pain and you are lit brilliantly for fifteen minutes and then discarded like an old match."

I felt myself consumed by that particular weariness that comes when you've slept too long or smoked too much dope or surrendered yourself to apathy. Left alone it drains you away. I was a whipped puppy there on the floor at her feet. A miserable day. I had failed my wife, failed my daughter, and most importantly, messed with myself. But all that was far from Anne's mind.

"I really think Bill misread that contracts question," she said. "I hope he did. Because if he didn't then I did." She paused and then added, "That was an awful thing to say, wasn't it?"

In the end I heated her a can of minestrone soup and brought it in with two pieces of toast. Then I ate most all of the pizza while she studied.

5

That night, another dream. Anne and I are in a huge building. She's searching for something; rushing down corridors, peering in doors. I have to run to keep up with her. Then I'm alone in a room that seems to be the hub for all the corridors. Phones are ringing. People are entering and leaving. They laugh and talk in loud voices that bounce noisily off the walls. Finally Anne enters from one of the corridors. She has her arm around the man who that morning had opened the door for her. On his T-shirt is the snake I had seen on the wall of the convenience store. They are beaming at each other, obviously much in love.

I stumbled to the ringing phone.

"Jason, babe. Fletzer on the horn."

"Fletzer?"

"You only been gone six weeks, you dumb shit. You forget me already?"

"It's five o'clock."

Jim laughed. He sounded a little drunk. "You own the place yet?"

"Jim, are you wasted?"

Another cackle. "I told Randy you said you were going to own Chicago. He thought that was pretty funny."

"Randy?"

"Jason?" Anne's voice was groggy.

"It's okay, Anne. Go back to sleep." Then I whispered into the phone, "What did you say about Randy?"

"Fucking Randy, man. He called a couple hours ago."

"Jesus."

"Same Randy, man. Four years, and what'd ya know. Same old Randy. Same voice, same everything."

I sat down on the floor and leaned against the wall. "Deep down I thought he was dead, Jim. Know what I mean?"

"A voice out of the fucking past, man. Brought back the good old-time feelings, I can tell you. Old Randy on the phone so clear. Like he was talking in my ear. Same voice, same everything."

"So where is he?"

"Wouldn't say. What can you say when you're on the run? Wanted to know where a few folks were. Sounded happy to hear you were in Chi-town. Wondered if you'd ever married Anne. No love lost between him and Anne."

"We were engaged before he left."

"Yeah, I couldn't remember. He didn't know I'd bought this place, of course. Had to fill him in on that one. He thought I was still just a bartender. Wish I was too. This bar's a loser, man. I shouldn't have sunk my money in it."

"You'll do all right, Jim. So, why you think he called?"

"Got me. Wanted your number, which I gave him of course, along with your address. I thought maybe he'd called by now."

As I contemplated the news, I could hear Jim breathing into the phone at the other end of the line. It was as if we were both in a state of shock.

"Well," I said, finally, "I guess I'll get off then. Thanks for calling, Jim."

"I wanted to talk about it but there's no one left around here. You were the last of the old crowd. Now you're gone and I'm all alone."

It was cool in the hallway, gray with pre-dawn light. After a while I filled the watering bottle and went into the living room. Finding my plants awake was a mild shock, like walking into a room you thought was empty and seeing someone seated in a corner. Only the prayer plant, its leaves folded reverently, feigned rest.

I was ravishingly hungry. In the kitchen with the door closed to keep the odors from reaching Anne, I prepared myself a breakfast consisting of four strips of bacon, two eggs and two slices of toast spread with butter and strawberry jam. All the wrong food and too much of it. I had known relatively constant hunger since we moved to Chicago.

The sun rose and a suggestion of pale morning filtered down the crack between the buildings and entered the room through the small window above the sink. My God, Randy. After all these changes.

"Who called?" Anne said, when I took in her coffee.

"Jim. He'd been drinking."

"I hope. It was still dark."

"He thinks he's all alone. Thinks he made a mistake to buy the bar."

"So he calls at five in the morning? I thought you said something about Randy."

"He wanted to talk about Randy."

"Great. Now there's a man who had a head for business. Most of it felonious, unfortunately."

I followed her to the bathroom. "You want a ride? I'll get Kim up."

"Thanks, but let her sleep. I'll take the El."

I knew I was right not to tell Anne about Randy's call. She had enough on her mind as it was. Still, I felt queasy about it. It was not my practice to hold things back. What I knew, she knew. Now I had this hot little ingot in my head and I had to be careful it didn't fall out on the floor.

Kim and I stayed home all morning but no one called. In the afternoon I took her to the doctor. I hate doctor's offices and as soon as we entered the building the skin on my arms began to prickle. The smell of antiseptic, the staff speaking in hushed tones, the racks of files with red and blue tabs. I wanted to pace, to rub my arms. We found a chair and sat down. Kim leaned against my chest. She sucked her thumb and rubbed the edge of her blanket against her nose.

The waiting room was crowded and relatively small. Toys had been scattered about, magazines. Soft music filtered from unseen speakers, a few plants clung to life. None of it did the trick for me. The room was filled with the precarious sick and nothing could hide the fact.

A small boy sat across the room beside his mother. The smooth waxy skin on his face was drawn tight against the bones. For some reason I could not understand, that tight and shiny skin disturbed me. I told myself the child might have been born with tight shiny skin. It might even be a sign of health to have skin like that. People with tight shiny skin might live ten years longer than the rest of us, win significantly more gold medals, compose the greatest music, head the most successful corporations. Still it frightened me, that skin. It held the chill of an omen.

Then I started thinking about how I should have brought Kim in the day before. Now I really felt guilty. My fears had given the infection more time to establish itself. The orange juice and the rest had not been enough. Yesterday she was feeling bad, today she was sick. I stroked my daughter's warm damp hair. Her pain, mea culpa.

A nurse appeared in the doorway and called for Aaron Levin. The waxy-skinned boy stood up and accompanied by his mother followed the nurse. He appeared practiced in the art of visiting doctors.

That boy Jimmie Rodriguez popped into my mind. Where had they taken him? I wondered. What had happened to him?

About then a baby started to scream. The mother, young and stylishly dressed, got up and began to walk him around. She stepped over the legs of the adults and the bodies of the children. She cuddled and cooed but her efforts did no good. Screaming had possessed the little fellow. It was as if everybody in the room had shifted their frustration to him and he dutifully funneled it into the air with a wail. We adults—all were women except for me—watched slyly as the mother's face went from tan to red. No one moved to assist or offered so much as a smile. She was alone with her designer labels and her flouncy hair, and they were powerless against the torrent erupting from her son.

"Kimberly Winter."

We followed a chunky, highly perfumed nurse to an empty examining room. Kim was set on the table, stripped of her clothing, rolled on her stomach and exposed of her temperature. This intimate figure was recorded in a folder which was placed in a slot on the outside of the door. We were left alone, unarmed and unrepresented in the camp of the medicos.

He arrived twenty minutes later, a giant of a man with a full beard and thick black hair covering his massive arms. Kim was awe-struck, reverent. He slipped lights and depressors into her orifices and cast his eyes and ears beneath the edge she held toward the world.

"Any infection in her ears?" I asked when he had finished. Wisconsin was on my mind, that distant paradise of my youth where the nights were cool and long needle pines rather than chunky nurses perfumed the air.

"The left one yes. The right seems clear. Is that a pattern?" The doctor was busy writing in the folder.

"It happens. Dr. Brown thought she might outgrow it."

"Hmmmm," said the doctor, the classic "hmmmm" signifying nothing. "I'll have Dr. Brown send up her chart." He wrote out the prescriptions. "Did he ever discuss a surgical procedure that is often performed in these cases?"

"Surgery? No, not with me."

Dr. Rubinsk placed a prescription pad against the heavy muscles of his thigh and began to sketch.

"The procedure is common enough. The problem is essentially drainage. Kimberly's ears happen to be constructed in such a way that fluid collects in the canal. By inserting a plastic tube here," he said, indicating with a pencil, "the fluids can escape."

There they were, Nora's tiny tubes.

"Dr. Brown thought she might outgrow it," I said again.

"I'll confer with Dr. Brown, but if this problem is constantly reoccurring—and here we are in mid-summer—you might consider the operation. It would save her a lot of misery and you a lot of time in waiting rooms."

I looked down at my sandals and saw there, suddenly, a black smudge on the big toe of my right foot. The bones jutting out from my heels would also be filthy; they always got that way when I drove. And my jeans, now that I looked at them, were stained from leather dyes, as were my hands. The strong overhead light seemed designed to search out and expose dirt in all its forms. Here I was, pinned like a beetle to a board.

"My wife and I were planning a trip to Wisconsin this weekend," I said, struggling not to mumble. "Up near Baraboo. Do you think we should cancel it?"

"Will you be leaving on Saturday?"

"We were thinking of Friday afternoon, but we could leave Saturday, I guess."

The doctor was standing near the door. "You'd be taking a chance in either event. What Kimberly needs is a few days rest so the medicine can perform its function." A smile emerged from the black fir. He was the objective but sympathetic observer. "I'd put it off a week."

At the main desk I paid the bill with a check. At the pharmacy I was not so lucky. Because I did not have an active card on file, the clerk would not take my check. This struck me, at that moment, as totally unreasonable. I showed her my driver's license, my Social Security card, an old student ID. She wasn't moved. She gave me a card to fill out and return. Once the information was verified, she said, I could cash a check.

"But my daughter is sick." I argued. I thought that if I could just explain the situation, she would change her mind. "Look, my wife's a lawyer, okay? We've just moved to town and my daughter's come down with this infection." I tried to hand her my checkbook but she refused to look at it.

"Look at the balance. It's more than enough to cover this. We're not the kind of people who bounce checks."

The clerk was becoming embarrassed. "I'm sorry," she said with a quiet iciness, "I'm just following store policy. There's nothing I can do." She looked over my shoulder. "You'll have to excuse me. People are waiting."

"Where's the manager?"

Relieved, she pointed to a man a couple of aisles away who was busy berating a stock boy. The employee had stamped the wrong price on a case full of deodorant sticks. I had to listen for five minutes with Kim heavy on my hip, before the manager would grant me an audience.

"Look, fella, you know how many times I been burned by the dying kid story? Your kid is probably dying, right?"

As a matter of fact I had been about to suggest that she could become very ill if she did not get her medicine.

"No, but she is sick and she needs her medicine." Again I offered my checkbook which he deftly brushed aside.

"I'd hate to tell you the stories I've heard. I got a drawer full of checks back there. It'd make you cry." The manager turned away.

"Okay, just give me back my prescriptions and I'll find someplace that'll take my check."

"Right," he said, spinning back. "And what do I do with the medicine, feed it to the pigs?"

I carried my docile daughter slowly back toward the pharmacy section. A line of people was waiting to pick up their orders. People with cash, people with major credit cards, people with active cards on file. Above the counter was a large window, and behind the window two men and a woman in white smocks were rolling pills down little chutes into white envelopes. They looked mechanical, lifeless, as if the automation of pharmacies, sure to come, had already begun to steal away their spontaneity. Periodically, the window slid open and another envelope or bottle joined the collection on the shelf behind the counter, two of which were mine.

Outside, a siren was wailing. The sound grew louder as I carried Kim to the car. Finally an ambulance roared past. It squealed around the corner and disappeared down the street. The sound of the siren was horrible, terrifying. I could not think of one more surely calibrated to dissolve what remained of my cohesion. It drew a small undirected prayer to my lips. Whoever the victim was—an old man faltering in the heart, a child shot by a motorist—I prayed that the poor bastard had an active card on file.

As the siren was still fading, a teenager approached with a portable cassette player jammed against his ear; the disco rhythm was so loud the air seemed to quake. Then a bus passed, its exhaust fumes slamming against my nose, while at the intersection horns blared in the wake of the ambulance. It was just a typical warm afternoon in the city but it seemed to me at that moment as though the earth had suffered a cataclysm the news had yet to report. Somewhere the tectonic plates had slipped and a sliver of hell had oozed through the crack and materialized on the spot, cleverly disguised as a normal street with normal people.

I had time to drive to the bank before it closed. I could easily cash a check and return to the pharmacy for the medicine. That was the reasonable thing to do, but reason was beyond me. A simple touch, a whiff of air, and I might be walking forever, back and forth, corner to car, a tape player lodged against my ear, or in some bloodless stupor beyond the pull of time, rolling endless pale pills down a gray plastic chute into countless white envelopes. In an hour Anne would be home, and that is where I went, like a rabbit rushing to its burrow.

That our dreary, colorless apartment, framed by equally humorless and unforgiving brick buildings, should have become a sanctuary, struck me as frightfully ironic. But there were doors to close against the world, familiar toys to pick up and put away, the smell of leather slowly permeating the walls.

When the buzzer announced Anne's return I didn't go to the door. Kim had just thrown her orange juice, cup and all, on the kitchen floor. Anne let herself in and found her way back to where we were.

"Ah hah, the orange juice rinse. Just what the floor needed. I thought it was getting too slick."

"Ms. Cheerful." I was on my hands and knees with a sponge in hand.

"Ms. Exhausted."

"That's progress, I guess. After what you went through yesterday." The sponge was full of orange juice. I got up to rinse it out.

"I'm too exhausted to be nervous anymore, but tomorrow it will be over." She sat down in a chair and placed Kim in her lap. "So, how's this one?"

"One infected, one not."

"I thought so."

I waited but heard no moral about how I should have taken her in the day before. Her refusal to twist the knife filled me with gratitude and lifted my spirits.

"You'll never guess what he recommended," I said, getting back down on the floor.

"My dear, I've been guessing all day."

"He wants to stick plastic tubes in our daughter's ears so they drain. Can you believe that? Dual exhaust pipes out the side of the head. Maybe for a few bucks extra we can get the chrome-plated model."

I thought Anne would laugh at this preposterous idea but she took it seriously. Dr. Brown had mentioned it to her when Kim was sick last spring.

"Maybe we should think about it," she said. "Dr. Brown said the tubes are so small you can't even see them."

I did not respond. Tubes in the ears—I didn't want to think about it.

Anne lit a cigarette and found herself a beer. She had spent the day under terrible pressure while all I had done was take our daughter to the doctor and fail to get her prescription filled.

I finished with the floor and glanced at my wife. She had smudged out her cigarette but her eyes still squinted and her beer rested forgotten on the table. She was miles away, dissecting a contract, analyzing a tort. Kim, too, seemed somehow stunned. She sat on Anne's lap with a finger absently caught at the corner of her mouth.

"You got any cash? The goddamn pharmacy wouldn't take my check."

The phone rang as Anne was digging in her purse. It was Nora. She wanted to talk to her daughter.

"Kim felt hot so I gave her a dose of painkiller and she went out like a light," Anne said when I got back. She had changed into shorts and a T-shirt and was watching the news.

I spread some burgers out on the coffee table.

"How's Nora?"

"Miserable. It wasn't enough that Charlie should abandon her. This afternoon her car broke down on the Stevenson and she had to be towed to a station. They won't even look at it until tomorrow."

"Jesus." My mouth was full. My hamburger was a third gone and I was out of control, eating faster and faster.

"She just bought that car a year ago," Anne continued, taking up her sandwich and helping herself to a small bite. "I told her the warranty must still be good. She's going to bring it over for me to look at."

The scene on the TV was a fire in one of the suburbs. Hoses were everywhere, smoke poured from the windows. I stuffed the last of the burger into my mouth and fell back on the couch with a groan.

Now an emergency squad was using a "Jaws of Life" to get a woman out of her car on the Eisenhower. She died in the ambulance.

"Maybe she doesn't do her maintenance," I suggested. "When your dad was home he probably saw to all that.

Your mom might not be doing it."

Anne thought for a moment. "Well, Dad always did take care of the cars. Would you help her?"

I agreed to talk with Nora about the car. I changed the channel and was lowering my teeth into a second hamburger when the phone rang. Bill Trowbridge again. Anne kept saying, "Bill, I told you. I'm simply not going to talk about it. Not until we're done."

The new channel was showing its version of the accident on the Eisenhower. Same results as before. Anne hung up and returned to the living room, waving her half eaten hamburger in the air.

"I can't eat this. My stomach's too tight. I haven't enjoyed food for days." She sat down and allowed her hand and the mutilated hamburger to dangle over the side of the chair. "Since we're not going to Wisconsin I've tentatively arranged a night out. Mom will be over after work tomorrow to take care of Kim and you can come downtown to meet us."

"Who's us?"

"Bill and his wife. Maybe Marty. He isn't sure yet. He's having a terrible time with the exam. Think you might enjoy it?"

"I guess." I knew I sounded apprehensive.

"I thought you would like a night out. You've been cooped up in here with Kim for weeks while I've been obsessed with this damn exam."

"It'll be fun. I just think I'm a little afraid of meeting these people." I was sitting on the floor beside her chair again. I began nibbling on her thigh, nuzzling up toward her crotch.

"Why?" she said, giggling. "They're only people."

"Not quite, dear. They're lawyers."

I felt a firm no-thank-you tap on the top of my cap.

"I do that," she said, "and I'd sleep for a week."

That night I awoke in a cold sweat remembering the bowl of waxed fruit on my mother's tall buffet. Tom Lingenfelter. They took him out of fourth grade and later we learned that he had died. We never learned why he died or how, or whether his illness was somehow connected with the strange waxy character of his skin. For a long time after that, whenever I looked at my mother's bowl of wax fruit, I saw the shining face of Tom Lingenfelter.

6

Early the next morning I was in my shop at the back of the apartment. I had drawn a pattern for the vest and I was cutting out the leather. Even at first light the roar of traffic was constant in the distance, a clear line etched on the environment and so familiar it might have been forming in my head rather than on the streets and expressways.

The leather brought Randy McGrath to mind. I met Randy near the end of my freshman year. At that time he lived in a cabin on the back of a flatbed truck that he would park along the strip between the campus and downtown. In the morning he would drop a set of stairs on the curb and be in the leather business. The police hassled him and his truck kept breaking down and he wasn't all that good with leather or much interested in it as a substance or a craft or, for that matter, as a source of income.

I used to go there to touch the leather and enjoy the smells and the rough-cut lumber and the people who stopped by, the cracker-barrel atmosphere of the place. But mostly I went because of Randy who was massive and unafraid, and who knew more about the world than I did.

One day he said, "Punch the holes in those belts."

I looked at him.

"You're just sitting around," he said. "Make yourself useful."

I looked at him.

"You've been here often enough. You know how to do it."

We were all getting into wheat germ and such in those days. A food co-op had started. Some folks had opened a natural foods restaurant in the basement of a church near campus. They sold dry tofu burgers, thick lentil soup with a dollop of sour cream floating in the center. Leather seemed a logical extension.

When I first started working with Randy, he and I went camping almost every weekend, which for us meant Sunday and Monday. We preferred winter camping, but winter or summer, whenever the mood struck, we would close the shop and set out. In addition to the truck, Randy owned a battered Renault that he had gotten from some guy as partial payment on a debt and that, precarious as it looked, always got us there and back. Usually we went alone, though sometimes Fletzer joined us and at other times the party was as large as six or eight.

We avoided designated campgrounds, those habitats of garbage cans, toilets and hibachis chained to metal posts. Randy had been born and raised in southern Illinois. He knew of secret, hidden places, places where the roar of traffic or even its whisper never reached. There were abandoned houses, one with a open letter lying in the dust on the table (the letter gave no clue to the mystery), a stream where a pair of eagles nested, an empty cache on the side of a sunny slope (a deep hole, narrow at the top and wide at the bottom that Randy speculated had been built by the George Rogers Clark expedition.) His preference, however, especially during the warm months, were the ponds and little lakes hidden amid the moonscape of abandoned strip mines. Here the earth had been gouged and heaped and cast aside. To the passing motorist the sight justified righteous anger, then repression. Like an injured animal it asked to be left alone. But Randy knew the abandoned mines. He had explored the terrain by foot and motorcycle during the first year after his return from Vietnam. It was, he had once explained in a phrase I never forgot, the place where he had felt "least uncomfortable."

On the radio Kenny Rogers was growling out his tale of "The Gambler." I was excited about the vest and working quickly on it. If Kim took a nap in the afternoon I would finish it in time for the outing that evening. The design was long and loose fitting; the seams would be hand-stitched with leather strips and the front joined by three frog fasteners. If I could convert my leather inventory into these vests and sell them at a reasonable price, I would pull in over seven hundred dollars. That amount—which once would have seemed like a fortune—was, I now realized, less than Anne made in two weeks.

I took her coffee when I heard the shower. Later she came back with written directions on how to reach our meeting place. She was wearing her soft green dress in deference to our night out. The dress was one of my favorites. It's lime sherbet color wetted my tongue and unchained my lust. After she left I studied the calendar; two and a half weeks had passed since we had last made love. To make matters worse I had caught Kim's cold.

The little lady woke up shortly after Anne left. Already she was better, though not enough better to want to eat. She came muttering out of her room, rubbing her eyes and saying she wanted to water the plants. I filled the watering bottle and got a glass. I poured small amounts from the bottle into the glass which she poured onto the plants, spilling and splashing and talking to them the way I did.

Nora called that afternoon. She wanted to know what time I planned to leave for the Loop.

"I'm supposed to meet Anne at six."

"I'll get there around five-thirty," she said. "Should I bring anything?"

"Not that I can think of. I'll have something here for you to eat."

"That's not necessary. I'll put together a sandwich and some soup. You needn't trouble yourself."

"It's no trouble, Nora. I was going to make some soup for Kim anyway."

"I'll be fine," she insisted.

The doorbell rang at a quarter to six. "I couldn't find a parking place," she said. She was wearing immaculate white sandals. The thought occurred to me that if I dared wear white shoes they would be grungy before I closed the front door.

Nora had stopped in the doorway. She stood staring at my leather cap. I recognized a judgmental squint in the eyes, a subtle but disapproving pinch of the lips.

I led her back to the kitchen where I had been trying to get Kim to eat some of the soup. "Do you like my vest?" I asked. "I made it today."

"It's nice," she said absently. "Do you think you'll have trouble getting into a restaurant without a tie?"

"A tie? Anne didn't say anything about a tie."

"Lots of places require them."

I wasn't going to give in to a tie. "There's a big pot of soup on the stove, if you want some, Nora. Real carrots, real cabbage, stewing beef."

"Thanks. I brought what I needed. I'm on a diet." She sat down at the table and tried to tease Kim into eating with the old "Choo Choo" routine.

A diet was what I needed. I had weighed myself after

showering. Twelve pounds since we moved to Chicago. I could barely button my slacks.

Nora did not need a diet. Time had marked her face and faded her hair, but she had a trim, attractive body. I was still staring blankly at her legs when suddenly she looked up.

"Don't you think you'd better get going? It's almost six o'clock."

Descending the stairs and then again more intensely when I reached the sidewalk, I experienced sudden anxiety. I did not want to go downtown or meet those people. I wanted to turn around and go back to the safety of the apartment. It was not the first time I had felt this sudden gripping at my chest. It was becoming harder and harder for me to go outside.

The late afternoon air smelled of the hot engines parked at the curb. A couple crossed the street in front of me and hurried into an apartment building. He had his suit coat flung over his shoulder like a politician. Her heels clicked on the pavement. At the dry-cleaners on the corner I saw my reflection in the window. The new vest looked gaudy, the sandals and cap absurdly out of place.

In the car I found a country station. The cultivated drawl of the DJ calmed me somewhat. I took the correct exit off the Kennedy, but at the top of the overpass, perhaps because I was busy singing "Sweet Memories" with Willie Nelson, I turned right instead of left. Ten blocks later I realized the mistake. Left turns were not permitted, so I took three rights in heavy, honking traffic, crossed the street I wanted and pulled into an alley to turn around. My heart was pounding. The radio said: "More than a hundred thousand items to choose from." I turned off the radio.

The cocktail lounge was dark and I stopped a moment

just inside the door to give my eyes time to adjust. Then I saw Anne waving. She was sitting with a guy in a horseshoe booth against the wall. He stood up when I came over. He was six inches taller than I and had the shoulders and chest of a gymnast.

"Did you make that vest?" Bill Trowbridge stuck out his hand. He was one of those people who squeeze your hand before you have a chance to tighten your grip and your fingers end up feeling like overly ripe bananas in the bottom of a packed grocery bag. "Cowhide, right? I've got one something like that." He sat back down and began to shuffle through the papers on the table.

Anne smiling up at me; the lovely green dress. I sat down beside her and squeezed her arm. She had rings under her eyes.

"Did Mom make it all right?"

"She's fine. How are you?"

"I'm all right. How's Kim?"

"Okay," Trowbridge said. "We both saw that one the same way. Now, I want to ask about you about the decedents' estates question."

"Kim's okay."

"Good." Anne picked a paper off the table. "We're looking at these questions, do you mind?" I said I didn't mind. "Okay," she said, "decedents' estates, first day." She read the question out loud. It made no sense to me. "I didn't answer that one," she said. "I did the crim pro one. Did you answer the crim pro one?"

"I did both of them. I didn't do the tort one. Let's talk about this one first."

"Okay." She read the question again, this time to herself.

Trowbridge looked at me. "What'd you want?"

"Want? What?"

"To drink. What'd you want?"

"Oh. Scotch and water with a twist. But I can get it."

"Bernadette!" Trowbridge had the voice of a line coach and Bernadette dutifully ran over. "Another Dubonnet for the lady and a scotch and water with a twist. What's your scotch?"

Suddenly I could not think of the brand name of a single scotch. Not one.

"The bar scotch is Black and White," Trowbridge said.

"That'll be fine."

"Did you get that, Bernadette? Black and White with a twist."

"Got it. Another of your usual?"

"Right." Bill Trowbridge turned back to me. "Carbondale, right?"

"Right."

"I've been there. We used to go down to Cairo goose hunting. Did you hunt geese while you were there?"

"No. We would go out to the refuge and watch them, but we never hunted them."

"Good hunting. Thousands of geese down there." Now he was talking to Anne again: "Of course the main point here is the at-death basis of the residence but. . . ."

"Let me finish reading it."

They both read the question, squinting in the dim light. When the drinks came I took the wallet out of my pouch, but Bill Trowbridge waved it away.

"I keep a tab," he said. "I been coming here for years."

I pondered the drink. Scotch and water with a lemon twist. I had ordered it because of Randy. He always drank scotch and water when he was catching a cold. He used to swear by it. I took a sip and instantly decided that I did not like scotch at all. Then I remembered that Randy had tried to get me to drink scotch once before. I hadn't liked it then either.

After a while a man approached our table. Anne introduced us. It was Marty Flanagan, the other new associate.

"Nice vest," Marty said, sitting down. He was also tall, though lighter framed than Bill Trowbridge. He had a complexion problem and a pronounced downward slant about the eyes.

"Thanks, I just finished it a couple of hours ago. You want to trade places so you can go over the questions?"

"I've had enough of the questions," Marty Flanagan said. He picked up his beer, turned the coaster over and scribbled a note on it. The note said, "Hang it up, Trowbridge." He flipped the coaster across the table.

Bill Trowbridge read the message, then scratched it out and wrote one of his own which he tossed back. Flanagan showed me the note. It said, "Fuck you, Flanagan."

Next to arrive was a tall woman with blond shoulder-length hair. What struck me at the time was that this was too trite. I wanted Trowbridge married to a short fat woman with a thick mustache. I wanted her to sit down at the table and crack her knuckles before yelling to Bernadette to bring her a beer. I wanted to smell sweat and see the butt of a pearl-handled pistol glinting beside her left breast. A tattoo on her thumb. Instead I noticed the way her hair shimmered for an instant in the brilliant outside light before the door of the cocktail lounge closed behind her.

She approached slowly, eyes narrowed by the lack of light.

"You're late," Bill Trowbridge announced, glancing at his watch. "I said six and it's a quarter to seven." Having said this he returned to the papers.

Liz Trowbridge paused and then greeted Anne with a smile. They'd met, Anne had told me that. She had a large mouth and when she smiled it spread from one side of her face to the other.

"Hi, Marty. I'm glad you decided to come along."

"You may as well sit here," Marty said after introductions had been made. "Jason and I are having fun. Those two are still talking exam."

Leaning toward me she smiled again. It was her announcement, I decided, her crest. It said, "I'm Liz and I mean no harm." Her voice said, "I like your vest."

"He made it this afternoon," Flanagan said. "Jason was doing something worthwhile while I was taking the bar."

"Was if awful?"

"That's a fair description," Marty said, lifting his bottle.

Liz began a soft intimate conversation with Marty Flanagan about how terrible it must have been, how he shouldn't get depressed, how most people pass, and so forth. At one point Bill Trowbridge summoned Bernadette for another round. I tried to change my order but he was so efficient and quick that she was gone before I could explain myself. I reached down in the dregs of the scotch and pulled out the twist. I did what Randy always used to do. I stuck it in my mouth and began to chew. It tasted terrible.

Later we agreed on dinner at a Greek restaurant the Trowbridges raved about. Then out on the sidewalk Flanagan changed his mind.

"I think I'll just go home," he said. "I'm really tired."

For a moment we all stood there in the swirl of passers-by, dazed by indecision. Then Anne put her arm around Flanagan's waist.

"No, Marty," she said, "you can't break up the three musketeers on a night like this." She let him off down the street with Bill Trowbridge in fast pursuit.

"That was so nice of Anne," Liz gushed. "I think Marty wanted to go. He's just feeling bad."

"Did you come on a motorcycle?" I asked suddenly, surprising even myself.

"No! I. . . ." She stared at me for an instant with a look of horror on her face, then she turned toward the nearest shop window and studied her hair. "Do I. . . ."

"You look fine. I just had this fantasy that you had ridden up on a motorcycle."

"Me?"

I nodded. "A big Harley hog."

"Me?" she said again.

Then something wonderful happened. Liz Trowbridge broke into a laugh and the laugh rose into a loud and unseemly cackle. It was a laugh to turn people's heads. I didn't know whether she was laughing at me or at the idea of herself on a motorcycle. It didn't matter much. I was entranced by the laugh. I saw it as a kind of miracle, an element of the two-year old Liz that had somehow survived into adulthood. I thought then of my own daughter. That was precisely what I wanted for her: to emerge whole and glowing into adulthood. To walk like a flame among the wilted.

Liz shut the laugh down as fast as she could, as though it were an ill-tempered dog that needed to be locked away, and we followed behind the others until we reached the window of a men's store.

"Bill has a birthday coming up," she said, pulling me over. "Do you see anything in there that might be right for him?"

The display contained everything from shoe-shine kits to three piece suits. No muzzles or strait jackets, unfortunately. I crouched down and examined a pair of sandals imported from Spain.

"Those aren't bad. I couldn't make them for any less."

"That's right!" She was bubbling again, grabbing my shoulder. "You're a leather craftsman. You made your vest. Your sandals, too? The little cap?" The three lawyers were waving to us from beside a car.

"I'm a walking commercial," I said as we started again.

At the restaurant we joined a line of people waiting to be seated. A waiter served us glasses of ouzo and Bill Trowbridge described a trip he and Liz had taken to Greece. When he finished he asked if I had been to Greece.

I hadn't. Mexico, I said, was the only foreign country I had ever visited. Marty wanted to know where I had been in Mexico.

"Juarez," I said. "I went with Randy, a guy I used to work with."

Trowbridge laughed. "Juarez! That's not Mexico. You got to the border, that's all. Whores and rip offs. When you said Mexico I thought you were talking about Mexico City. The Mexicans call Mexico City, Mexico."

"I was in LA once," Anne said, coming to my aid. "Now that's a foreign country."

We were soon seated and then served a large marvelous salad. Very hungry and slightly looped from the ouzo and the two scotches, I began forking it into my mouth.

"This is wonderful," I exclaimed between mouthfuls. "I love salads with artichokes."

Trowbridge stopped eating and looked at his salad. He poked around with his fork. "I see feta cheese," he said. "Olives. I see anchovies, but I don't see any artichokes. You got artichokes in yours?"

Everybody was poking through their salads.

"Anchovies," I muttered. "I meant anchovies."

When the laughter stopped, Marty Flanagan said,

"Language, that's what it all comes down to. Even the bar. It's all language. Wollan told me that he was in court with a lawyer one time who kept arguing that his client's check had been improperly garnished when he meant to say garnisheed. Finally the judge leaned over and asked whether the creditor had been paid off in parsley."

"Actually the judge was wrong," Anne explained. "You can use either verb, garnish or garnishee, to indicate the taking of property by process to satisfy a debt." Then she slapped her forehead. "God, I'm still taking the damn bar. Anyway, Wollan does tell funny stories. The last day I was in the office he told me about a guy who threw up all over his bar exam. Wonderful sense of humor, Wollan."

"The guy should've turned it in," Marty said. "He probably had as good a chance as I have."

"Flanagan, would you stop moaning about the bar? You passed the damn thing and you know it." Trowbridge turned to Anne. "You should've seen him in law school. Every exam you'd think he'd flunked cold. Then he'd end up with an A or a B. That's true, Marty. Every goddamn exam. I got to expect it after a while."

Bill Trowbridge called the waiter and ordered two bottles of wine, one resinated and one not. He knew this waiter too.

"Who's Wollan?" I asked when the entrees were served.

"I'm sorry, hun," Anne said. "Marshall Wollan. He's about to be made partner. And speaking of Wollan, he said we're expected at work tomorrow."

"Bullshit!" Trowbridge was pouring wine for everyone. "Hell with Wollan. I'm going sailing tomorrow and Friday."

I had a vision of it suddenly. Bill Trowbridge was standing at the wheel of a large yacht, legs apart. He was wearing white from head to toe and had a pair of binoculars hanging from his neck. Slaves worked the sails.

"Are you going in, Anne?" Marty Flanagan asked. "If you go, I'll feel like I'll have to."

"I'm just telling you what Wollan said."

"He was joking," Trowbridge said. "Wollan's always joking."

"Are you?" Flanagan persisted.

"Yes, I think so. I'm not saying you should, but, yes I am."

I was disappointed. I had assumed Anne was going to stay home the rest of the week. She could tell what I was thinking. She glanced at me over the rim of her wine glass. Her expression seemed to say there was nothing she could do about it.

By the time dessert was delivered, Anne's and Marty's resistance to talking about the bar exam had collapsed completely.

"Res ipsa locatur," she announced at one point.

"Of course, but nunc pro tunc," Marty cautioned.

Et cetera, I thought, ad infinitum. I glanced across the table. The baklava was sweet but the lovely eyes of the effervescent Mrs. Trowbridge, I noticed, had glazed.

"I embarrassed you, didn't I?" I said when Anne and I were finally alone in the car. "Artichokes, Juarez. All this old hippie leather. I felt like a fool."

"You didn't embarrass me. Now that's silly. It was Bill who was embarrassing."

"That guy's an asshole! I'm glad I'm not locked up in a cubicle with him every day." The presence of Bill Trowbridge still rang in my ears, the unrelenting force of will. It was like having spent too long at the base of a waterfall. I turned the radio to something Anne might prefer, innocuous strings. "He kills geese. When he thinks of southern Illinois, that's what he thinks of: killing geese."

"Do you feel better now that you've met him? I've had the feeling you were getting a little jealous of this Bill character who keeps calling up." She was teasing, nudging my ribs.

"Trowbridge?" I wheeled onto an entrance ramp of the Kennedy and pushed down the accelerator. "Jesus." I ran it up to forty-five and shifted into fourth. "Yeah, well, lock yourself up with a two year old every day and your mind would begin to wander too."

Anne giggled. "A wondering mind I can tolerate. A wondering eye . . . that's not permitted. What'd you think of Liz? Pretty, huh?"

"Bill's mannequin. Stand her in the right place and she'll stay there smiling. Isn't that what you'd expect? Another piece of the show. Anyway, if I'm jealous of anything it's that damn office. I don't see why you're going in. Asshole is going sailing."

Anne sighed. "Bill and Marty are men, but there's more to it than that. Have I ever talked about Gil Patek?"

"Don't think so."

"Patek is a senior partner who lives in the Internal Revenue Code.

"Sounds homey."

"Take any section to him, no matter how complex or obtuse, and he'll masticate it for you. Anyway, Gil is Bill's uncle on his mother's side. And Harold Trowbridge— that's Bill's old man—Harold has supposedly sold insurance to about half the old boys on the top floor. Country Club thing. Then there's Seamus Flanagan."

"That one I've heard."

"Senator Seamus Flanagan, that's Marty's dad. Seamus pulls a string and the better half of Springfield begins to grin and babble."

"Nepotism."

"Not in the way you mean it. Bill and Marty deserve to be there. They went to Northwestern and did well, and they're expected to produce. It's just that there's a familiarity. An acceptance."

"And Anne Winter?"

"Ah, that one. The woman. The Czech-Irish mongrel. And from SIU no less. But one who just happened to wow the recruiting committee. It's not that I'm running into hostility, just a lot of wait and see. I have to do what's asked and more."

Now I sighed. "Well, we got through this one."

Anne slammed her fist down on the dash. "Your damn right we did! I think I aced the bastard, if you want to know the truth."

That was my baby and I hugged her with my free arm. "When do you learn the results?"

"Months. Let's forget about it." She slid the back of her fingers along the side of my face and lay back against my shoulder. "Let's just forget about it."

Traffic was light on the expressway; the night warm. I felt peaceful and at ease. I reached down and began to stroke her hip and thigh with my palm, the only part of my hand that would not snag on the fabric of the lovely green dress. In the old days when we came north to visit Nora, we used to travel in this position from Marion to Chicago, three hundred miles along Interstate 57 without a stop sign or a sharp curve, and little to observe but soybeans and corn. I used to stroke her belly for fifty miles then slowly, languorously, slip my hand beneath her jeans- —she always wore jeans in those days. It went on for hours, slippery, tender, cornfield hours. Then somewhere north of Champaign she would lower her head between my stomach and the wheel and tease and toy with me until the traffic thickened in the suburbs and the truck drivers started to leer.

We reached our street with her tongue in my ear and there I discovered an occasion of some magnitude: a parking place within a block of the apartment. I would not have to drive around for half an hour or walk ten blocks. I took it as an omen. Soon we could remove the lovely green dress and get serious about celebrating the conclusion of the bar.

Nora was sitting on the couch watching television. On the coffee table was a half finished drink. The glass rested primly on a coaster. She must have had the bottle in her purse because we had no hard liquor in the house. And where she had found the coaster was beyond me. I had not seen the coasters since we moved. Still, she could have rummaged through everything we owned for all I cared. All would be forgiven if she would just accept our thanks and be quickly on her way.

"Well, you two are home early," she said, looking moderately cheerful. She suggested we have a cup of decaf before she left. Not a good sign.

In the bathroom I emptied my bladder of wine, both resinated and unresinated, of ouzo and of scotch and water with a lemon twist. From the medicine cabinet I removed a thousand milligrams of vitamin C. On my way out to the kitchen I heard Anne say something about the papers on the car. I poured myself some orange juice and swallowed the tablets. As I watched the pot of heating water I thought of Anne's father, the man who should have been taking care of Nora's car. Frank was a mediocre artist who resented the fact that he was dependent on his very capable executive skills to make a living. I knew him well enough. He had come down for Anne's graduation from undergraduate school and he gave her away at the wedding just a few weeks before he gave himself away to his secretary.

Frank had studied sculpture and painting at the Art Institute early in the fifties. His work, which demonstrated considerable technical skill, featured harsh edges and deep shadows; it was bold in technique, definite in statement. Unfortunately there was little market for unrelieved and angry arrogance. The failure of his work to sell caused Frank to paint and sculp with more arrogance and more anger resulting in continued obscurity and ever more resentment of his white collar job.

Then on a Tuesday morning in October, 1976 Frank and Nora planted brief kisses on each other before leaving for their respective jobs. Frank veered off the appointed path, picked up a rental truck and returned to the house where he exercised a rough justice dividing up twenty-five years of marital possessions. The temptation was probably to feel guilty, leave the bulk, take only what you need. Frank resisted. He took his share, maybe a little more just to give Nora yet another bone to pick. Job transfer it was, and off in the rumbling truck to Kansas City, his secretary—whose age was similar to his daughter's—close behind in the new family's car, she having sold hers that morning to make things a little less complicated. Back at the house Frank had left a note on the dining room table. The note was held secure by a bottle of Nora's favorite gin. The bottle Frank undoubtedly saw as a touch of class, the wrap on the tale when he related it to the boys in the years ahead. A "how it's done" tale, when it's time to do it.

The water boiled. I made two cups of coffee and delivered them to the living room. Anne had kicked off her shoes, hoisted her dress and was seated on the couch, knees apart, lovely legs folded beneath her. She was studying the papers.

I went back to the kitchen and slipped a slice of bread into the toaster. It was astonishing that I could be hungry. I covered the toast with margarine and strawberry jam and ate standing at the counter, not bothering to slice the toast, just devouring it from one end to the other. The jam was wonderful. It was the best jam I had ever eaten. I could have eaten three more slices, and would have except I wanted to save the jam.

When the toast was finished I poured myself a second glass of orange juice and started back toward the living room. I was resigned to a late night discussion of automobile maintenance. But the papers lay forgotten on the table. Mother and daughter were talking in soft voices about Charlie. Nora had an expression on her face I had not seen before. Perhaps she wore it while driving alone at night or walking through the empty house her husband had been unkind enough to leave her in. I had not seen it, but I recognized it. It was the weary, frightened look of a person who knew she had crossed the high ground and was starting the long descent alone.

Nora looked up then and I realized that I had just trespassed in my own living room. I paused and the conversation stopped.

"I'm beat," I said. "I hope you don't mind if I hit the sack."

Anne winced. She looked toward her mother and then at me. Her eyes tried to apologize but I could see she was trapped.

I closed the bedroom door and then turned on the radio. I finished drinking the orange juice and crawled naked into the empty bed. The Statler Brothers were singing a tune and the Statler Brothers made me sick. I turned off the radio and the light and snuggled down against the pillow, only to discover that I had forgotten to take off my leather cap.

7

I lie awake in the middle of the night, unable to sleep. To relax I try to place myself inside the barn that my great-great-grandfather and his son built a hundred years earlier and which still stands on my aunt and uncle's farm. The walls are massive, constructed with thick slabs of Joliet limestone hauled a hundred miles by rail and wagon. The great beams are oak trunks still in their bark. The milled lumber forming the stalls is thick and smoothed and rounded by the throats of large animals. I think of the pulleys, levers, fulcrums used to erect the frame. I watch the men cluster in the evening light, moving a massive stone into place. The plumb line drops untouched. The fine ears of the Belgian horses pivot to the heavily accented voices; a huge rear hoof lifts and bends at the fetlock. The tip settles in the dust. From the porch a woman calls: "*Schon Nacht!*"

"*Noch nicht!*"

The men have lit a lantern to better see the level. They knew what they were about, I think, lying in the dark. They finished what they set out to do.

In spite of my resolve, I was bothered when Anne got up the next morning and went to work. Some part of me took it personally. I did not want to take it personally but I did. During the next few days I found myself waking at five. Anne and Kim were still asleep. The room was cool, the street relatively quiet. Down the hall my leather work waited. I knew I should get up. I was certain I would feel better if I did. Yet I didn't do it. The husky voice had settled into an enduring summer cold. Get well first, I told myself; take what rest you can. I would fall back into disjointed dreams only to wake with the alarm, feeling drugged and dispirited.

On Friday night Anne and I went out to dinner. We had paella in a restaurant decorated with a lot of black wrought-iron and a swarthy guitar player. She suggested we go out every Friday night. She would talk to Nora about taking care of Kim. And she would keep Sundays free for the family. Saturdays she would probably have to work. At least in the mornings. She looked exhausted.

"And I think we should consider child care," she went on. "We've been here almost two months now. Kim is adjusting, don't you think? That would free you to do some leather work during the day."

I realized that I had been wolfing down the food. My table manners of late had taken on an element of exercise —aerobic eating. I caught myself, took a deep breath and tore off a piece of bread.

"I still got some money left."

She frowned, perplexed. "It's not a question of money. Don't you see? I don't know why you feel obligated to pay half our expenses. It's not like it used to be. I got this big bucks job and you're home all day taking care of Kim. That's valuable. It doesn't bring in money but taking care of Kim is at the core of what our family is about."

In Carbondale we had each had separate accounts. Then at the end of the month we would tabulate our expenditures and one of us would write the other a check to make it even. It worked because our incomes—mine from the leather shop and Anne's from the part-time secretarial position and a scholarship—were roughly equal. Now she was making twice what before we made together.

"I don't think she's ready yet," I said. "She's sucking her thumb more than she used to. And having some accidents. She seems less independent to me. Let's give it another month."

She seemed relieved. "Yes, I'm sure you're right and I'm so glad your willing to take this on. I feel guilty about the time I'm putting in at the office."

"It's not a problem, Anne. . . ."

"And, I'm worried about you," she added, above the guitar. "You're having a hard time, aren't you?"

"Me?" I felt a sudden panic. "I'm all right. We're going through a period of adjustment, that's all. You're the one doing the work. The stress you been under, Jesus. Sure, I'd like to do more leather, but I just need to get up earlier. I can't believe how lazy, I've become. Fat and lazy." I broke off another piece of bread and began to smear on some butter. "You want some of this, you better grab it."

She laughed, but I had the sense I was failing her. She had set this Friday evening up for me. As if I were the one needing a break. And yet in the drama our family was presently staging, my part was so minor, so simple relative to hers. That she should have to worry about me bordered on the obscene.

I woke that night thinking about Kim and how Anne had deferred to me on the subject of child care. I had become the front line parent, the one presumed to know the status of things. But had I been honest? The idea of Kim spending her days outside the home scared me. Who would we trust to do this work? How would we select the person? I thought about the neighborhood beyond the walls of our apartment, all those blocks of apartment buildings and corner shops. It seemed faceless and disturbingly alien. How would I feel working here at home, knowing that my two-year old was out there somewhere? On the other hand, would she really benefit from more time with me or was I holding her here out of my own fear?

The awful wakefulness drove me from the bed. I wandered into Kim's room where I ended up kneeling beside her crib. The night-light shone through the little fuzzy-looking plastic lamb face. The room smelled subtly of damp diaper. It would not be accurate to characterize my behavior as a prayer, nor the crib and sleeping child as a form of alter. If not a prayer, then a plea.

On Sunday we went to Lincoln Park for a tour of the zoo. Kim thought this quite the occasion. She wanted to show her mother everything and she ignored me throughout.

During the week, life remained pretty much the same. Anne had to be at work by eight and was rarely home before six-thirty, usually with a briefcase full of papers which she spread across the dining room table after we had eaten. The reports I delivered during the meal were brief. I was embarrassed by how little I seemed to accomplish during the day. Hers—when she was not staring off in space or fiddling with her food—were filled with tales of conquest and plunder. Though a raw recruit, her allegiance to the firm was complete. Our lovemaking was crowded into those moments when we were most weary.

I was not prepared for what happened the following Wednesday.

Anne failed to set the alarm and we woke an hour late. In her eagerness to adjust the spray she broke the shower head. As she rushed toward the door she shouted back to the kitchen that I should run a load of laundry through the washer.

It was after lunch and Kim was down for her nap before I carried the laundry basket down to the utility room. I put the clothes in the washer, waited until it filled with water and added the bleach. Then I stepped out into the tiny back yard. Except for a few tufts of grass cowering against the walls and bits of rubble scattered here and there, the black dirt was barren. The day was hot and smelled of tar. The sky had a grayish, green color, as if it were covering a bruise or a bad local infection. From somewhere the sound of the Bee Gees blared. A black customized hardtop rumbled through the alley, its exhaust pipes gurgling.

I unscrewed the broken shower head and took it into the kitchen. I poured myself some orange juice and sat down with a catalog that had come in the morning mail. The models all looked angry. Both the men and the women were staring belligerently from the pages as if to say that no one was going to push them around or criticize the color of their Dacron. On some a thin line of white had slipped in between their irises and lower lids. They had been looking tough so long their minds had wandered.

I phoned the Pyramid Lounge in Carbondale. Randy had never called and I wanted to find out if he had ever gotten back to Fletzer.

"Nope," Fletzer said, "and I'm here all the time. I'm thinking of putting a bed in the stock room. Give up the apartment. I might as well be living in this damn place for all the time I spend here."

"I can't figure why he hasn't called."

"Who can figure Randy? He might call tomorrow or he might never call. You never know about Randy. He might be knocking on your door next thing."

"That could be a problem," I said.

"Yeah, he'd be crazy to come back to Illinois."

"I was thinking more of Anne. She being a lawyer and him wanted and all."

"Put her in a funny position, I guess." Fletzer set down the phone and I could hear him talking with a customer. "I put in a small microwave," he said a moment later. "Shiny little devil, sitting here, bouncing around with electrons. I'm selling sandwiches, pizza slices. Frozen stuff, but the pizza's not bad if you been drinking. You should come down and try some. I'll zap a pepperoni for you, on the house."

"We're going to Wisconsin as soon as Anne can get off. I've always loved it up there."

"Yeah," Fletzer said, "there's no reason to come down here. This place is the pits."

I pulled out the heavy sheets and stuffed them into the dryer. One of Kim's socks fell to the floor where it immediately acquired a layer of crud that had to be picked off. When I got upstairs Kim was waking. She was puffy and petulant and I released her to amble about the apartment, giving her time to push back the shadows and fit the pieces of her world together. When I figured the time was right, I asked if she wanted to go to the store. Enthusiasm filled her face; my daughter had returned.

We brought up the laundry and found her purse beneath the couch along with two building blocks and a violet crayon.

On our way to the car there were leaves and weeds and alleys. We discovered a long brick wall. It was seven or eight feet high and ran half the length of the block. In the center was an iron gate. Kim wanted to climb on the gate and I stood there a while so she could do that. Just inside—the gate had been left partially open as if to permit passage but not encourage it—was a thicket of bushes and small trees. I took Kim's hand and we followed a curving ill-defined path through the thicket until it opened onto an expanse of lawn that stretched a hundred or so yards to a wall and gate on the next street. On our right a similar wall was covered with vines and broken in the center by a gate that opened into a churchyard. On our left the wall met the back of a two-story house with a gray porch that ran the length of the building. The enclosure contained several carefully maintained flower beds, a few benches and nearby, to Kim's delight, a slide and swing set. The grass was lush and around the playground only slightly worn. The slide and swing set had been constructed years before of sturdy graying metal. The air was rich with well-watered vegetation. A little bit of paradise.

Kim pleaded and I consented to a few runs down the slide. She insisted on squealing with each descent and I could not resist hushing her each time. I did not want to be discovered. I wanted to slip out, leaving the dream intact. Finally I had to take her arm and pull her fussing from the slide.

On our way back to the gate, at the edge of the lawn near a line of juniper bushes, I saw something that for a moment my mind would not accept. A rabbit was hunched down feeding on the grass. How, I asked myself, had it come to be there? Unless I assumed someone had brought it in, or that it somehow had migrated across expressways and down thoroughfares from an environment less hostile, I had to acknowledge that this rabbit was the successful product of a hundred or more generations of urban rabbits. Thousands of dogs and cats, horse-drawn wagons, cars, trucks, fires and fire engines, boys with BB guns, malevolent drunks and the desperately hungry had not succeeded in breaking the thin line of life leading from the first joining of molecules down to the fat contented animal we saw before us. The rabbit flicked its ears, pink and translucent, stared at us for a moment with a large brown eye and then returned to its meal.

Two uniformed guards stood at the entrance to the discount store. They looked official, done up in blue, fat and bored. Inside, the walls were spotted with convex mirrors and red signs stating that shoplifters would be prosecuted to the fullest extent of the law. High in the corners small cameras scanned the aisles.

It took a long time to locate and then reach the hardware section. Kim wanted to examine everything and somewhere a temptress was pouring caramel over popped corn. I could not find what I wanted. Too much stainless steel grinning at me to see anything clearly.

We approached a clerk, a man who was ripping open cardboard boxes and pouring their contents into the display bins. The one he was tearing apart at that moment contained hundreds of toothbrush racks, each with its little plastic bag taped to the ring, each bag containing four screws. There were so many toothbrush racks in that one box it seemed inconceivable they would ever be sold. I mean, how many homes do not have a toothbrush rack? Or need one?

"Excuse me."

"Yeah?" The man did not pause. The next box he attacked was brimming with soap trays.

I took out the broken shower head. "My wife broke this this morning when she was taking a shower. The alarm didn't go off, you see, and she was in a hurry and it broke. I guess she pulled. . . ."

The man grabbed the shower head and took off down the aisle. "It was probably old or something," I said, lifting Kim and trying to catch up. "You can see it just pulled loose at the joint there."

The clerk stopped at a bin full of shower heads. He matched up the diameter of the orifice and handed me both the old and a new one.

"Don't leave that old one lying around here so someone buys it and then comes back bitching to me about shoddy merchandise." Returning to his boxes the clerk added over his shoulder, "The alarm clocks are in the appliance section."

"Pardon?"

"You said the alarm didn't work, right?"

"Oh, she forgot to set it." I chuckled. "The alarm's all right."

"Broads," the clerk said and bent over to convert another box to trash.

I scooped up my daughter and walked to the checkout counter. I entertained the insane thought that one of the security officers was scrutinizing me. I tried to explain to the cashier how the one shower head was broken and how I had brought it in with me. I even offered to demonstrate but she was busy with the cash register, one of those new ones that buzz and hiss as if it were tabulating the federal deficit. She placed both shower heads in a paper bag and stapled it shut with the receipt on the outside. When we walked out the guard smiled and said hello. I was another good customer with his tightly stapled package.

Daytime was best for finding a good parking place. Spaces two and three car-lengths long were scattered along the block. I pulled into one directly in front of our building. We had stopped for ice cream and half of Kim's was drying on her chin and T-shirt. I led her up the stairs, careful to keep her from touching anything, unlocked the door and guided her into the bathroom. She stood patient, squinting, and her skin reddened beneath the pressure of the wash cloth. I screwed in the new shower head and tried it out. Good spray, a job completed. Then, on my way out past the bedroom, I noticed that the laundry was on the floor. It trailed from the bed to the door as if someone had grabbed the bottom sheet and pulled it out from under the stack.

"Dammit, Kim," I said, "what were you doing in here?"

She was several steps in front of me. At the sound of my angry voice she began to cry and ran into the living room.

"Come back here. Help me pick this up." I went after her, swept her up and was turning back toward the bedroom when I noticed that the television stand was empty.

I held my breath and turned in a slow full circle. The two building blocks and the violet crayon were resting on the coffee table. My parents' clock ticked on the mantel. Everything was normal except that where the television set used to be, our new color television that we had bought with Anne's first check, there was a hole.

Kim was complaining. She was thirsty and she wanted down.

"Hush!"

She continued to fuss but I held her tightly. My heart was pounding at the base of my throat, my scalp contracting against my skull. We went slowly from room to room. I peered into all the closets. I poked at the dark corners with the handle of a broom. No one. Nothing seemed to have changed in any of the rooms. I ran back to the living room half thinking that the TV would be there. I dropped down on the couch with Kim still in my arms. It was gone. It was really gone. Broad daylight.

The phone receptionist at Anne's firm had the same nasal voice as the receptionist at the doctor's office. There was a long wait.

"Anne, we've been robbed!"

"What?"

"We've been robbed! The TV. We just got back from the store. You know, the shower head, and the TV is missing."

"The TV?"

"Yes! I think everything else is all right, but the tube is gone. We've been robbed!"

"Burglarized," Anne said, correcting me. "Robbery is when they take it by force or by threat of force."

"Anne, Jesus Christ!"

She groaned. "I just can't believe this. You must have not locked the door."

"I locked it, Anne. Dammit, I remember locking the door. And it was locked when we got back."

"What about the back door?"

I ran to the back door. It was closed but not locked.

"That must be how they got out," I told her. "It was locked when we left."

"God, I just can't believe this. Our new TV, four hundred bucks."

"I'll call the cops."

"Well, don't touch anything. They may want to take fingerprints. Jesus, and no insurance."

I poured Kim a cup of apple juice. I came back to the phone and picked up the ponderous directory. I felt myself sinking down along the wall until I was sitting on the floor. The sensation was not loss so much as violation. The picture in my mind was the harsh urine-stained stairwell in the housing project where the tourist had been raped. The crazies. I had known they were out there, but until that moment I had considered us secure inside the apartment. The TV had served as a kind of voyeuristic device, a one-way window that allowed me to peer out at them safe and unseen. Now they had stolen the window and had jumped back through the hole. They had disappeared but in a real and fundamental sense they were not gone. What had divided outside from inside and kept us safe no longer existed.

The officer at the police station was not much excited about the burglary. He said he would try to get a unit over there that afternoon to make a report, but if not then, one would be there in the morning.

"I sort of thought you might look around the neighborhood," I said. "I just returned home a few minutes ago."

"How long were you gone?"

"About an hour."

"They were in and out of there five minutes after you left," the man said. "Your TV has been sold and the bastards are already shooting up what they bought with it."

About an hour later two officers arrived. They were large men with thick necks and heavy thighs bulging from their tight uniforms. Accouterments of capture and death hung from their wide, black belts. Their speech was formal, their features smooth and unsmiling. Their presence charged the room with an aura of contained aggression. Kim sat on my lap, her finger pressed against her lip. The officers collected the information necessary for their report; one seated on the couch asked the questions and wrote down my responses, the other stood legs apart near the doorway.

"Do you think you'll catch them?"

"Not likely, sir. Though the set may turn up some day. I'll need the serial number."

Later, the other, still standing at parade rest, turned his

head and looked out the front window. "From where your set was situated, the screen could be seen from the sidewalk across the street. I'd suggest moving your furniture around before getting another."

It took only a few minutes. The officers had no desire to obtain fingerprints, no sense of pursuit. They behaved more like reporters recording what had happened than participants in an ongoing event.

It was only after they had gone and Kim and I were alone in the apartment with the shades drawn and everything too quiet, that she finally understood.

"Daddy," she said, "Mr. Rogers gone."

8

"It's a cloud machine," the man said. "I've got it set on billows." It was a manhole and there were puffs of cloud coming out the grate. I heard a gurgling noise down in the hole and the clouds were coming out. They pushed against the manhole cover, making it rattle in its casement. Running to the bathroom I held my mouth closed. I vomited, kneeling before the toilet. Outside, through the darkened windows I heard a car door slam, then another. Two men were talking, unafraid of the night. One of them laughed.

Kim and I were up early the next morning. We returned to the discount store where we waited among the bargain hunters for the doors to open. A man wearing a Chicago Cubs baseball cap and a green jacket that advertised a bowling alley was talking about car wax. The new stuff, the man said, the sprays, the liquids, they were no good. If you didn't have to rub it in it wasn't doing any good. I bought two dead bolts and two heavy chain locks.

A woman sat on the sidewalk beside a cardboard box with her back against the store front. She was wearing a muslin, hand-embroidered blouse and a full skirt that lay in gentle folds around her. A sign on the box offered free kittens. I paused. She smiled, recognizing a kinsman.

The woman dealt in portents, stars, the configuration of planets. Kim pulled a kitten from the box. It was white and it had something wrong with its tail.

"A birth defect," the woman said. "For some reason

she has no control over it beyond the first couple of vertebrae."

I lifted the tail which was dangling over Kim's arm and then watched it flop when I dropped it.

"It probably drags in everything."

"Not really." The woman brushed her long hair back from her eyes. "She's a very clean little lady, but she is the one I'm most worried about. People will be reluctant to take her because of the tail. If I can't give them away, I'll have to take them to the pound. It's that or be evicted."

The kitten cuddled against Kim's chest. Her eyes were very green.

"What I really need is a large dog," I said, rattling the locks in their tightly stapled bag. "Something to keep the crazies out."

The woman smiled benignly. "The kitten will permeate your home with such good vibrations no one will think to harm you." She lowered a well-ringed hand into the box and the three remaining kittens writhed around it, meowing, their tails in the air.

The store had everything you could ever need for a cat. The store, it seemed, had everything. We named her Emerald for her eyes and decided to call her Emmy. She traveled well, crawling onto my lap to escape Kim's enthusiastic clutches. At a stoplight I took my daughter's hand and together we stroked the kitten's neck and back. Its fur and skin hid nothing. We could feel its bones, its thin muscles, life itself pulsing just beneath the surface.

We set out bowls of food and water in the kitchen and placed the litter box beneath the bathroom lavatory. Kim, herself having only recently mastered the craft, was intrigued. She picked the kitten up, held it firmly in the box and demanded a performance. "Gentle," I kept saying. "Gentle."

The doors already had locks of course. They were the standard locks built into the door handles; I had thought them secure until one of the policemen demonstrated how they could be breached with a credit card and five seconds. Working on the doors, I found holes that had been filled in and painted over. A former tenant had taken along the heavy locks when he moved. The locks themselves had been stolen.

That afternoon Liz Trowbridge called. She was still thinking about a birthday present for Bill. She wondered if she could stop over to discuss a project. An hour later she arrived carrying a clothes bag and spreading her broad smile.

"I thought you were just coming for a few minutes," I said, taking the bag.

She giggled. "It has a vest of Bill's. I thought you might be able to estimate his size from it." Kim appeared in the doorway of her bedroom. She was holding the kitten in front of her. Her hands encircled its middle as if gripping the handle of a suitcase. The kitten hung limply from either end and stared with woeful eyes.

"This is Kim," I said. "She's learning to be gentle." I had to pry loose her fingers. The kitten raced down the hall and into the living room with Kim in screaming pursuit. "And that was Emmy. We just got her today. I don't think Kim realizes yet that the kitten is alive and has feelings like she does."

Liz Trowbridge wrinkled her nose. "Don't cats make you nervous? They do me."

Here was a woman who had chosen to live with Bill Trowbridge and cats made her nervous. I followed her into the living room where she admired the Swedish ivy.

"Anne's plants are lovely," she said. "This ivy puts mine to shame."

"Actually, they're mine." I was somewhat embarrassed.
"Really?"

I nodded. "Yep and late at night I put on Anne's underwear and prance around the house watering them."

"Oh, God. I'm sorry." She covered her eyes. "It did sound like that, didn't it?"

We walked back to the shop. I hung the bag on a dowel rod and pulled down the zipper.

"I didn't know exactly what information you'd need." She was looking at the handbags. "His shirt size is sixteen and a half/thirty-four, if that would help."

A bull, I thought. All neck and shoulders, pushing his way through the world. Inside the clothes bag was a vest from a very lawyer-like three piece suit.

"I was so impressed by that vest you had on the other night. I thought maybe you could make one for Bill. But more in the style of one of these." Her face was always doing something, eyes squinting, nose wrinkling, tongue slipping quickly over her lips.

"You mean a dress up thing?"

"Well, with a sports jacket say, or maybe a corduroy suit. I thought you might use a light-weight cloth on the back like on this one to make it cooler and less bulky."

I told her I needed to make a pattern. I spread the vest across a strip of butcher paper, tacked down the edges and flipped on the work light.

"It *is* kind of gloomy in here," she said, sitting down in the old caned-bottom chair. "Do you always keep your shades down?"

I had pulled the shades after the policemen left. On the windows with drapes, I had drawn them as well. She was right; it was gloomy. The light in the apartment had taken on a yellowish tint, like aged paper. I told her about the TV.

"God, that's awful! Did they take anything else?"

"A sheet to cover it with." I bent down over the vest and began to trace the outline with a pencil. "The cops figured the bastards saw the TV from the sidewalk across the street. That's why the shades are down. The next guy might decide he wants Kim, or Anne."

I could feel Liz Trowbridge looking at me. "It must have been terrible to realize that someone had been in here," she said. "But don't you think that your reaction is a bit exaggerated? Do you really think someone would bust in here and steal your child?"

I felt a sudden irrational anger. "Do you read the papers? Watch the news?" I told her about Jimmie Rodriguez. Then I described what happens to the wives of men who stop to read road maps. "They decide to come in here, am I going to stop them?"

I had been more graphic then I intended. I glanced at her. She was looking down at her boots, expensive riding boots that I had noticed the moment she walked into the apartment. She was chastened, I thought, or else she had decided that I was crazy.

My pencil reached the bottom, crossed to the side seam where I made a notation and then started on again. Kim entered the room on shy quiet feet. She was carrying one of her favorite toys, a brightly colored wooden duck that lurched and quacked when you pulled it. She handed the toy to Liz and without a word turned and ran out the door.

"She'll have all her toys in here pretty soon, won't she?" Liz seemed happy to change the subject.

"Probably. Why, is she bothering you?"

"No, of course not. I work with children."

"Really?"

"I'm a guidance counselor at a grade school. This will be my fourth year."

She probably put the old boy through law school, I thought. No, people with yachts are not put through law school. Probably a rich do-gooder occupying her mind until a family occupied it for her. I wasn't sure I wanted this woman in my apartment. Her perfume disturbed me, her nervousness agitated the air. Everything already seemed too fluid and permeable.

I handed her some leather samples and told her to pick out what she wanted. I liked the way she took her time at it, touching them, raising them to her nose. Finally she selected a fawn-colored suede. Her lap by this time was covered with toys.

"Anything special with the buttons?" I asked. "Maybe horn or bone?" I noted the darts and the pattern was complete. "Somewhere around here I have a collection of buttons."

Liz was examining my old sewing machine.

"My friend Randy bought that at an auction in some small town along the Ohio river years ago. It's a treadle, must be fifty years old. Used to belong to a cobbler." I could not find the buttons anywhere.

"Randy." She was petting the machine as if it were a great dane. "The fellow you went to Mexico with."

"Juarez," I said, correcting her.

Liz Trowbridge winced. "I'm sorry. Bill can seem awfully rude. He's not really that way."

I did not respond, not being as optimistic as she. The buttons were on a loop of wire and I always kept them in the center drawer of the cabinet. I rummaged into it again but found nothing. When I looked up she was holding out a check for fifty dollars. Elizabeth Irving Trowbridge, was the name in the corner. "To get you started," she said. Also on the check was a picture of a horse and rider jumping a fence. I took down the clothes bag and carried it back toward the front door. The kitten chose that moment to reveal herself and with a squeal of delight Kim was after her.

"Bill wants to have children," Liz said, watching the spectacle. "Actually, Bill wants me to have children."

"And you don't?" I was surprised.

"Some day. But I'm really into work now."

The kitten paused to slide under the couch and Kim grabbed its useless flopping tail. Whimpering with a kind of fiendish ecstasy, she pulled it out, secured it around the middle and shoved it toward Liz.

"Hasn't quite got the gentle part yet," Liz said dryly. She held the kitten at arm's length, as though it might possess hazardous fangs.

"It's like a wonderful toy," I suggested. "No batteries and you never have to wind it up."

"I wonder if its tail was stepped on or something. There was a litter of kittens born at the stable this spring. One of them was stepped on by a horse. Not the tail, the whole thing." The wrinkled nose.

"You have a horse I take it. The check, your boots, kittens being squished around stables."

"Yes, Ariel. A jumper. That's where I'm going now. I've been neglecting her, I'm afraid. The stable is up near Lake Charles."

It sounded wonderful to be out in the fresh air riding a horse. I exchanged the clothes bag for the kitten, and holding Kim's arm, let it down. We watched it flee to the couch and squirm underneath.

"Do you think you'll have the leather by next week? I thought I might drop by and take a look before you cut it."

"Sure, and I'll have found the buttons by then."

We were standing at the door when Liz's nose began

to twitch. I ran to the couch, pulled it out. A puddle of very fresh, very soft kitten shit was rapidly soaking into the carpet. It was a large puddle for such a small kitten.

The smell was astonishingly potent. It seemed to fill the room instantly. It permeated the furnishings and the walls. I filled a pan with hot soapy water, and while Liz and Kim watched in silence, began to scrape it up. The smell conquered the sponge, invaded the water, coated my hands. Cat shit was everywhere.

"Does it do this often?" Liz asked, eyes squinting.

"Don't know. We've only had her a couple of hours."

"Well, I hate to leave you at a time like this, but if I'm going to get up to Lake Charles. . . ."

"It's okay, Liz."

"You might try vinegar."

"Thanks," I said, and then went back to wiping up the good vibrations.

Anne called after lunch. Nora had yet another problem with her car and she wanted me to check on it.

"She met a new man," Anne said, "and she wanted to talk about that. I don't know how she thinks I can sit on this phone and talk to her when I'm supposed to be working." She sounded exasperated. "Maybe you should pick up something simple for dinner. TV dinners or something. I'm not going to have time to do the chili rellenos. I had a rough experience here this morning and I'll have to put in some hours tonight."

"Big problem?"

"I really can't talk to you right now either. We'll talk tonight, okay? I'm sorry about the chili rellenos."

Anne's chili rellenos were one of my favorite foods. I had been hinting about them for weeks.

Kim and I drove to the bank where Nora worked as a

loan officer. The problem with her car was that she had left the lights on and the battery ran down. I started it with my jumper cables. Then Kim and I took it for a short drive to recharge the battery. On the seat was an open purse-sized package of facial tissues. The ash tray was half full of butts, each filter stained with lipstick. A small mirror hung from the inside of the sun visor. Otherwise the interior was empty, as was the glove compartment which I flipped open and examined at a stoplight. Nora's car had a sterile, unowned feeling about it, as if it were part of a rental fleet. I had the sense she never occupied her car in any real sense but simply used it to move from place to place as one would a cab or bus.

At the bank, on the other hand, Nora seemed at home. She was wearing a light blue dress with white trim, a pair of small white earrings. A white sweater hung neatly over the back of her chair. I could not help wondering if loans were granted or denied in accordance with the amount of dirt visible beneath the applicant's fingernails.

Probably thirty people were working behind desks and counters and yet the space was virtually silent. The carpet, walls and ceiling soaked up all sound; even the telephones announced themselves with a muffled buzz. It was a spotless world, soundless, where only numbers talked— everything else whispered.

Nora took back the key. She had only given me the one key, having removed it from her ring with one perfectly clean fingernail, as if fearing I might slip off with the others and have them copied.

"You left the lights on," I whispered.

"It was foggy this morning, I may have."

"They were definitely on, Nora. It runs down the battery to leave the lights on if the engine isn't running."

"Yes, I know." She offered me a brief, hesitant smile.

"Anne told me what you said about the maintenance." She looked away and straightened a stack of papers that to my eye had already looked perfectly plumb. "It is true that Frank took care of the cars. So last night I read through the owner's manual. It's embarrassing that the very next day I should leave the lights on."

"It can happen to anyone," I felt compelled to say. "I once parked my car, jumped out and locked the door only to realize that not only had I left the key in the ignition but the engine was still running."

Nora started to laugh, then quickly placed a hand over her mouth. Not becoming of a loan officer to be seen guffawing at her desk. But for a moment there, she had actually laughed.

Later, in the frozen food section of the supermarket, I was attacked by a craving for cherry pie. I remembered my mother seated at the kitchen table seeding cherries with a hair pin. Her heavy arms rested on the edge of the table. Her thick fingers moved with remarkable speed. Sometimes she would mutter to herself when she was lost in her task. My mother would not have been comfortable in the bank either. She would have stopped just inside the door and placed her hands together in front of her as if she were at once both parent and child.

A tall woman in a tight elegant dress and long sharp heels was rummaging through the frozen pies. Three, four, five frozen cherry pies disappeared into her shopping cart. It was ludicrous, like a dream, and I did not bother to see if she had missed one. I selected the frozen dinners and then wheeled Kim through the produce section just to look at the vegetables and enjoy the smells. They had fresh cherries! We filled a bag and on the way out picked up a pie crust and a quart of ice cream.

Anne looked tired when she got home; her mouth was working. She saw the kitten right away.

"My, God," she said, "we can't keep it."

"Why not?" Kim immediately began to cry.

"It's the lease." She dropped her briefcase and we followed her to the bedroom closet where she pulled out the metal file box. "You should have called first. Now Kim will be brokenhearted."

"But. . . ."

"Here look." She withdrew the lease and unfolded it. 'The party of the second part shall keep no animals of any kind on the premises neither temporarily nor permanently.'"

"God, Anne that would outlaw a goldfish."

"That's right! That's what we agreed to. We violate the lease and they can throw us out." She returned the document to its proper place and closed the door. "Do you remember how hard Mom looked before she found this place? They're converting every liveable structure into condominiums."

It baffled me. What was the problem with a little cat? "I don't understand. We pay our rent, we keep quiet. What more to they want?"

"They want no pets!" Anne groaned and placed a hand across her forehead. "This is such a mess. I don't know why you didn't call first."

There was a sense of resignation in her voice that encouraged me.

"I guess I should have called, Anne. I just had no idea that a cat. . . . She's a nice kitten. Housebroken. . . ." If she smells the shit, I thought, and the smell, it seemed to me, was everywhere. "I just thought it would be good for Kim. She's away from her friends. This place is still new to her. I thought a kitten. . . ."

Hard to tell how long I might have blubbered on in a similar vein with Anne holding her head in her hands, had the phone not conveniently rang. It was Nora. She wanted to talk to her daughter.

Anne came into the kitchen when she got off the phone. "Mother said we could borrow the old black and white set that she keeps down in the basement. That way we won't have to buy one until we see if the police get ours back."

"I don't know why she didn't tell me that when I saw her this afternoon." The cherry pie was the first pie I had ever made and I had three recipe books open on the counter. Each one had a different recipe for cherry pie.

"What kind of dinners did you get?" Anne took a beer out of the refrigerator.

"Turkey and ham."

"I want ham!" Kim was certain.

"I got chicken for you, hon. A pot pie. You like pot pies, remember? I'll run over for the TV if you watch this for me." I showed Anne the cherry pie. "Put it in as soon as the temperature is up."

"Okay, where are the dinners?"

"In the refrigerator. Kim's got a chicken pot pie."

"I want ham!"

"I can't drink this," Anne said. "I'll just fall asleep." She returned the beer to the refrigerator and pulled out the dinners. "I had a terrible day at the office."

The temperatures in the different recipes were confusing. I closed two of the books and decided to go with the third. "Try and watch the clock real close, Anne. After twenty minutes the temperature must be turned down. I don't know if I'll be back."

"Okay. How far down?"

I took another look at the recipe. The kitten was boxing

with the cuffs of my jeans.

"It doesn't say how far down."

"That's weird. I'll put it down to 350, then I can stick the dinners in."

"Are you sure that's not too hot?"

"Mommy, no chicken!" Kim stomped her foot.

"Jason, I'll take care of your precious goddamned pie, all right?"

"All right," I said, and turning toward the door nearly tripped over the cat.

The dinners were out when I got back and the pie was cooling on the sideboard. Anne was finishing a beer. She must have reconsidered. More and more it seemed to me she regulated herself through chemicals. When she was tired or dull, she drank coffee; when too wound up she turned to alcohol. Then there was tobacco and whatever it was she got from the flesh on the inside of her mouth.

"Did you see Norman?" Anne asked as we were eating.

"Norman?"

"Mom's new friend."

"No, he hadn't arrived yet. She was all dressed up, though. She had a bar set up and a dish of appetizers on the table. Good stuff, I sampled one."

"I'm encouraged that she met him at work. He manages a tire store or something and came in for a business loan. She's had real bad luck with men she met in bars. She met Charlie in a bar."

"She was having a drink when I got there. Getting ready I guess."

Anne asked if I would put the coffee water on. I cut the pie and covered the slices with mounds of ice cream.

"You think Mom drinks too much, don't you?" she said when I carried the pie and her coffee into the dining room.

"Well, I don't know. Sure, she likes a drink. But I don't know that it's too much."

"You're always making insinuations about it. 'The bar was set up,' you point out. She was 'getting ready,' you said, 'by having a drink.'"

"Well, she was. I didn't mean anything by it."

"It's the way you say it, Jason. I have the feeling you really dislike my mother. I've had that feeling ever since we moved up here."

I had no idea where all this had suddenly come from, but I wanted nothing to do with it. I wanted to eat my pie. The ice cream was melting.

"Your mother's all right," I said without much conviction. "She laughed when I told her about the time I locked myself out of the car with the engine running."

"Just now?"

"No, this afternoon when I jumped her car."

"Oh, right." Anne had forgotten that I had gone to the bank to fix her mother's car. She looked apologetic now. "What was the matter with it?"

"She left the lights on," I said with a certain relish. "Ran down the battery."

"I see."

We cleared the table and Anne spread out her papers and lighted a cigarette. After I had Kim in bed I went back to the kitchen, closed the door and turned on the radio softly. I rolled a fat joint before facing the dishes. It wasn't just Anne who was turning more to chemicals. In Carbondale I used to smoke a joint once or twice a week. Now it was a nightly ritual and that one time I had started before noon.

I finished the dishes, then went into the living room

and set up Nora's ancient black and white. I was careful to position its back to the windows even though the shades were down and the drapes pulled. Colorless television. When I woke the news was on, and I had decided to stop watching the news.

Anne was still at the table. Her coffee cup rested on a paper towel. Smoke curled around her hair. I realized that I had never learned what had happened at the office. I had been too involved with the silly pie to ask.

I placed my hands on her shoulders. The muscles running toward her neck felt taut as cables.

"Would you like another slice of pie?"

"I don't think so. I've just about got this." She began to roll her neck in response to my massage.

"Piece of toast?"

"With your jam on it?"

"You drive a hard bargain," I said. I had resisted opening the last jar of strawberry jam.

I brought the snack out on a dishwasher's service: the toast on a paper napkin and one large glass of milk for us to share.

Anne looked up with a tired smile. "The most they would probably do is ask us to get rid of her."

"I should'a called first. I'm sorry."

"A cat. Mother is terrified of cats."

She broke off a piece of her toast and dipped it into the milk. Then tilting back her head she lowered the sodden mess into her mouth. She had done that the morning after the first night she stayed with me in the little cabin I had on Washington Street. And she had done it so innocently, so child-like, that my perception of her had changed forever. She was an intelligent and beautiful woman who in the morning sat on folded legs and dunked her toast in her coffee.

I took a drink of the milk and wished that I had used two glasses. The surface was speckled with crumbs of toast and blotches of strawberry jam.

"So, what happened at the office?"

It was a long story having to do with a confusion of assignments, contradictory instructions and office politics. In the end something that needed to be finished wasn't, and she having the least seniority had swallowed the blame. I listened as patiently as I could; an attentive ear was one of the few things I felt I had to offer. As she spoke, intense, caught in the turmoil, I became acutely aware of how the responsibilities of her work had served to sharpen and narrow her and point her away from Kim and me. And I wasn't making it any easier by moping around the house, smoking dope and getting fat. Snide comments slipping out about her mother. Another thing to worry about, that's what I was.

9

The cat being contraband, so were its droppings. I thought
of the superintendent down below with his bass guitar. I
double-wrapped the litter in plastic bags and placed the
bags in a paper sack which I topped with trash. It was
absurd.

I began to watch a lot of animal shows on TV. I watched
them in black and white. Then one afternoon I went out
and bought another new color set. My half the cost took a
chunk of my savings but it was worth it. Anne wanted to
pay for the set herself but I resisted. I wanted to feel I was
making some contribution other than child care.

I tended to watch any animal show that came on. I saw
shows about mallards and porpoises, penguins and moose,
giraffes, wolves, mountain goats and mice. Sometimes it
was hard to imagine that there exists a single lion in all
Africa that has not spent hours on national television. Did
you know that a mouse can fit through a hole the size of a
dime? That an adult male elephant weighs six tons and
eats 400 pounds of vegetation a day?

Some things were impossible when Kim was awake.
Pick up a book and she was all over you with questions
and demands. Start a project in the workshop and she
made life impossible until you gave it up. I could lace a
vest or a handbag while playing a game or watching her
show off some skill like jumping from the couch arms or
trying to do a somersault. Sometimes pieces of leather
entertained her briefly. But she always knew where my

head was. My attention was a great protective shield that hovered over her as she went about the apartment, and she could tell when it wasn't there.

I kept the TV on. She let me watch so long as she did not believe I was seriously watching. She became quite knowledgeable about the animals. "Flamingos," she would shout, as though we had just come across a rise and below was a lake filled with them.

I felt guilty about the TV. I didn't want her getting addicted to the daily drivel or becoming a happy little consumer who demanded to possess each useless new product with a clever ad. Or worse yet, taking as role models those obnoxious children in the sit-coms. Except on the worst days, I limited us to the public channel, though I would travel anywhere to watch animals or aboriginal people, or any show having to do with nature. These were educational, I would tell myself. Also they were shot out of doors, often with great expanses of sky or water, mountain or grassland. Still, I felt guilty. So I read to her. We would go to the library weekly and come home laden. It was exciting the way phrases appeared in her speech from books we had read days before. She came to love stories; she would insist on them and I was called upon to invent, to speak for her many stuffed animals, telling stories of their lives before they had come to live with us.

I also felt bad about the dope. What lesson was I giving her? I became furtive, sneaking into the bathroom, opening the window and taking a few puffs. I knew the smell clung to me. I had it in my hair, on my clothes. I couldn't smell it, but I knew it was there.

It struck me on one of the trips to the library, how flat the landscape was. This levelness formed a horizon from objects close at hand, buildings, utility poles, a few trees.

If you were higher up the horizon became vague and ill defined, lost in the haze, in the imperceptible curving of the earth.

One afternoon while the washer was spinning through its cycles, Kim and I decided to collect the junk that was scattered around the back yard. There was a broken tricycle, some sparkplugs, a milk carton, bits of plastic, cardboard boxes weakened by rain and sun and no longer able to maintain their shape.

While we were working the building superintendent entered through the back gate. He was pushing a shopping cart and in the cart was a case of vodka. He stopped his cart at the door of his apartment and began carrying the bottles in two at a time.

"Back's out," he explained. "Two is all I can carry."

I carried in the remaining bottles and then used the cart to haul the junk out back.

"I thought of throwing some grass seed around," I said when I came back. "Think it'll grow?"

"Probably will," the superintendent grumbled. "Then I'll have to mow the damn stuff."

"Got a mower?"

"Somewhere." The superintendent opened a bottle and filled the bottom of a glass. He sat down on the couch with a groan. "If you want some, pour your own."

"I'll mow it," I said.

"You'll move," the superintendent said, "and the damn stuff will go to seed."

"Nothing's forever."

"Ain't that the truth." The superintendent made a motion with his hands, palms up. I took it to mean I could plant the lawn if I wanted to.

Kim liked the guy. She went out again into the back

yard, found some more junk and brought it in and gave it to him.

Liz Trowbridge called again. I had just finished cleaning and Kim and I were in the kitchen with the vacuum bag resting on some newspapers. We were poking through the contents in search of a plastic ring Kim had lost. Liz wanted to know if I had gotten the leather yet.

"Yes," I told her, "and I found the buttons."

"I wish I could come over but a friend's moving and I promised I would help. This is the only day she could get a truck." I had a visions of dairy cattle and rolling green hills.

"Where's she moving?" I asked.

"Just another apartment in Rogers Park. She and her boy friend broke up. That's why she's moving."

"So when's Bill's birthday? Maybe we can do it later, if there's time."

"The end of August. Will you be able to finish it if we wait a few more days?"

The end of August was a month away. It seemed likely she had someone else busy working on his Christmas present.

Kim had emptied the contents of the vacuum bag on her self and across the floor. The ring was back on her finger.

In the bathroom I took off my cap and examined my hair. Anne had been cutting my hair since a couple of weeks after we met. In Carbondale we always did it on Sunday mornings out in the back yard, weather permitting. There was something unreasonably reassuring about the process. She would pace around me, checking the angles, pressing the sides of my head with her hands, issuing commands with the comb in her mouth: "Sit up straight," she would say. "Don't move now."

She had last cut it just before we left for Chicago. More than two months had passed and the thick red hairs spiraled around my collar and scratched at my neck. When I pulled my cap on it felt too tight.

Outside it had begun to rain. I could hear it slipping down the shaft between the buildings and caroming off the bathroom window. Because the glass was frosted, it was the one window whose shade I had not bothered to pull. I forced the window up and looked out. A bathroom window in the next building was only inches away. A bar of soap was melting slowly on the wet sill. People, it suddenly struck me, lived right next to us and I did not know who they were. We showered side by side. We made love only a few feet from each other's bed. And yet if they chose to walk into my apartment and grab my television or my daughter, I would not recognize them. I reached a hand out and felt the cold drops. I closed the window and locked it.

The rain reminded me that the wiper motor on the car was acting up.

I was beginning to learn how to make telephone calls in the city. I knew now to avoid friendly chatter and long explanations.

"Service," I said to the voice that answered when I called the dealer. "I need an appointment for a valve adjustment, a tune up, oil change and lube," I said to the second. The wiper motor was more difficult; I wanted to talk about it. I resisted. "Our wipers squeak when we turn them on. I think it's the motor."

"We'll check on it," the voice said, respectful of this conciseness. He appointed the time. "It should set a couple of hours before we do the valves."

"I'll have it there."

Kim came to my side with paper and crayons. She begged me to color with her, and to demonstrate her eagerness emptied the contents of the box on the coffee table. Some rolled off. Emmy chased them down and tumbled with them across the floor.

A slow day, rainy day. "I think I'll draw a flower," I said, yawning and picking up a green crayon.

"No, Daddy. Draw a cat. Draw Emmy."

Cats are easy to draw: big circle, small circle, eyes, ears, a few long whiskers, the tip of the tail sneaking around from behind. It didn't take long to draw a cat.

Liz showed up that afternoon with her friend. Gretchen was a plump blonde wearing a T-shirt across the front of which was written, "Love is where you find it: I'll be home all afternoon."

"We decided not to move," Liz said. "The rain." Her hair was pulled back and tied. She was wearing jeans, a denim jacket and a Greek fisherman's cap. The cap angled jauntily above her right ear.

"If the bastard wants to be alone that bad, he can move himself." Gretchen had a broad flat face with a short thick nose. She held her cigarette between her thumb and index finger and cupped in her palm the way men do when smoking in the wind.

"Would you like some coffee?" I asked when they were seated among the toys.

Gretchen nodded but Liz could only tolerate de-caffeinated. She wrinkled her face as if to demonstrate what caffeine did to her stomach. I served the drinks and then brought in the leather and the ring of buttons for Liz to examine. Knocking the ashes off her cigarette with the tip of her little finger, Gretchen looked around the room.

"Jesus, is this place gloomy!"

Liz was embarrassed. She explained about the television.

"Eric's previous woman was raped in her apartment," Gretchen said to no one in particular. "The bastard came right through the window one hot July night. Eric used to love to describe it. He told me about it so many times I began to think he was the one who did it." She snuffed out her cigarette and coughed. "I'm lucky to be rid of the bastard when you think about it."

"Do you like it?" I asked Liz, hoping we might change the subject.

"Yes," she said, "it is just what I had in mind." She began to consider the buttons.

"I bought Eric a leather coat shortly after we started going together. It was in the fall and I wanted to buy something he'd use. It's a lovely coat. Pigskin, sort of yellow. Very soft and sensual." Gretchen lit another cigarette. "The bastard loves that coat. He'll be wearing it everywhere as soon as the weather cools." She had started to cry.

Liz was embarrassed again. "Maybe I can pick out the buttons another time." She smiled weakly. "Gretchen and I are going to a movie since its too wet to move." She stood, adjusting her cap. "We should be going, Gretchen."

"So, when are you going to do the move," I asked walking with Liz to the door.

"That'll depend on the weather and when we can get the pickup. We'll have to see."

"Well, if I can be of any help, just call."

"Hey, that's great! Really. Neither of us is comfortable with stick shifts." She looked back at Gretchen who was still sitting in her chair, smoking and staring at the drawn shades. "We have to go, Gretchen. We don't want to be late."

"What are you going to see?"

"'The Amityville Horror,'" Gretchen explained, coming to life. "After Eric it'll be a comedy." She wiped her eyes with the back of a thick wrist.

Anne called at five-thirty to make sure I had set up the Crock Pot and plugged it in.

"Are you leaving now?"

"Not right now. In about half an hour. I sat in on my first deposition today." She had just been a spectator but she was excited about it. The attorneys had gotten into a long argument over a line of questions one of them wanted to ask the witness. My wife had become enthused at the sight of two men arguing.

"Well, call me when you're ready to leave."

"Do I have to? I'll leave in about a half hour."

"Indulge me, Anne. Things change. Just give me a ring before you step out the door."

She sighed. "Are the shades still down?"

"Anne. . . ."

"I don't like it, Jason. It's not healthy. I am worried about you."

"It's a phase, Anne. My way of working through it. It's not going to hurt anything to have the shades down awhile. Or to give me a call before you leave. So call, okay?"

She agreed, reluctantly. Since the burglary I had been unable to relax until I knew she had reached her destination. So she called every morning when she arrived at work and every evening just before she left. It took between twenty-seven and thirty-five minutes for her to get from the office to the front door depending on whether she had to wait for a train. It was another burden I had laid on her, and I had no idea what I would do if one evening she was late.

The next day Kim and I went down to the Loop to have lunch with Anne. I wasn't crazy about the idea. A similar scheme shortly after we moved had been a disaster. I almost had an accident when a bus pulled in front of me while I was trying to keep Kim from climbing out of her car seat. Then I could not find a parking place. Lunch was late and sour. Exhaust fumes, horns, the whistles of traffic cops that seemed to come from all directions at once. I had neurotic a sense of myself that I could not dismiss. I was odd and thus observed; disoriented while everybody else knew where they were going. Alone I could handle it, but with Kim I felt vulnerable, far extended from my home base.

Over dinner Anne persisted in her proposal. "You can leave the car at home," she said. "I'll give you directions for the El. It'll be an adventure."

On our way to the El-stop Kim and I paused at the iron gate. It was the third time we had returned to what in my mind I had begun to call our private park. I loved placing her in the presence of these growing things. We had become more bold and Kim ran along the path ahead of me and out onto the lawn. I caught up with her. She was standing very still, her hand at her mouth.

A man was crouched before a flower bed, a bushel basket heaped with weeds and grass clippings at his side. Heavy set and balding, he looked to be in his late fifties with large thick hands and a wide smooth face. He was clothed for work in loose denim trousers, a blue work shirt and heavy boots. For a moment we all stared at one another, Kim with her attention pivoting between myself and the other man. Then the man smiled and motioned toward the slides and swings.

"Is it all right?" I asked. "We don't mean to interfere."

Still smiling the man nodded his head. Then he returned to the flowers. Perhaps he was foreign, I thought, or had taken a vow of silence. Kim needed no more encouragement. At his nod she ran ahead to the swings. The man continued to work, seemingly oblivious to our presence but I was not comfortable. I swung Kim a few times and then convinced her we had to leave. As we were going the man looked up and smiled briefly; whether the smile approved of our coming or our leaving wasn't clear.

At the savings and loan across from the El-stop, I withdrew $750 from my account. I pocketed fifty and mailed the balance to my checking account. It would cover the rent check I had just sent the company that managed the apartment building.

The tracks dropped below the ground as we approached the Loop and the sound of the wheels on the rails rose to a scream. I pressed my face to the grimy window in an effort to read the signs. Many mornings and evenings Anne had to ride standing up in a crowded car and I wondered how she could manage to exit at the right stop—and where she would end up if she didn't.

We came out on a cement island in the center of a long dreary tunnel. A train was approaching from the opposite direction. The shriek of its wheels caused Kim to cover her ears. I picked her up and hurried toward the stairs. Halfway up the crowded stairwell a man stood, legs apart. He was urinating against the wall. The people descending did not look at the man. They did not glance at Kim and me either as we passed beside him and the strong sudden smell.

I held tight to my daughter until we arrived on the crowded sunlit sidewalk. I was confused and stopped to determine our direction. A large man carrying a package in front of him like a shield nearly knocked us over. Without a backward glance the man regained his stride and moved way. I carried Kim to an eddy of calm beside a store window.

"Is Mommy here?"

"Somewhere," I said, looking around. Either we had gotten off at the wrong stop or we had gone up the wrong set of stairs. Nothing made sense according to Anne's directions. An old woman wearing a black coat was standing beside us. She had two shopping bags leaning against the wall of the store and a red perfectly round circle of rouge on her left cheek.

"Excuse me," I said to the woman. "Do you know the direction to La Salle Street?"

The woman did not respond. I was mumbling.

"Excuse me. Do you know the direction to La Salle Street?"

The circle of rouge crinkled and the old woman turned and stared at me. Her lips were folded in at the corners and the pupils of her moist eyes seemed to have faded as if they had been a long time under water.

"La Salle?" She reached toward me with her hand.

I stepped back, tightening my grip on Kim. Then instantly I felt shamed. The woman had been reaching out to Kim; her lips had begun to unfold into a smile.

"Three blocks." The reaching hand pointed and the face turned away as the lips folded back in like a flower retiring for the night.

"Thank you," I effused. "Thank you very much." The circle did not respond.

Anne's firm occupied the 19th, 20th and 21st floors. Anne was on the 19th, the bottom of the ladder. The elevator door swung open and we were standing in front of a receptionist who was seated in an arched alcove, like a saint awaiting her candles.

"May I help you?"

"We've come to see Anne Winter. I'm her husband and this is Kimberly, her daughter."

"Pardon?"

"Anne Winter, please."

"Your name, please."

"Jason Winter."

She picked up her phone and said something. "She'll be with you in a moment, Mr. Winter."

She seemed to be staring at my cap. Her voice was not nasal, I noticed. Perhaps they kept the one who answered the phone in a cage out back.

Anne was in a good mood. Descending in the elevator with Kim in her arms, she said to me, "Well, do you want your surprise now, or after we eat?"

"Surprise?"

"Oh, just a little something." She winked, and then after a moment added, "Now that I think of it, we should eat first. Yes, definitely. Let's eat first."

We chose a small place around the corner, a busy nook with clattering dishes, with cigarette smoke and people entering and leaving and talking about debentures. Anne ordered soup and a salad, as if she were trying to lose weight when to my eyes it was obvious she needed to put some on. I had a hot beef and half of Kim's hamburger, when I should have had soup and salad.

"You should stay down this afternoon and go to the Art Institute," Anne suggested.

"Where is it from here?"

"Not far. It's over on Michigan. You've always talked about going."

"I know, but I don't think I'd enjoy it much with you-know-who. She gets fussy in the afternoon."

"They might have strollers to rent. Maybe she would just fall asleep."

The place had me spooked. I had been reading a book about the history of Chicago that I got from the library. I thought now of Armour and Swift, the McCormicks, Marshall Field and Montgomery Ward. Ambition was the wind for which this city was famous. Acquisition, manipulation, control. I looked toward the street at the people passing with hurried strides and certain direction. Around this corner had walked men whose wills were so alloyed with audacity they had dared to corner the world's flow of grain. Sometimes they succeeded. It was relentless. It blew cold in all seasons and in this clattering establishment with the smell of the grill I felt beaten by it. I wanted to put cotton in my ears and hoist my collar up around my neck.

"It was just a thought," my wife said, looking up from her salad. "That's all."

"We get out," I said without conviction. "We shop. We go to the library. Sometimes we walk around." I wanted to tell her about the private park we had found, about the strangely quiet man and the wonderful grounds, but I decided against it. I had the sense suddenly that she wouldn't understand, not the way I would want her to. She would ask questions; her mind would insist on analysis, as if it were a problem that needed solving. I did not want it solved. The longer it remained unsolved the better. "I wrote a check for the rent this morning," I added.

"From your savings? You don't have to do that. I'm making plenty of money. I can pay that stuff."

"You've always paid it before and I want to make a contribution."

"But you take care of her all day. That's worth a tremendous consideration. It's not just the money we save in child care. It's the fact that she's home."

"I know. I just feel better when I help pay. What I really should do is sell some work."

Anne was unconvinced. "I don't feel good about you spending your savings on that. It was the same with the TV. We're in this together, love. I wish you would accept the fact that what you're doing is as valuable as what I'm doing. The money I make is the result of both our efforts, don't you see?"

"I just want to pay my share."

Anne sighed. "Well, I still think we should consider a sitter three or four hours a day. That would give you a chance to do some work and peddle your things in the stores."

"I was hoping to approach a few stores when we go up to Wisconsin."

"Okay, but there are thousands of stores around here. The market must be virtually limitless." She blew on a spoonful of chowder and nodded toward Kim. "More time has passed and I think she'll be all right. What do you think about a sitter?"

"It might be a hassle," I said absently. In Carbondale we had a sitter; she was a friend and she had two small children of her own. It was like a second home for Kim. It seemed natural there.

A man at the next table was talking about something that had happened on the bus that morning. At a busy intersection the driver got out and walked away leaving the engine running and everyone sitting in their seats.

"Finally we all got off and walked to the next bus stop," the man said. "It was crazy."

"Nobody gives adequate notice anymore," said the man seated across from him.

"I'll think about it," I said, stalling. "About a sitter."

"Jenny was a sitter." Kim looked up from the scribbles she was making on her place mat.

"That's right," Anne said, smiling. "Jenny was your friend, wasn't she?"

"Todd too, Rosie too." Kim named Jenny's children.

"That's right," Anne said again. She looked at me and winced. "Sometimes I feel like I dragged the two of you up here just so I could pursue my own selfish goals."

"Anne. . . ."

She leaned forward. She was wearing a pale blue-colored blouse open at the throat and the delicate silver necklace that I had gotten for her years before. My eyes were captured for a moment by the little tear-shaped pendant that rested just below the base of her throat. I had gotten the necklace in Centralia at a fair I was working the summer after we met. She was in Chicago visiting her parents and I was lonely and thinking of her. I traded two pairs of sandals for it, one pair for the woman in the next booth who made the necklace, the other for her husband. All this came back to me in the second it took for her eyes to lift from the table to my own.

"Are we lost, hun?" she asked, suddenly.

Her manner was dramatic, intense and I started to stammer.

"No. . . ." Then I found myself laughing nervously. "No, of course not. We're together aren't we?"

"That's what I need to know. Are we?"

I took her left hand in mine and held it. I felt the wedding band and turned it gently with my thumb.

"You graduated. It was time to move on. We agreed on it. I believe we did the right thing. We're going to make it here."

"Tobey too, Chiss too," Kim said now. She had passed on to Jenny's pets. It is true that she loved Jenny and her family.

"I keep telling myself that, but I'm not sure I'm convinced." Anne withdrew her hand and lit a cigarette. "I'm scared."

Husband as burden. As lump of clay that needs to be moved about, set up and shaped to fit the occasion.

"That's my fault, not yours. I've just been kind of . . . jolted, I guess. Stunned. But we're on course. We're doing what we should be doing. I just need some time to work my way through it."

A man at the counter turned around and was talking to the two men at the next table. "If Bryne was a man," he said, "she'd fire all of 'em."

Anne frowned through the smoke. "I hope you don't take this present the wrong way."

"Present?"

"The surprise I was talking about. I wanted to get you something and I know there are going to be situations where. . . . Oh well, lets go do it."

The surprise was a new suit, and that was a surprise. I had not worn a suit since our wedding, and that had been a rented tux. We crowded together in front of the triple mirror. My sandaled feet protruded pale and lumpy from the slacks. Kim admired herself. I was examined from all angles. The salesman, looking smug and slapping the end of his tape against the perfect crease running down his right thigh, said to Anne: "You're absolutely right. The blue in the fabric does set off his eyes."

By now Anne had lost all her reservations. "You can wear the coat with your gray slacks," she said enthusiastically, "and if we get you a light-blue jacket you could have three separate outfits." She tugged at the hem of the coat and then straightened the lapels.

Back on the crowded sidewalk, after we had told the

salesman we wanted to think it over, she was concerned again that I was going to misunderstand.

"I don't want you to feel pushed. Am I doing that? Am I making you feel like I want you to change? That's not what I want, Jason. You should do whatever you're comfortable doing and wear what you want. It's just that I remembered how the other night you said you felt embarrassed. I wasn't embarrassed, but I just thought you might want the choice, that's all."

"Yeah, you're right." A siren wailed and at the corner a policeman was directing traffic with his whistle.

"I can't hear you," Anne said. We were walking back toward her building.

"No, you're right," I said again. "I should have the choice. It's a nice present. A nice suit."

"Then I should call and tell him we'll take it?"

"Yeah, let's do that."

Moments later she was gone, sealed behind the sliding elevator doors.

I thought about when my dad got religion. Some born again type at the proving grounds had convinced him to go to a revival meeting and my dad bought the store. For about a year after that we went to church every Sunday, and Dad was off on Wednesday nights to prayer meeting. He was always carrying his Bible around, struggling with the language of King James. He bought us suits and snap-on ties so we would look proper at Sunday service. My father had a ruddy outdoor look. With the white shirt tight at the neck, the shiny tie, he appeared choked and crimson, as though the struggle to overcome a life-time of imagined sin left him no time to breathe properly.

I carried Kim back to State Street and then down into the tunnel with a rush of people. At a stand near the tracks I bought a package of red licorice which I shared with her. Usually I didn't give her candy but I knew it would occupy her during the trip and if she stayed awake until we got home, I could work while she napped.

10

Saturday morning Liz called to say that she and Gretchen had the use of a truck and were going to move. It was not the best of days. Anne and I had so little time together as it was. And there was laundry to do.

"Give me a second, Liz." I covered the speaker and explained the situation to Anne.

"I don't see why Bill can't do it." Anne was not happy.

"I don't know. Maybe there's something he had to do. There's not much stuff. They're not comfortable with the truck."

Anne frowned. She held Kim's blanket and the bedding from her crib. "It can't be done another day?"

"The truck's on loan, from a friend. I think I'd like to do it. Want to come along?"

"No, I'll straighten up here. You'll be back by the afternoon, won't you? There's the dinner at Mom's."

"If it's a problem," Liz said. "The trouble is Eric. He has a new friend and he's putting a lot of pressure on Gretchen."

"It's okay," I said, looking at Anne. "We just have to organize a few things."

The two women were waiting in front of the apartment. They had managed to park the truck only two doors away. Gretchen was sitting on a red bean-bag chair at the edge of the sidewalk drinking a glass of orange juice.

"You'd think he'd offer to help," she said, "if it's so goddamned important to him."

The apartment showed signs of the severed union: gaps on the bookshelf, a few albums leaning sadly in the rack, drawers in the bedroom and bath hanging open and empty. The space smelled of cigarettes and cooked cabbage. On the walls were posters of dead gods stroking their power sticks: Hendrix his guitar, Joplan her microphone.

"I haul them around," Gretchen said. She removed the thumb tacks with my knife and carefully rolled the posters. "I tell myself that some day they'll be valuable, but really, I think I just enjoy carrying old pain."

The brass bed was hers, a double. We wrestled down the mattress, heavy and tricky on the landings, and stowed it against one side of the truck bed. Most of the kitchen equipment went, including a set of copper-bottom pans a handsome salesman sold her the first week after she left home at the age of eighteen. Gretchen related the incident wryly as another guidepost on the trail to her present understanding of the human male. Since Eric's stereo was the more elaborate we found hers dusty and buried in the back of the bedroom closet.

"I did these curtains," she said. "Shopped for the fabric, everything." She had a sewing machine, shopping bags full of yarn and cloth. Her art was soft sculpture and samples hung from fish line around the apartment.

We were descending to the street in single file, arms filled, when I encountered a couple at the foot of the stairs. I moved to one side so they could pass. From behind me Gretchen began to shout:

"Eric, you son of a bitch! I said four and it's two fucking thirty. Get that twit out of here!"

Eric, thick lipped, his dark hair severely parted with Elvis sideburns and an aura of after-shave, was reduced by this blast to looking smug. His companion appeared terrified.

"You always did come too soon, you useless prick! Get out of here!" Gretchen raised a box of books above her head as if to heave them down the stairwell.

The woman tugged at Eric's arm and they moved backward toward the door. He behaved solicitously toward her, as if to say, "Now you understand what I've been talking about."

"Get a vibrator, twit," Gretchen shouted as they left "You're going to need it!"

Later when everything was moved into the new apartment we sat on folded blankets on the hardwood floor of the living room and shared a six pack. We were enjoying that easy camaraderie that comes after shared physical work. I knew Anne was waiting and I should get back to her but I couldn't bring himself to move. It seemed that I had been doing nothing but waiting lately; waiting for her to come home from the office, waiting for her to stop working and come to bed.

Gretchen was being philosophical. "Changing digs," she said blowing smoke out the corner of her mouth. "I should write a book. Rule Number One: Never hold a yard sale before you move in with a man. Pack everything in there I don't care how cramped. Maybe after ten years you could sell it off, but not before. You'll want it back, believe me, you'll want it back." She tossed an ash in the direction of an empty beer can. "Everything I own is in here and the place looks empty."

"It'll be fun," Liz said. "We'll do the second-hands."

"You wouldn't believe the things I sold off for a song just so I could move in with that creep. I had a platform rocker, walnut. I had a couch that an old lady only sat on on Sunday afternoons. Really," she added when I snickered, "this couch had been recovered twelve years before and it looked like new. I had a floor lamp with a marble base that lit up. There was a three-way bulb in the center, three one-ways set out below that could be turned on individually; their bases had this fake wax dripping down the sides and the shade had a little fringe around the bottom. It was a goddamned carnival, that lamp, but Eric said it would jar with his track lights."

"Where'd you meet Eric?" I asked. I was thinking of what Anne had said about Nora meeting men in bars.

"That's Rule Number Two. Never move in with a man you meet at a rock concert. I knew that before but I made an exception. Bad mistake. Rock concerts lead to disaster. I prefer galleries and art museums. I go to the Institute and stand in front of the Ivan Albright's. The comparison does wonders. Or you can discuss the social significance of Calder. What does it really mean to suspend things not from a wall but from the ceiling?" She shook her head. "But Eric liked my sculptures. He's the one who wanted to hang them around. It probably would have ended the same way if I'd met him in church."

During this last sentence her voice trailed away. The cigarette paused inches from her mouth. She stared at a barren corner of the room and allowed a canine to sink into her lower lip.

Liz put a hand on her shoulder and I suddenly became aware of what Liz had obviously known all along: The whole thing had been a sham, from the rage to the detached acceptance. Courageous and convincing, but a sham none the less. Still, Gretchen was not defeated. I watched as she sipped her beer and drew on her cigarette. She had a sense of solid persistence about her. You could leave her at mid-task and know it would be finished.

"The real problem was his hollandaise sauce," she said now, more to Liz than to me. "Eric makes a great hollandaise sauce and on Sunday mornings he would bring me eggs Benedict in bed. The quality of that sauce confused me. Unconsciously I assumed that a man who could cook like a woman would have the sensibility of one." She snuffed out the cigarette and slowly shook her head. "He was a disaster in the kitchen. He walked away like a surgeon and I was forever after him to clean up his messes." She sighed and looked at me. "I was probably getting too much cholesterol anyway."

About four-fifteen I bounced out of Gretchen's new apartment feeling pretty good with a couple cans of mover's juice under my belt and the knowledge that I had done a good deed. Plenty of time to return home, shower and get the family over to Nora's by six.

Then I ran into the parking problem. Chrome against chrome wherever I looked. Exhaust pipes sticking out into the street, bumpers edging into the redzones. Even the little secret nitches I had stored in my memory for desperate times were jammed. I circled and wove patterns through the three or four block area around the apartment building for a half hour. Finally I pulled into a service station and called Anne from the pay phone.

"Where are you?" She was clearly exasperated.

"At the Shell. I been in a holding pattern for half an hour."

"We have to leave in twenty minutes, Jason. There were plenty of spaces right outside most of the day."

I took this as a commentary on my late arrival and decided to let it pass.

"I'd say, grab me some clothes and come on down, but I have to shower. I been working."

"No, Kim, you can't do that!" Then to me: "She's driving me nuts. I haven't had a coherent thought all day long."

"She's probably a little gassed at having you to herself all day."

"Is that it?"

"Got me. Are you ready?"

"We're both ready. That's part of the problem. She's wearing the new dress Mom gave her, the pink and white. She insisted on putting it on an hour ago. And white-tights? In the middle of summer? The knees are already brown."

Her dad's grunge gene, I thought, alive and well.

"Look, Anne. Why don't you bring her out to the curb? I'll come over and you can wait in the car while I run up and do my thing. Do a couple of laps if you have to. Okay?"

"Jesus, that's crazy."

"Best I can do. Five minutes?"

"All right."

When I pulled up Kim, brown knees and all, was jumping up and down and laughing in the middle of an empty parking space. Right in front of the apartment. Anne looked sullen. I noticed two other spots further down the street.

"It was packed ten minutes ago," I said lamely.

"Jason, this is important. Mom wants us there on time." Then, as I was running toward the door, "She said to dress 'appropriately,' whatever that means."

Anne and Kim were standing around in the bedroom when I came out of the shower.

"I sure hope Norman turns out all right. But I'm worried. He seems a little weird."

"Weird?"

"The whole thing has developed so quickly and he wants to be with her all the time. Of course Mother finds that flattering, but deep down I think she's bothered by it. The other day he sent flowers to the bank. Can you believe that? And every night he has a different plan, a movie, a dinner theater. He's already talking about season tickets to the Lyric Opera."

"The opera?"

I told myself not to be annoyed by Nora's comment about appropriate dress. The evening was obviously important to her and to Anne. The suit wasn't ready yet. I took down the green double-knit slacks Anne had gotten me one Christmas. I tried them on but they were very tight. Maybe, I thought, with a wide belt I could leave the snap open.

"He's into high culture," Anne was saying, "and, according to Mom, very handsome."

"He owns a tire store?"

"He manages it. It's his brother apparently who owns it. It's all kind of hazy in my mind. And here's something else that bothers me. Whatever he wants to do involves drinking in some way. Not a lot, but some. The night they went to see 'Manhattan,' he passed Mom a pint of Southern Comfort while the Gershwin introduction was still playing."

I decided to not respond to that, though it did occur to me that Nora could have refused.

I was strapping on the belt when Kim entered the room, carrying Emmy. The cat always went limp whenever Kim picked her up; she hung there now purring.

"Can Emmy go too?"

"No, honey," Anne said, "Grandmother does not like cats."

"Is grandmother allergic to cats?" I asked.

"No, it's just that they always climb all over her. There can be twenty people in the room and if a cat walks in, it goes straight to Mom and jumps up on her lap."

"They always pick the most uptight person in the

room," I said without thinking.

"Jason, that is ridiculous."

We stopped at a liquor store on the way. I picked up a bottle of wine and a stick of beef jerky. I ate the jerky before returning to the car. Nora's food was always good and it was attractively arranged, but it was never enough. My mother used to cook huge amounts of food. Then she served leftovers three or four nights a week.

The man standing in the doorway beside Nora had the look of a United States Senator. Not a real United States Senator but one you might see in a soap opera, a man with silver hair, a straight nose, square jaw and something horrible hidden in his past. In addition to the magnificent head, Norman possessed a rich baritone voice. I could tell that Anne was charmed. She was suddenly more animated, pulling out a cigarette (which Norman lit—he had the fastest hand on a lighter I had ever seen) and saying with a quick smile, "Mother has told me so much about you."

"Your mother has swept me away."

Nora wore an uneasy smile as she made the introductions. "And this is Jason."

"Ah yes, the craftsman. Did you fashion that cap I saw you wearing before you got out of the car?"

Apparently I had not taken it off soon enough. We stood in awkward silence for a moment, as if honoring our coming together. Finally Norman suggested martinis. It almost made me laugh. Martinis had been the epitome of "Them" to Randy, the suburban golf-playing Babbitts of the world.

Norman poured and stirred, as ritualistic as a priest at Mass. He served the drinks and then glided toward the stereo.

"Let me offer a side or two of Vivaldi."

Vivaldi? I had poked my way through Nora's record collection. It consisted of Percy Faith, scores from a few musicals and a couple of old Mitch Miller sing-alongs. No Vivaldi. Take Norman, it seemed, and you got a record collection and a bartender's guide to good drinking.

Anne was off and running with the *Thayer* case. That was the one involving the rotten heads of lettuce in a line of semi-trailers piggy-backed on flat cars on a siding outside of Lincoln, Nebraska. The question was whether the fault lay with the shipper, the purchaser, the trucking company or the railroad. Anne's firm represented the purchaser. I had heard the details a dozen times and so I concentrated on the martini. It was surprisingly delicious. I wanted to gulp it down. To control myself I bobbed the olive up and down a few times and watched the tiny bubbles adhere to the sides.

Nora came out of the kitchen with a platter of hors d'oeuvres which she placed on the coffee table near Norman and five feet away from where Kim and I were curled up on the stuffed chair. I put the olive in my mouth and chewed it as slowly as I could. Norman asked Anne if she knew Frank DeSilva. She didn't.

"Brian Cohen?"

"No, I don't think so."

"Lawyers," Norman explained. "They're all lawyers. You'll meet them."

My eyes kept returning to the platter of hors d'oeuvres. There were strips of celery (their cavities filled with what appeared to be a soft cheese), olives, sandwich wedges and a few tiny sausages speared with toothpicks. No one was paying any attention to them.

Norman said that he once worked for a railroad and that it was not uncommon for a flat car to get misplaced. "It could sit on a siding for days and no one would know where it was."

The first martini I had ever drunk was nearly finished. Norman's was gone. Norman was chewing his swizzle stick.

"Those martini's are all right, Norman," I said during a pause in the conversation. "Any drink that tastes this good and in the process gives you something to eat is hard to criticize."

Norman smiled. "A splendid concoction, I agree. I'm ready for another if the rest of you are."

"I'm fine thank you," Anne said, "but please help yourself."

Nora handed over her glass. She was seated beside Norman on the couch wearing a bright-yellow, sleeveless dress. She looked happy, and it occurred to me as I looked at her that Nora was all right. I have to watch myself, I thought. I tend to get paranoid about things. Why should I be irritated because of where she had placed the platter of hors d'oeuvres? Nora had been through a lot and I should be more tolerant. I got up, a little unsteadily, and grabbed a celery stick and a couple of sausages.

"Nora," I said, "you look very nice this evening."

Nora positively blushed, and in the charged atmosphere of an unexpected compliment, Anne beamed at me. I tilted back toward the chair. Yes, I decided, Nora was all right, and it was good to be here in Chicago meeting different people and drinking things like martinis. Everything would work out just fine if I could only relax behind it. That was my problem. I just had to relax and go with the flow of things. We had left one life behind and we had started a new one and it would be fine. I sat down and looked at my lovely wife. Her legs were sheathed in dark hose and she sat there with them crossed so damned erotically that Norman was continually glancing at them.

She was a wonderful woman and I loved her and wanted her. I felt bad now that I had run out to help Gretchen move and then sat around drinking beer while Anne was home working; she had to work so hard all week.

"My dear," I said now, "why don't you tell Norman and your mom about the interrogatories and the other work you've been doing in the *Creative Builders'* case?" I had heard even more about the *Creative Builders'* case than about *Thayer*, but it was more interesting. It seemed wonderfully funny, especially in my present state, that some rich bastard had built an eight story office building on a piece of land that it turned out he didn't own.

Anne explained how she had been preparing a complex set of interrogatories that she was going to present to Ed Peterson on Monday. Ed Peterson was a senior partner.

"I spent several years as a realtor in South Shore," Norman said as he served the second round. "I can believe anything."

"Well, you can believe this, Norman," I said, taking a sip, "you make a great martini."

Anne laughed happily. "How can you tell? You've never had one before in your life."

"That's exactly why I decided to have a second, dear. I wanted to be sure." I could not help giggling at the cleverness of my comeback. It was as if someone were running around inside my body turning on all the lights.

Midway though the second martini Anne and Nora departed for the kitchen. I wanted to go out to the back yard to check on Nora's old apple tree. Norman agreed to join me, but before we left he refilled his glass.

"I sometimes wish we had a house instead of an apartment," I said when we were outside. "Just a small yard like this would help. An apple tree, maybe a plot of garden."

"I had a lovely place up near Elgin," Norman said. "Full acre, circular drive. Twenty-three oaks on the property. Squirrels running around. It was lovely really."

"Did you have a garden?"

"Flowers. Every spring and fall out there with the bulbs. My ex-wife let it go to hell when she got it. An absolute crime, really, the way she let that place deteriorate."

"Divorce?" We reached the apple tree. It felt better if I held onto a branch.

"Yes, she ended up with most everything. I was going through some difficulties at the time and let it all go. Eventually she sold the place but she didn't get what it was worth. Beautiful woman, but hard, and not all that capable when you come right down to it. The way she abandoned that lovely yard. That saddens me more than anything."

"Nora has always let these apples rot," I said, "but I hope to make some apple butter and a few pies this fall."

"Scrimp on the water," Norman volunteered. "That's the secret of a good crust. Chill everything before you start and be a miser with the water." Norman scrimped on water, and he scrimped on vermouth, but I doubted just then that he ever scrimped on gin.

Dusk was coming on and the lawn smelled wonderful. I dropped down onto my knees to smell the grass and nearly fell over. Not every part of me was arriving at the same place at the same time.

"Jason, do you mind if I ask you a personal question?"

"No, Norman, of course not." I had rolled over onto my back and stretched out my arms and legs. I could look up through the branches toward the sky. The apples hung there like promises, like the way when you were a child some future event, a trip, say, or a birthday, would hang untouchable before your vision. I thought that thought, then I thought how strange that thought was. Then I tried to remember what the original thought had been.

"Are you acquainted with this Charlie fellow whom Nora was involved with for a while?"

I told Norman that I knew Charlie. Norman had taken a position against the trunk of the apple tree. His martini was gone and he was converting his swizzle stick to rubble with his teeth. It was hard, once you looked closely, to think of him as a senator. He had removed his sport coat when we came outside and his arms were pale and thin with bulging veins and absolutely no hair. From my position on the ground, his neck seemed gaunt and weak. It was as if he had devoted so much energy to creating a large impressive head that the rest of him had been neglected. And there was a studiedness about the man. He was, I decided in my semi-blotted state, frightfully aware of what others might be thinking about him.

"Do you think Nora was in love with him?" Norman asked after a moment.

"I don't know, Norman. She was sad when he left. What can I say?"

"Well, I intend to marry Nora in the next few months, but if she's in love with Charlie. . . ."

"Marry?" I started to sit up, but then lay slowly back in the grass. It felt better if I lay still. "How long have you known each other?"

"Two weeks, Tuesday," Norman said.

"Isn't that kind of short? I mean to be talking about marriage?" My mind was trying to calculate whether the strangeness of all this was coming from the alcohol or from what Norman was saying. Supposedly, some people can drink a couple of these things at lunch and then go back to work.

"Nora's a wonderful woman. It's hard at my age to

find a woman with her qualities." Norman had pulled out his lighter and was flicking it on and off. As the evening light faded the orange flame became more predominate. The man must go through a lighter a day, I thought.

"Well, all I know is that Charlie went back to his wife. So I guess the field is open."

"I like to think I have qualities that Nora could value." A senatorial smile appeared on Norman's face. "And I'm not aware of any other contenders, are you?"

"Not at the moment, Norman." A couple of crickets had begun to perform nearby. If I had not been so hungry and were Norman not continually flicking his lighter on and off, I could have spent the night in that spot. The smell of damp grass, the sound of crickets. I saw myself lying beside Anne at the edge of a pond on a warm evening in southern Illinois.

"I have set my goal," Norman said, "and I intend to achieve it. I plan a late October wedding. October is a beautiful month."

October, the month of the bar results. I let that thought slide. The sounds had become a symphony: Norman's voice lyrical and rich, the crickets, and behind it all, deep and unforgiving, the distant roar of traffic. Then, just before Anne shook me, there was a moment when I saw the music being made. Maybe it came from the martinis, or maybe it was a dream, but Norman's voice had become a rich brown, the color and texture of fine leather, while the crickets' song was lavender, like the clouds above a setting sun, and then, just for an instant, the sound of the traffic melted into the action of the earth turning green and free on its axis.

Her strongest prejudices confirmed, Nora said, "Go back outside and brush the grass clippings from your clothes."

I must have looked miserable; even Kim offered to help. When I returned the lights were so bright I had to squint.

Norman was pouring large glasses of wine. He announced in his modulated voice, as though I were not present, "I would never have realized what was happening, had he not started snoring."

They were all seated at the table. Nora had served my portion of the stroganoff. It was minuscule.

11

On Monday night the trip home took Anne exactly thirty minutes. In addition to her briefcase and purse, she was carrying a box that she set on the armrest of the couch and a bag containing the new suit.

"Beer?"

"Sounds wonderful."

I brought in two, and because Kim had snuggled onto Anne's lap, I retrieved her cigarettes and lighter.

"Mother called today," she said, kicking off her pumps. "Right when I was getting myself together for the conference with Peterson. I couldn't get her off the phone. She's all depressed."

"The car?"

"No, it's Norman. After we left Saturday night, Mom told him she wanted to spend Sunday alone. She didn't mean anything by it. She was just tired and she had a few things to do before going back to work. Well, last night about midnight he called. She was sound asleep. He was drunk and he wanted to know who she was with."

"Did he suspect Charlie?"

"How did you know?"

"Just a guess."

"He made an ass of himself and she came very close to hanging up on him. Then this morning he called her at work; very apologetic of course. He said he'd been out with friends and the more he drank the more he missed her. Apparently he hadn't seen these people in a long time.

His drinking just got away from him. But it bothered Mom. Tonight they're going out to dinner to talk."

"I told you it wasn't just the martinis. The guy is strange."

Anne was unconvinced. "Well, I liked him. He's intelligent and cultured. Maybe it was just a bad night."

"Just check out his arms. They're the palest, thinnest, most hairless things I've ever seen. Forgotten, that's how they look. Forgotten. The contrast between that man's face and his arms is astonishing."

Anne giggled. "You sound like Vincent Price. What do his arms have to do with anything?"

"The guy's weird, Anne, that's what I'm saying."

Anne didn't want to talk about it anymore. "Maybe it's nothing," she said, turning toward the TV. "You and I were jealous when we first met. Everybody is."

The news had come on and I had to decide whether to stay or leave. The agenda sounded innocuous enough. Chicago had survived a rather quiet day. The weather had been decent, both the Cubs and the Sox had the day off and thus couldn't lose; no one had smeared himself across a major expressway. Another movie was being made in the City and the news people were on the scene filming the filming. In this one a police car crashed through a window of the Civic Center. The news folks never let you down. If there's no actual gore, they run out and film some fiction.

"So, how did it go with Peterson?" I asked during the next commercial.

Anne shrugged. "It was kind of funny, really. I was all excited, but he was on the phone when I got there and didn't even look up."

"That must have been depressing. I know how much time you put in on those interrogatories."

"He'll get back to me after he looks them over."

We ate when the news was over. I finished the dishes and then tried on the new suit. Anne had also gotten me a shirt and tie. The colors matched perfectly. She helped me tie the knot and then hovered around me, tugging and nudging.

"Next we'll get you a pair of shoes," she said.

"What I really need is a haircut."

Anne was on her hands and knees studying the length of the slacks. "I've been thinking you should have it styled. Most men are doing that now."

"I've always liked your haircuts."

"They were crude, and I don't have the time anymore. Put your feet together."

Kim and I left early the next morning for the store. We bought grass seed, fertilizer, a hose and rake. We scuffed up the ground, pulled out the most offending weeds and scattered the goodies around. Then we scuffed it up again and soaked it down. Amateur job all around, and the wrong time of year. The super though seemed pleased. He sat in the doorway strumming his guitar. He let Kim pluck a few strings while I did the work.

The service manager at the dealership was a gravelly-voiced bald-headed man whose defense against the exhaust fumes was a fat, well-chewed cigar.

"Winter? I've got you down for 8:30. It's now 9:20."

"I've been waiting in line," I claimed. That was true, at least for the past twenty minutes. Before that I had been struggling with Kim. She had sensed my urgency and realizing her power had dallied over breakfast. When I tried to put her shoes on, she kept kicking them off. Finally, she had screamed in my ear as I carried her forcibly down the stairs, her shoes in my hand. Now she was tugging at my jeans and telling me she had to pee.

"I've got you down for points and plugs, oil and lube."

"And a valve adjustment."

"What?"

"A valve adjustment. It needs a valve adjustment."

The man looked at his chart. "It says nothing here about a valve adjustment."

"Well, I said that when I called." Kim was squirming beside me. She crossed her legs and used her finger as a plug.

"You're going to have to speak up. I got a line of cars waiting here."

"I said 'valve adjustment' when I called."

The soggy cigar returned to the man's mouth and he scribbled another line on the work order and handed it over for my signature.

"Keys in the car?"

I signed the order and was reaching in my pocket for the keys when I remembered the wiper motor. Engines were roaring, tools clanked against cement. The service manager stared at the line of cars as if they were tanks approaching his bunker. Kim was pulling again at my leather pouch. "Daddy, pee!" I handed over the keys.

The morning passed the way mornings used to pass in grade school during the month of May. We walked the neighborhood, a down-in-the-mouth industrial area, dreary with its buildings of blackened brick, its windows gritty behind cast-iron grates. Kim wanted to be carried and fussed when I insisted that she walk. At a small park a group of boys monopolized the swings. She was intimidated and refused to go down the slide even though it was not in use. I ordered a cup of coffee in a cafe and tried to read the paper. Kim spilled her milkshake. She was embarrassed and burst into tears. We returned to the car dealer. We sat for an hour on the floor of the showroom where salesmen bored and slick waited like web-weaving spiders. Kim exhausted my supply of pennies on the gum machine. She stuffed the bright pieces into her mouth until they formed a lump of greenish-gray corrosive that bulged her cheek.

I was defeated. I consented to her every demand just to keep from having to face her frustration. She was as bored as I was, as ill at ease, and she could sense my distraction. The damn wiper motor; I could not get it out of my mind. That was the main reason I had made the appointment in the first place. I had told them about it when I called and it was not my fault they had not written it down. In Carbondale I wouldn't have let it pass, and I knew I shouldn't let it pass here. I got up and looked through the door into the service department. The service manager was waving his cigar and yelling at a mechanic. I turned away. I could not bring myself to walk in there and deal with it.

We got the car shortly after two and drove to a supermarket. In the parking lot Kim begged for more candy.

"No. You've had a milkshake and too much gum already."

I picked up three packages of frozen vegetables, a ten pound bag of potatoes, some pork steaks, two pounds of hamburger and a bunch of bananas. I had decided to assume more responsibility for the evening meal. I was home. I had the time, and it would free Anne to play with Kim while I cooked. Maybe I wouldn't feel so useless after the day was over.

I pulled into the express line behind a tall old man who was wearing a shiny black suit and a bow tie. The sign above the checker said seven items or less. Surely, I thought, everyone considers a bunch of bananas to be one item. Still, it gave me pause. Just before Kim had spilled her milkshake, I had read an item about a man who had honked his horn at the driver in front of him when the driver failed to move as soon as the light turned green. Instead of driving off, the driver had gotten out of his car, walked back and shot the honker. It sounded to me like the same nut who shot Jimmie Rodriguez. Or were there more than one? And did they shop in supermarkets? And what happened if they decided that a bunch of bananas was eight items instead of one? I could not resist turning to look behind me. A man in a business suit stood with a package of sandwich cookies. Dour, but he hardly seemed the type.

The old man's blotchy hands shook as he counted out his money. His purchase consisted of a box of Ritz crackers, a cube of cheese, a bottle of apple juice, a can of prunes to counteract the cheese and three cans of dog food. I didn't want to think who was going to eat the dog food.

Watching the old man had been a mistake. Kim slipped an arm past my wondering gaze and grabbed a Tootsie Roll from the candy rack. The damn thing looked delicious to me too, but I couldn't let her have more candy.

"No, Kim, you can't have that." She tightened her grip and began to whine. "Dammit, you've already had too many sweets today." I wrestled the candy away and placed it back on the rack. I was furious at the people who stack rows of candy at the checkout line. They know how difficult it is for a parent not to buy something. That's why they do it.

The old man tottered away and I pulled Kim, who was crying now and reaching for more candy, out of the cart so the cashier could slide it into place.

"Nine-thirty-eight," the cashier said a moment later, sultry and bored. To extract my billfold from my pouch I had to set Kim down. While I was paying the cashier, she slid behind me, grabbed a Heath Bar and escaped behind the business man.

"Kim!"

She was grinning happily, tearing at the wrapper. "Little bit, Daddy? Little bit?"

"No!" I grabbed my change from the cashier and jammed it in my pocket. "Dammit, give me that."

Kim stepped farther back into the store; the epression on her face appeared gloatingly smug to me, as if she were thinking: I don't have to listen to you. I saw how you cowered in front of that service manager.

"Dammit, Kim!" I squeezed past the business man who had turned sideways so he could watch the action at both ends of the court. Kim began to run. She was four aisles away by the time I caught her and she had managed to pull the candy free of its wrapper.

"Mine!" she shouted, and defiantly stuffed the end of the bar into her mouth.

There was a moment, just before my hand made contact with the side of her face, when I saw in her eyes and felt in my own a common terror. Never in my daughter's life had I hit her in anger, not a spanking, not a slap on the wrist. But the force of this blow hurled her to the floor and sent the candy bar skittering beneath a display of panty hose on special. Kim lay still for a second and then began to scream.

Two women stood near us. "Poor child," one of them said to the other. "He didn't have to beat her."

Suddenly, my finger was shaking uncontrollably an inch from the woman's nose. "Lady," I shouted, "you shut the fuck up! You hear me? You just shut the fuck up!"

I turned around, people backed away. They looked into their carts or pondered the colorful boxes on the shelves. The business of the supermarket had stopped, stifled by an eerie silence that seemed to hold independent of Kim's wail. I lifted up my daughter and then my groceries, and through that great chasm of silent space, I walked out the door and into the heat of the parking lot.

By the time we reached home, Kim was surprisingly at ease and ready for a nap. I, on the other hand, was filled with a feverish energy that sent me pacing back and forth through the apartment. In the kitchen, and then again in the bathroom, I scoured the porcelain surfaces. I took down the new suit, tried it on, walked around, and then took it off and hung it up again. I returned to the bathroom and through a convoluted ordeal of mirrors and angles, managed to cut my own hair. I marched through the apartment again. I pulled back the drapes and raised the shades, letting in the light. Finally, I pushed up a front window, chipping off the paint seal, and sat down on the sill. The sounds of the street met me with a warm rush, as though all this time they had been waiting, pushing against the glass.

I was still sitting at the open window when Anne got home. She didn't notice the raised shades, the open window or the haircut. Ed Peterson, senior partner, had demolished the interrogatories that she had so carefully prepared. The muscles around her eyes were thick bulges. Her mouth worked with relentless determination.

Except for Kim's chatter and the commerce necessary for the sharing of food, we ate in silence. Until a few weeks before I would without question have confessed to her that I had hit our child. Now I hesitated. The edge that had come between us seemed too sharp to cross with such shameful information. I was baffled myself. And her mind was elsewhere. Her fork made idle work; her responses to Kim were rote, empty of presence. My confessions would only be a burden to her, I decided. I gathered up the dishes and started toward the kitchen.

"Mommy, can we play?"

"Not tonight, honey. There's important work I have to do. Maybe tomorrow night."

"Mommy." Kim was whining.

"Play with her a little bit," I said from the kitchen doorway. I was suddenly irritated at her refusal. While I had cooked the pork steaks she had sat in front of the TV focused on the news. Kim had been in the kitchen with me. "Just play with her a few minutes. Is that too much to ask? You hardly said a word over dinner and now you can't play with your daughter for a few minutes?"

Anne looked to be in sudden pain. "Honey," she said to Kim. "I'm really sorry. I am. But I have to do this." She turned toward me now, eyes pleading. "Peterson wants the interrogatories back in the morning, and he wants them right this time."

We stared at each other a moment. Then I said, "Come on, Kim, you can pour in the soap."

"Thank you." Anne seemed on the brink of tears. She hugged Kim. "Tomorrow night we can play all you want. Maybe we'll paint or build towers. Whatever you want, all right?"

Kim was noncommittal. Tomorrow night was a long way off.

The dishes were finished and Kim was in bed. I went to the kitchen for a beer. Anne was still at the dining table, her papers spread before her. On my way back she reached out and touched my arm.

"I'm sorry."

"You don't have to apologize."

"I haven't had much to give lately."

"She'll survive. We both will."

Anne reached for my hand and held it. "You're being wonderful." I could only shake my head. The pain of what had happened that afternoon caused me to close my eyes.

"You're pissed," she said, "and I can't blame you. You have every right to be pissed. Kim too."

"You should get your work done now." This is the time to tell her, I thought. But I didn't. Something had moved inside me. Something new and strange. I was uncertain, unwilling to trust my reactions. I was not up to heart-to-heart discourse. I wanted to forget the whole thing.

"It's that damn suit, isn't it?" Anne brought up her hands and covered her face. Her body was suddenly quivering in silent undulating sobs. "You think I want to change you. I'm making a terrible mess of everything. You're miserable. Mom's not happy. Kim feels abandoned, and Peterson laughed at me. He sat there reading my interrogatories and laughed." She picked her cigarette off the ash tray, took a drag and snuffed it out. "Why am I putting us through all this? What's the point?"

"Anne, you had a bad day, that's all. You'll show the bastard."

"Well, I do think I'm on the right track now," she said, calmer. "I talked to Wollan and he gave me some clues."

"Then get it together. And let me know when you're done. There's something I want to show you."

"What do you mean?"

I started back toward the living room. "Do your work, Anne. I'm going in here and drink my beer and watch the tube."

It was nearly eleven when we stepped quietly out on the landing and gently closed the back door. The sliding dead bolt had a reassuring heaviness about it. The alley smelled of dew and faintly of exhaust fumes.

"Lead forth, oh great explorer." Her work finished Anne was in high spirits.

Cars were jammed bumper to bumper along the curbs, their colors distorted by the street lights. A figure hurried into an apartment building. A cat ran across the street a half block ahead of us.

The gate was ajar just as it had always been in the day time. Anne was teasing, coy. She snuggled close and we passed through together, and then down the darkened path. I moved ahead cautiously to keep from tripping in the dark while from behind Anne fondled the seat of my pants and chortled breathily. At the edge of the bushes, I stopped. There was a yard lamp in the center set on a pole. Its rays reached out and touched one of the benches and a portion of the swing set. Her arms around me, Anne peered over my shoulder

"What's that?"

"The rabbit," I said. "It's part of the scenery." It was feeding at the dim edge of the light, seemingly secure.

"Have you named it?"

"We call it Rabbit." The house was dark, the gray porch empty. I wondered if the man lived in the house.

"You guys are filled with imagination," Anne said. "So, what else do you do here beside name rabbits?" She had loosened the belt of my pants; now her hand slid inside my jeans.

"Well, Kim swings and goes down the slide. I sit on the bench, enjoy the smells."

"There must be more than that." Her fingers were cool velvet, her voice urgent.

"Well, there's the rabbit. We look for the rabbit. Kim's gotten very good at spotting it. And there's the caretaker, Michael. He doesn't speak but once he wrote his name on a piece of paper and gave it to me. He may be foreign. We smile at each other. I think it pleases him to see Kim here." My being had come to center on her fingers.

"So, that's it?"

"I'm afraid that's all I have to offer," I said as we moved into the deep shadow off the path.

"Well, I'm impressed," Anne said, and we both tried to stifle our giggles.

Desire had focused my discordant energies and made me strong. I recognized that there was an element of compensation in all this. Anne was in a crude sense rewarding me for keeping Kim off her back, but for the moment at least, I was beyond tabulating accounts. It was fine outdoor love with the senses tuned and set out like sentinels. The range of temperatures on the surface of her body was dramatic: cool at the shoulders, warm inches away at the base of her throat, cool again across her back, damp and heated around her breasts. I told her I loved her and it was true.

Afterward we lay quietly looking toward the pole lamp. The rabbit had moved closer; it was less than twenty feet away, secure in its sanctuary. I remembered then killing many rabbits as a boy. We had hunted them, and for a while my brother and I had raised domestics in hutches with wire floors at the back of the garage. Father taught us how to kill them quickly by stretching them across the knee and snapping their necks with a single jerk.

It was time to tell her. I wanted to tell my wife that I had bashed our daughter. I wanted to get it off my chest. I was thinking about how I would phrase it when Anne broke the silence.

"I think I'm beginning to understand."

"What's that?"

"This is Peterson's little trial by fire. His interrogatory torture. You see, the thing about a written interrogatory is that the person responding has days to think about his answer. He can discuss it with his lawyer and together they can fashion a response that both answers the question and reveals nothing of value. It's not like a question on a deposition or in a courtroom where the person has to answer on the spur of the moment. That's why an interrogatory has to be so carefully worded. Otherwise you get no information. And Peterson uses this device to test new associates."

"I see." My face was inches above the grass. Looking toward the light I could see that the leaves of grass were covered with tiny glistening drops of dew. My mind flashed now with particular kills; a rabbit hurtling across snowy corn rows, another tumbling bloody into the bank of a hill. Each picture raised a small wave of nausea, like dust long undisturbed.

"Peterson's mind is like a razor. In all the firm he may be the best trial lawyer. Some say Huntley's as good, maybe better. Huntley's got this easy charm that goes well with juries. But Peterson's a lawyer's lawyer. His mind is like a razor. He started reading my interrogatoies out loud and he just laughed. Just sat there and laughed. The bastard's good and he's got no mercy, none." The realization seemed to please her.

12

Days passed. They passed without regard for what I thought of them, or the use I made or failed to make of them. We decided to go to Wisconsin over Labor Day weekend and I worked sporadically on leather to build my inventory. I did the work during odd hours. Sometimes I worked in the early mornings and often during Kim's afternoon naps. I rarely had the discipline to work in the evenings after she was in bed and the dishes finished. I accumulated a modest stockpile but I possessed no inclination to venture into what I thought would be a rough and tumble Chicago market. Nor did I place an ad that would encourage strangers to come to our home. We reached the middle of August and my savings continued to drop.

I thought about Wisconsin while I worked, and in the idle moments a bulbous fantasy formed and dissipated, re-formed and disbursed again: Maybe when Anne saw Wisconsin she would want to move there. No, the idea was ridiculous and I put it aside. Then later I would find myself thinking about it again. We could rent a building. One side would house her law office, the other my leather shop. No, the idea was totally unrealistic. Anne was at home in Chicago. Her mother was nearby. The firm a great opportunity. This was where we were going to make it.

On the tube one afternoon I saw a film about wildebeests. It had to do with the migration of a herd of what was said to contain a million animals. I came in after it had started and Kim lost interest before it was over, so I never learned where the migration had begun or what its destination was. It was just footage of this seemingly infinite number of animals moving like a running cloud across the landscape. The proportions were staggering: the size of the herd, the speed at which it traveled, the devastation of the environment, the death, the raw vitality of exposed life. At one point a number of animals were caught in a flooded river. Many were swept away in the brown waters. Some managed to reach a crowded bit of land, where, while the water rose, their efforts to free themselves sank them deeper into the mud. I was struck that they never thought to not struggle. They struggled until they freed themselves or died. Their struggle was magnificent. I sat in the lazy comfort of my living room and I thought about what separated me from the wildebeest: Among the wildebeest there was no evidence of self pity.

The new grass began to emerge in thin little blades. It rose from the earth, pale and sturdy, vulnerable and brave. As Kim and I stood and looked at it, I felt an unreasonable delight.

One afternoon while Kim was napping and I was working with leather I heard a pounding outside. There was the super hobbling around with one hand on his back and a hammer in the other. He was putting in stakes and stringing a line to keep people off the tender blades.

When I went down, he said. "Speaking of grass. You got any?"

"What do you mean?"

"Dope. You know, fucking, mari-jew-wana."

"Me? No. Why?"

The superintendent did not believe me. "Come on man. We're into landscaping here. You can trust me." He came close and made exaggerated sniffing sounds around my neck. He had me. He knew what I was about.

The superintendent smiled slyly. "Have I complained about the cat?"

"What cat?"

"The one with the broken tail."

I stammered and the superintendent chuckled gleefully.

"If you want to hide a cat, man, you got to shut up the kid. The kid likes to talk about the cat. And if you're going to smoke you're going to smell. Now, what about the dope?"

I had begun to like the superintendent. I sold him a lid out of my precious stash, and he said that if I thought the grass needed water to pour it on. No charge.

One hot morning more than a month after our TV was stolen I called police headquarters to see if anything had turned up. I explained what I wanted and was transferred; I repeated the explanation and was transferred again. Then I was told to call the precinct. A voice there took down my information and put me on hold. I stayed on hold for a long time. Then the voice returned and asked if I knew the exact date of the theft and the names of the officers who made the report. I didn't and was returned to limbo. When the voice came on a third time it wanted a description of the officers. Beyond color and an appreciation of size, I wasn't very helpful; I had been in shock. Finally, the voice revealed what I had begun to fear: The department had no evidence of any such report having been filed.

"But if there was such a report," the voice said, "I will locate it this afternoon and call you back." The sweaty afternoon slid into evening. The phone never rang.

The following afternoon was hot and humid and Kim was napping on damp sheets when Liz Trowbridge came over to pick up the vest. It was finished except for the buttons which she had never gotten around to selecting. I led her back to the shop. She made her choice and we sat down and I began to sew them in place.

"So, how's your friend Gretchen?"

"Lonely. Bearing up. And she has her job to worry about now. They're threatening to cut back on teachers' aides and she might be laid off."

"I understand Marty's bummed out too."

Liz nodded. "Anne told you that?"

"Bill told her that Marty was moping around your place. She understood you were counseling him."

"It's not counseling, exactly," she said, irritated.

Emmy strolled into the room. It was a favorite spot for her. The belts and strips of leather hanging from the wall were ideal for swatting. I picked her up and she rubbed her face against mine.

Liz asked whether I had my own shop in Carbondale.

"Yeah, I had a little place on Illinois Avenue. Not a bad location. You know Carbondale?"

"No, I've never been there."

"Why'd you ask?"

"Oh, I was just wondering. You must have had some arrangement for child care, with you working and Anne going to school."

"Yeah, we did. A family."

"I was just thinking on the way over how big an adjustment this move must be for you." She was watching me, eyes wide.

It occurred to me that Liz Trowbridge was hungry for a client. Marty was not enough. The woman wanted to do some counseling.

"My plants are getting light again," I said. "I guess you haven't noticed."

"Hmm." She smiled rather coyly as if we shared a secret. "You don't want to talk about it."

"No, I don't."

She looked embarrassed. "Well, it didn't seem to hurt them any," she said. "The plants, that is." She touched the leaves of the piggyback beside her chair. "This one looks wonderful. What's the trick? Mine all die. I go through the whole process with the leaf in the water until it sprouts new leaves and roots. It all proceeds perfectly through the potting. Then a few weeks later it starts to die." Her face assumed a grimace.

"Are you sure Bill doesn't get up at night and choke them?"

And there it was, suddenly, the cackling laugh. "You really dislike my husband, don't you."

"I do," I agreed joyfully. "I find your husband obnoxious."

My enthusiasm had hurt her. "He can be very nice under the right conditions."

I decided to let it go. "I'm sure he can, Liz. And it doesn't matter, I'm not married to him."

"No, but it would be nice if you were friends. He and Anne may be working together for years. It'd be great if the four of us enjoyed doing things together." She mused, eyes squinting.

"It's just that if I had a china shop and I saw Bill Trowbridge coming down the street, I'd lock the door and turn the sign, know what I mean?" I had to force myself not to laugh. The image of Bill Trowbridge walking down the sidewalk and all the shopkeepers closing their stores seemed, at that moment, very funny.

But Liz only frowned. "A bull in a china shop, well there's some of that for sure." She paused, as if the analogy were a revelation. "Part of Bill's attraction is his vitality. He has great energy and he's full of ideas. You would have a fun time on the boat with him, or skiing. We do cross-country and downhill. It's frightening to watch Bill do downhill. He just goes to the steepest slope and plunges down."

The conversation was beginning to fatigue me. "He obviously has his good qualities, Liz. You married him after all. And you're happy, right?

She nodded, and I was surprised to see she was verging on tears. I felt terrible.

"God, I didn't mean to make you feel bad," I said, looking around for some tissues. Liz pulled an unopened packet from her purse and began to fumble with the wrapping. I took it from her, opened it with my teeth and handed it back.

"He has lots of friends," she said, wiping her eyes. "He knows people everywhere."

"I know. The night we were out he knew all the waiters."

"Part of the problem is that the people who I like don't like him. Gretchen told me once that if they want to understand the stone age they should forget fossils and study Bill. And he bribes the waiters. His tips are lavish. Bill has money, you know. His dad made a fortune selling insurance. Now he plays golf every day and gets richer and richer. Every premium that comes in he gets a little portion. He just plays golf and the money keeps rolling in. Old customers come to the clubhouse and beg to buy insurance. They can't get enough."

"Sounds nice."

Liz wiped her nose. "He's helped us. Bill's used to it.

Do you know the first thing Bill did when he met me?"

I could not imagine.

"Well, not the first thing." She looked toward the ceiling. "I was working in the student center cafeteria. I worked the cash register three days a week. That's where I met Bill. He used to buy gigantic lunches. I thought he was a football player."

"He bought you lunch?"

"He bought me braces."

"Braces?"

Liz exposed her teeth. "He used to come through the line with his heaping tray and while I was totalling it all up he would talk to me. And he'd always say the same thing. He'd say, 'You know, if it wasn't for your teeth you'd be beautiful.'"

I expressed surprise.

"It was a compliment in its way."

"Yeah, I suppose so."

"I had a . . . well . . . a dramatic overbite."

"Buck teeth?"

"And a gap. My teeth were ugly, but I always thought that I was ugly and my teeth were just evidence of it. Bill taught me that wasn't true. While I was adding up his ticket he'd say, 'You're not your teeth.'"

I had to laugh. "Bill Trowbridge said that?"

"Every day. 'You are beautiful,' he'd say. 'You're not your teeth.'"

"So, he had your teeth fixed?"

"Eventually. My parents were scandalized but they'd never done it. That's the way Bill is. If something doesn't work, if something's not right, you fix it. It seemed perfectly sensible after a while. He had he money, there was an orthodontist at the country club. Bill had him look at my mouth one day on the tennis court. 'No problem,' he said. 'Call my office and make an appointment.' Bill took care of it."

Her teeth were beautiful. The guy had done a good job.

Liz looked weary but then brightened. "Well, maybe you'll get to know him better at the party."

"What party?"

"His birthday party, Labor Day weekend. I give him a party every year on the weekend closest to his birthday. Bill was supposed to have told Anne about it."

I hadn't heard. "That's the weekend we're going up to Wisconsin. It's the first three day weekend since the bar exam." I was not ready to give up Wisconsin for an evening with Bill Trowbridge.

Liz paused. "We could have the party on Friday, I guess. You wouldn't be going up until Saturday would you?"

"Probably not."

"Then that's when we'll do it," she said, pleased.

The heat was terrible. Kim woke. She was less shy now around Liz. She played the big girl and helped Liz mix a quart of frozen lemonade. By the time they brought the clinking glasses back to the shop, I had finished with the buttons.

Anne called later that afternoon. She was leaving work but she was not coming home. She said she was going to spend the night over at Nora's. "It's Norman. He's calling her all the time. She's broken off completely with him."

"I don't see why that means you can't come home."

"Mom's real nervous. We don't know what he might be capable of. Toward the end he was threatening suicide. He said that if he couldn't have her he would kill himself and it would be her fault. Last night he claimed to have a knife; he said he was going to cut his throat and she could listen to him gurgle to death."

"Jesus."

"Then he called her at work today and asked if he could take her to lunch. He said he could explain everything. The man is crazy and Mom's a wreck. I'll call you when I get over there. Okay? You would not believe all the work I have piled up here. This is the worst possible time for this to happen. Wollan wants a memorandum by Friday on some obscure connection between tort and admiralty law, and McIvers dropped an appeal on my desk this afternoon. He wants a draft by next week. . . ."

"Anne, why doesn't your mom come over here? Or we all go over there? The guy is obviously a nut. What can you do if he shows up?"

"We'll be all right. You and Kim would just make more work for Mom. And I know she would never impose on us. That's the way she'd see it." She groaned. "Do know that loan Mom arranged for him?"

I hadn't heard.

"That's how she met him. He applied for a loan for the tire store business. Mom processed it."

"Okay."

"Well, supposedly Norman took the papers and got his brother's signature. Now it turns out his brother never signed anything and never received the money. Apparently, it was this money that Norman has been spending on Mom. It's very embarrassing at the bank."

"I can imagine."

The night was long and it brought no rest. My dreams were tormented. I kept groping for something familiar to lodge against. In the middle of the night I masturbated. I told myself I was doing it so I could sleep. For inspiration I studied the bodies of the angry women in a catalog but in the end I was thinking of my wife.

The oppressive heat lingered into the following morning. Anne left for work without calling and Kim threw her cereal on the floor in an argument about bananas. The heat and her mother's absence had her on edge. Something was wrong and her little instinctual antenna was picking up every nuance.

"Nothing happened," Anne said, when I reached her at the office. "I just overslept. You may remember that you called every hour until eleven."

"Senator Norman probably decided it's a lost cause."

"God, I hope so. But I'll have to go back tonight. He tends to be sane one day and crazy the next."

I did not want her going back. I wanted her to come home. I also wanted her to stay away several days. I wanted to prove to myself that I could be relaxed and comfortable, taking care of our daughter while she was gone.

"Why doesn't Nora call the cops?" I said. "There must be something they could do about this."

"Mom believes she's partly responsible, I think. Like she led him on or something. She doesn't want to call the police. I tried but she absolutely refuses."

That evening Anne called to say she was safely back at Nora's. Kim and I were eating macaroni and cheese topped off with watermelon. I did the few dishes and went into the living room. I lit a joint and turned on the TV. The meal had given Kim a kind of manic thrust and she was running around opening drawers and emptying out the contents. Finally, I got her to sit down and draw with me. My own creations were monstrous bird-like creatures with huge bat-shaped wings and great hooked beaks and talons. Anne called a few minutes after eight.

"He's here," she said. "We're fine, but Mom's very upset."

"What's he doing?"

"Right now he's sitting on the porch step. He's very drunk and I think he's crying."

"I'm coming over."

Anne did not object.

Norman was no longer seated on the porch step when I arrived. He was lying on the welcome mat before the door, curled in the fetal position, facing the house. In the evening light the elastic band of his white undershorts formed a bright strip across the exposed patch of his lower back. I carried Kim around to the back door and Anne let us in. She was wearing one of her mother's house coats and she appeared to me somewhat unknown like a person I had come to visit. She was in the midst of explaining Nora her rights.

"All I am saying, Mother, is that you do not have to put up with this. I will look into getting an injunction against him in the morning, but for now I really think we should call the police."

"Well, he really hasn't done anything wrong, has he?" Nora's voice indicated not so much disagreement as bewilderment. She stood in the doorway between the kitchen and the dining room. Her arms were crossed and her hands gripped her shoulders. She glanced periodically toward the front door. She was, I realized, a woman to whom these things simply do not happen. She dressed well, she bathed daily, her teeth were always brushed and she discarded her nylons at the first sign of a snag. For twenty-nine years she had been the faithful wife of one man and her daughter was about to become an attorney. She had never collected any kind of welfare. Her lawn was manicured and she paid the boy who mowed it a decent wage. She never had anyone arrested, nor dreamed she ever would.

From the living room window I looked down on Norman a few feet away. His noble head lay on the rough cement and he was weeping. He appeared anything but dangerous.

Kim had clasped herself around her mother's legs. Anne and Nora were standing a few feet apart and not looking at each other. It occurred to me how seldom and how fleetingly they touched or looked directly into each others eyes. When we still lived in Carbondale they would always embrace when Anne and I arrived to visit or prepared to leave. But the act was been formal, ritualistic, required by the time and distance that separated them. Now that they saw each other every few days, such displays of affection no longer happened.

Anne finished explaining the legal requirements for a case of trespass.

"We should demand first of all that he get off the property. You told him he couldn't come in, but you never really told him to leave. We should do that to make the case stronger."

"I just wish he would leave," Nora said, glancing again at the door. "If I call the police, the whole neighborhood will know."

I volunteered to go out and talk with Norman.

"You don't have to go out," Anne said. "You can talk right through the door. Just tell him to get off the property. If he hears it from you, he may be more likely to do it."

"I think I'll feel better if I went outside."

"I've been here twenty years," Nora said. "That's a long time."

"Well, be sure and tell him he has to leave. And if he

comes back we'll have him arrested." Anne was intense. She had a pen in her hand and she jutted it toward me as I was about to close the back door. "And tell him he'd better not call her any more, not here, and not at work."

It was nearly dusk though still very warm. I could hear crickets in the back yard. My feet lifted the aroma of grass. Norman was still, breathing quietly and I had the impression he had fallen asleep. I sat down beside him and rested my back against the wall. The great white head rose from the cement and two wet and smeary-red eyes gazed up at me.

"Ah," he said in a thick voice. "It's the craftsman."

"Hi, Norman."

"I guess it is my turn to lie down while we talk."

I relaxed a little. He may be drunk, I thought, but at least he's coherent.

Then Norman suddenly turned on to his stomach and began to smash his face against the cement floor of the porch.

"Oh, God," he cried, "it hurts. It just hurts so bad."

He repeated this litany for a minute or more while crunching his face against the porch floor. I could not move; I had no idea what to do. Anne rustled at the window behind us. She wanted me to convey the essentials and get out of there. I said nothing. Gradually, Norman's voice subsided into sobs and his head came to rest again on the cement. Slowly night permeated Nora's street. A car passed, then another. Two boys, their forearms resting on the handlebars, peddled slowly past, lost in deep conversation, and their voices soft and clear in the evening air. No one walked the sidewalks, and no one seemed to notice that a man was lying on a front porch crying into the cement while another, who since he could not think of the correct thing to say, sat beside him and said nothing.

I kept my silent vigil for an hour. At one point Anne opened the front door a crack and said, "Just tell him, Jason."

"Shut the door, Anne," I said. She did, with more force than was necessary.

It was fully night and slightly cooler when at last Norman raised his head. His hair had fallen across his face and in the glow from the street light I could see a dark crust of blood around his nose.

"Is there anything at all that I can do?" he asked.

"Nothing. It's over. Absolutely."

"I'll pay back the loan."

"Doesn't matter, Norman."

"There's no hope?"

"None."

Norman slowly sat up and looked out at the street. Then, as if he were about to depart a casual party, he said, "Well, I guess, I'll be going."

"Do you need a ride?" For a second as we stood up my head felt light. I started to place a hand on Norman's shoulder, then redirected it to the wall.

Norman said he was all right to drive. He descended the stairs without tripping, negotiated the sidewalk and leaned on the car while locating his keys. I had the sudden thought that the car would not start, or if it did, Norman would plow into ours on his way out. But this was undoubtedly not Norman's first such exit. After starting the engine, he adjusted the rearview mirror to better see himself. He wiped away the blood and combed his hair. Norman looked noble again. Then competently, if a little slowly, he drove away.

We stayed the night at Nora's. Kim slept on the couch. Anne and I commingled in her old bedroom. It had always been good for us there, as if love were being stolen from under Nora's watchful eyes.

In the morning, Nora insisted on taking us out for breakfast. She seemed pleased, though stunned, when I consumed half a cantaloupe, two eggs, bacon, hashbrowns and a short stack of buttermilk pancakes.

"I suppose he's gone for good," Anne said, as Kim and I were driving her to the El, "but I'll be nervous about going to Wisconsin. What if he shows up while we're out of reach?"

"Nora can always have him arrested."

"Yes, but they'll probably let him out in a few hours."

"I doubt it, Anne. Remember the TV. Once the police get hold of Norman you won't hear from him again. After a couple of hours the police themselves won't know where they put him."

I was in a good mood. I had been useful and Nora was grateful. I had enjoyed good loving with my wife. I was filled with food and well rested. The face of Chicago held a crisp cleanliness that morning as we drove along that I had not noticed before. Trees lined the streets of Nora's neighborhood, the pavement had been swept. I had the sense it was all right. I could just go along and everything would work itself out.

13

Wisconsin. We were leaving on Saturday morning and I made lists, laundered clothing. Kim emptied her shelves and drawers into half-filled shopping bags while I did the real packing and stashed it out of reach.

I was filled with energy. On Friday morning I cleaned the house. Then that night we went to the Trowbridge party. Bill greeted us at the door. He was wearing the new vest and had a thumb hooked in an arm hole.

"Not bad," he boomed. "Good fit." He looked like an auctioneer, needing only a cane and an array of musty junk. Marty was there. Gretchen was playing badly at the piano but not too loud. She had the look of someone determined to ingest more alcohol than was good for her.

Anne introduced me to everyone she knew including the legendary Marshall Wollan, a squat gray-eyed man with a dry humor and a rolling southern voice. He was addressing a cluster of associates and drinking from a bottle of beer.

I found a fifth of Jack Daniels on the kitchen counter. I did not want to begin the trip with a hangover so I paced myself by focusing on the heaping trays of food Liz had spread throughout the apartment.

Wollan was the newest partner and the only member of the firm's upper floors to put in an appearance. He had come apparently to give out the firm's history, the party version. I had a flash of the assembled partners: Their feet dangle in the Jacuzzi; they scratch their hairy bellies and discuss the invitations they have received from Bill Trowbridge. "Wollan," they say in unison, "one of the honors of the newest partner. . . ."

We learned about the associate who had committed suicide, about the wives who had become alcoholics while their husbands were becoming judges and politicians, about the shuttle between Chicago and Washington during the Johnson years when a partner had been prominent in the Justice Department.

I drifted away to my third bourbon and water and finally to the sofa and a magazine. Liz came over a few minutes later. She kicked off her shoes and crossed her ankles on the coffee table

"I hope you know he likes it."

"Well, he's wearing it."

"It fits perfectly. Did you notice? He really likes it."

I sipped my drink. "Party seems to be going well. A lot of lawyers for one apartment but there's no sign we've reached a critical mass."

"Gretchen's miserable," Liz said, as though she were responsible. "And you're reading."

"Actually, I was looking at cartoons."

She shrugged. "Anyway, they seem to have good appetites. Except for this dip." She scooped up a chip full and delivered it to my mouth.

Marshall Wollan left and the lawyers and their ladies gathered around the piano. With Gretchen playing they began to sing "Country Roads."

"Oh, that's good for Gretchen," Liz said, her voice mushy.

I found myself staring at the feet of my hostess. They were different from Anne's, larger, but also smoother, fleshier. Anne's feet were angular. They reflected dramatically the shape of bone and tendon beneath the surface. It was true of all of her, I thought, as I looked over to where she stood beside the piano. She was thin, angular, exposed. She had no buffer to set against the world and I was always afraid the world would chew her up—if she did not chew herself up first.

My eyes cruised the people in the room and returned to my wife. She was the most attractive person there, it seemed to me. She had chosen her thin, navy blouse with the high neck and long sleeves above a muted plaid skirt. In the soft light with the blouse and her dark hair and lashes, her skin had a pale clarity that I found beautiful. She looked refined, delicate, especially in the mouth and nose; her hands seemed almost fragile. At the same time you sensed a certain vitality, an intelligence crackling in there. Even more than Bill Trowbridge, she was the focus of the party. A kind of power had come to her. Maybe, I thought, she did have a buffer, or maybe she did not need one. Maybe it was all in my head.

Liz sat forward and slipped on her shoes. "I'm going to fill the trays."

I helped her gather them up and we took them to the kitchen. Marty Flanagan was refilling his glass.

"Just the man I was looking for. Got any dope?"

We went back to the bedroom and closed the door. I brought a packet out of my pouch and rolled a joint.

"Makes Anne nervous when I carry this stuff around."

"Most lawyers I know smoke a little. At least the young ones."

"It still makes her nervous."

Marty blew out a cloud of smoke, nodding his head. "Anne's into her career. She doesn't want anything to jeopardize it."

The walls were covered with photographs of the Trowbridge family at play on the decks of boats and the backs of horses.

"What do you think about her career, Marty? How's she doing down there?"

"She's leading the pack," Marty replied without hesitation. "Anybody out there will tell you that. She's dedicated. She does good, thorough work, and she's sharp. Damn sharp. She makes connections I can't make."

"I worry about her. Some nights she can't get it out of her mind. It seems to obsess her."

"They drive us. That's the way they shape you into the mold. I had a law professor used to say that the law sharpens the mind by narrowing it."

I found myself taking a narrow look at a photograph full of Bill Trowbridge. He was holding a fish whose head was at his waist and whose tail nearly touched the pier. Trowbridge glared at the fish with a ferocious expression. One move, the look said, and you'll be clobbered.

"Good dope," Marty said, taking back the joint.

"I brought a kilo with me from the south. Easy buys down there."

"You be willing to part with some? Even a lid would last me for months."

I thought about my stash. "Not more than that. I don't know when I'll get back down there."

"Anything," Marty said. "I'm down to seeds and stems."

We smoked.

"She's all right," Marty said, after what seemed a long time. "She just wants to be a good lawyer, and she's willing to devote herself to that. I wish I had her dedication."

Across the room I noticed a painting of a herd of horses grazing in a pasture bordered by a white fence. It was a wonderfully peaceful scene; the kind of thing you might find in Wisconsin.

"Did Anne tell you I'm doing a play?"

I had a vague recollection, something shouted over the roar of the hair dryer.

"Just some walk-ons. A cab driver, a messenger, a drunk that wanders on stage and off again. A few lines in a neighborhood theater, but it's going to be fun."

"Sounds like it."

"My dad thinks I'm crazy. Course the Senator is always on stage."

"I don't know where you get the time, knowing the hours Anne puts in."

"I don't have the time. I just had to do it." Marty pushed himself up on one elbow and looked at me. "Did you see the 'Invasion of the Body Snatchers,' the last one?"

I nodded, sucking the roach.

"Remember how people would go to sleep as one person and wake up as another? The change would be complete, total, and they wouldn't know it. They wouldn't even remember! Every time I get on the elevator I'm afraid that's going to happen to me. I say to myself, 'Maybe tonight when I come down I'll be Marty Flanagan, lawyer. I won't be Marty Flanagan, whatever. . . .'" He waved an arm in the air and let it drop back onto the bed. "Whatever I am now, which is pretty fucked up I can tell you, especially at the moment."

"Whew. I wish you hadn't said that. That is exactly what I'm afraid is going to happen to Anne. One night she'll come home, same as she always does, only it won't be Anne. It will be someone else. Someone who looks like Anne, but different, not her at all."

Marty shook his head. "No, you're wrong. With Anne it's different. She loves it. I don't love it."

Marty rushed through a sequence of quick drags. He dropped the last spark in the heel of his shoe and extinguished it with the handle of the clip. My eyes returned to the painting. The white fence embraced the pasture and the feeding horses, nudging them together. I could see the rich green grass flowing up and becoming brown horses. It flowed up not only through the gracefully curved necks but also through the legs. Far away in the State of Wisconsin.

This time it was Liz Trowbridge who wakened me. She was laughing and pulling at my shoulders and saying something I couldn't understand. I gathered myself on the edge of the bed and she clamped my leather cap down over my head. She put it on too far back and pushed down as if it were something pressed rather than pulled into place.

"I didn't hear you."

"Gretchen and Marty. They left together." Liz gave a final pat to the top of my head. Wasted and muddled though I was, I recognized that pat as the unmistakable mark of a grade school teacher. "Isn't that wonderful?"

"Where's Anne?"

"Still at the piano. I told her I would track you down. She has a very nice voice. Bill's playing now that Gretchen left. Gretchen and Marty have known each other for years, but peripherally, at different edges of our circle of friends." She laughed happily. "I know what you're thinking, but I had nothing to do with this."

She had no idea what I was thinking. "Do you believe she loves her work?"

"Gretchen?"

"No, Anne. Marty says she loves it."

"Bill says she's a wonder. The other day he held Anne up to me as an example of someone who could raise a child and still have a demanding job. That was after I told him I was not ready yet to quit work and have a baby."

From the other room I could hear voices announcing that Bobby had slipped away somewhere near Salinas.

"I told him Anne wasn't raising the child. You were raising the child." Her voice was somber.

I took off my cap, rubbed my scalp and put it back on so it felt right.

"I looked at your piggyback. It probably has mealy bugs or red spiders. I was too obliterated to see clearly."

We sat at opposite ends of the bed and stared at the far wall, our elbows on our knees. Two strangers on a park bench.

"The thing about a baby," Liz said after a moment, "is that a baby is forever. You can't undue a baby." She raised her head and looked at me with a half smile. "So what should I do?"

"Tell him to have his own goddamn baby."

She laughed. "I was thinking about the piggyback."

"The piggyback." I stood up and tucked in my shirt. "Soap solution. Spray it with a solution of soap and water and call me in the morning." I began to fumble in my pouch for the car keys. I knew I was wrecked. I had been filled with good news and it had made me sad.

My mother stood beneath the awning of the old green and yellow tent. She was cooking fish and I was aware of her arms. They were large, the skin oily and smooth, and they swelled out from the sleeveless house dress and dimpled at the elbows. I could smell the fresh fish cooking in batter, hear the hiss. It did not seem a dream so much as a visitation, a scene I might step into had I the strength to hold it in my mind. But it was just a flash and then it was gone. Much too early. Jack and weed still gurgled in my streaming blood. My stomach felt lousy. Without moving I went back to sleep.

The next time it was light. The curves of the brightly colored bedspread covering Anne's body suggested something abstract, elemental. Tints of amber escaped her mussed hair. I moved carefully against her. We were both naked from our love-making the night before and my cock rose and pressed itself against her bottom. I wanted her again. More and more frequently I wanted her. I felt competent when my cock was hard. It made me hungry and alive.

"I'm still sleeping," she muttered, and moved closer to the edge of the bed. I got up and took a shower.

Marty Flanagan stopped by as we were eating breakfast. He had come to claim his ounce of dope. "I heard you were going away," he said to justify his early arrival. I took him back to the shop and measured it out. I had not given a thought to money but he paid a good price.

After he left I returned to the table. My wife was smoking a cigarette. She sat clutching her robe to her throat and I noticed a burn on her sleeve.

"Is that new?"

I looked at her face and it suddenly stuck me.

"I'm sorry. I wasn't thinking. But Marty's all right. Right?"

"It's not Marty," she said. "It's the idea. We don't need that kind of money, Jason. We don't need money at all."

"It wasn't the money. It was for Marty. He said he was out."

"And you somehow have responsibility for that?" She looked pasty, hungover. She turned away, mouth tight. "Let's just forget it, okay?"

I did not want to forget it. I had never dealt the stuff.

That had been Randy's occupation and I stayed far away. Before this I had always bought a lid at a time, nothing more. She knew all that.

"What I resent is the idea that I did it for the money. Marty's a friend. He's your friend. Money had nothing to do with it."

We had walked into the bathroom and Anne was busying herself with packing her personal things.

"Okay, I'm sorry about the money. Let's do just forget it."

We stopped at Nora's where the idea was to run in, pick up Kim, drop off Emmy and run out again. Nora was wearing a white blouse, light blue pleated slacks snug at the hips and perfectly creased. She might have been going to a reunion or a potluck in the park. She had a pot of coffee on the table and a dozen old fashioned donuts. Kim was halfway through her second when we arrived.

The cat made Nora extremely uncomfortable. Her condition for this boarding was that Emmy remain in the gloomy basement. I set her up with food, water and a litter box while Nora stood at the head of the stairs, doing nervous things with her hands.

"You don't think he'll do any damage down there, do you?"

"Emmy's a *she*, Nora."

"I have some valuable things stored in the basement. I hope he doesn't claw them up."

"*She* won't, Nora."

At the bank parking lot a large digital clock informed us that it was 11:37 and 85 degrees. I had hoped to leave by nine.

"I'll just be a minute," Anne said, getting out. She had intended to get the traveler's checks downtown the day before but had been too busy.

"Me, too, Mommy."

"No, you stay with Daddy. I'll just be a minute."

Anne passed in front of the car and I watched as she entered the bank. She was wearing a T-shirt I had bought her, a pair of jeans and her lace-up leather boots. The T-shirt said, "Have you Hugged Your Lawyer Today?" She would have had a sort of racy outdoor look if she hadn't been so pale. We waited. By now it was 11:48 and one more degree. Still no Anne. I decided to run to the supermarket next door and pick up some snacks.

Saturday morning and the aisles were packed. I grabbed apples, bananas, a quart of orange juice. Kim wanted yogurt. The cashier in the express line was remarkably efficient and within a few moments we entered the gleaming sugar canyon—temptations beyond words that caused Kim's eyes to glow and her hand to reach for a luscious looking roll of Life Savers.

"No, Kim. You've already had three donuts, and you can eat this yogurt when we get back to the car. You love blueberry yogurt."

"Little bit, Daddy?" The familiar refrain and her voice laced with the sugar whine.

"Yogurt. You said you wanted yogurt." I let her hold it for a moment, hoping the weight would add substance to the promise.

No luck. Kim glanced at the container and then heaved it to the floor. Splat. The lid popped off and rolled to the next aisle where it came to rest, yogurt side down, next to a pair of elegant, high-heeled shoes.

I took a deep urgent breath. The owner of the elegant shoes stooped gracefully and picked up the lid which she wiped with a tissue from her purse. She retrieved the container of yogurt, wiped the rim and snapping the lid in place, handed it to me with a smile. I was reminded of those ads on TV: A pill is dropped into a beaker, dissolving the acid and neutralizing the threat.

Kim was still crying when we got back to the car. It was 12:07 now and 87 degrees. Anne opened the door on the passenger side and took Kim into her arms. I shoved the groceries onto the floor of the back seat, closed the door and walked around to the driver's side. Kim had stopped crying. She was sitting on her mother's lap and she was tearing the wrapper off a yellow sucker, a little token from the generous folks at the bank.

Wisconsin, I told myself. Forget the candy. Just go to Wisconsin. With careful determination, I inserted the key in the ignition. I started the engine. Then I reached over, pried the sucker out of Kim's mouth and tossed it out the window.

Things got noisy as we drove out of the bank's parking lot. Mel Tillis was singing on the radio. Kim was screaming, pausing when she had to catch her breath to also lick her lips. Anne was shouting at me. In three short blocks we entered a tollway ramp where an automatic station demanded a quarter. I slowed down, digging into my pouch, but then just as I reached the basket, I jammed the transmission into second and drove on through. Now to the general din had been added the clanging of a bell.

Anne moved up against the dashboard. Her head revolved as if it were the turret on a tank. "You just committed a crime back there for a quarter! One lousy quarter!"

My ears felt very hot and I knew they were bright red. For the moment I chose not to speak. I felt quite wonderful actually. Let the world roar, I thought. I was driving I-90 and I-90 will take you from Chicago to Wisconsin where the nights are cool and the air smells of conifers and farms.

I rolled down the window and let the wind pour through.

"My head is killing me," Anne confessed after I had mumbled my apologies.

"I bought orange juice. It's right behind the seat." Soon my wife was asleep, as was Kim in the back seat, her chunky arms and legs dangling, her cheeks blue with her favorite yogurt.

A while later Dolly Parton came on singing her version of "Mule Skinner Blues." It was an old song, one of Randy's favorites. We would be driving along in his ancient Renault with the sun roof open and the insects buzzing and he would start to sing about the water boy bringing the bucket down.

14

North of Janesville, Wisconsin I left the expressway, took 14 to Madison and then picked up 12. The decision slowed us. I had originally planned to reach our destination in time to approach a few stores, but I wanted to get us into the country. Outside Madison we passed a sloping pasture with a herd of holsteins. I stopped when I noticed an old farm implement parked near the fence. Anne did not want to get out, but Kim was excited. I took the camera and we ran over.

"Now," I said to my daughter, "do you know what this is?"

She stood with her hands on the wire fence and peered intently at the object for a few seconds before shaking her head.

"Well, that is a hay rake, very old. Your great-great grandfather had a hay rake like this. I remember seeing it when I was a little boy. Of course they were no longer using it. Now, see those beautiful curving tongs? That's what raked the hay."

"Tongs?"

"Yeah, those wire things in a row. They're called tongs or teeth. You can call them teeth."

"Teeth?" Kim put her hand in her mouth.

I just loved the way such things delighted her. "Want to know something funny? That long thin thing up in the front. That's called a tongue. That tongue is for a tractor, but I'll bet when this rake was new it had a longer tongue and was pulled by horses."

Kim's fingers went back to her mouth and Anne stuck her head out of the car.

"Jason, tell her to stop putting her fingers in her mouth. That fence is filthy."

I climbed over the fence, careful to avoid the electric wire. I lifted Kim over and placed her on the broad metal seat of the rake. The air was hot, heavy with humidity. A few clouds had begun to form in the southwest. The smells were wonderful.

I took the camera and began dancing around, trying to entertain my daughter while I snapped a couple of shots. It worked for a few moments but then she became more interested in exploration. She made her way over to one of the large metal wheels and slowly descended using the spokes as a ladder. She was agile for a two year old, adventuresome. I watched with pride until her foot sank into a pool of fresh cow manure.

"Did you have to bring her back to the car before you cleaned that off?" Anne said, her nose twisted.

"You know, Anne, it really does surprise me that you should think this stinks. It smells, I grant you. But you can sit in that cubicle all day smoking one cigarette after another and think nothing of it."

"Cow shit may be organic, lover, but it still stinks."

I finished rubbing the small shoe in the grass and returned it to Kim's foot. In a way I was happy that my daughter had some cow shit on her shoe. She came from a long line of people whose shoes had smelled of cow shit.

"Why are we fighting like this?" I asked once we were back in the car.

"I'm not aware that we're fighting, but we do seem to have a difference of opinion. I say that cow shit stinks and apparently you say it doesn't."

"And you think fences are filthy."

"And you don't? Look at her hands, her pants. They're covered with rust."

I started the engine. "That's just it, Anne. That's not filth. That's rust, just rust."

"Right," she said, sarcastically, "and cow shit is just cow shit. If rust is just rust and cow shit is just cow shit, then what the hell is filth?"

Anne apologized and complained again about her head. We were at that stage of a marital disagreement when both sides wanted it to go away but neither could quite forget it. Our glands were secreting toxic juices and our lips spouting nonsense. Best then to drive on in silence.

I saw photographs everywhere I looked: a round barn, an old silo bound to the earth by a massive stone foundation, a red-tail hawk poised on a utility pole. I wanted to take Kim into a corn field. I wanted her to feel the silk, see how the roots supported the stalk, smell the fertility in the shadows of the leaves. I used to play in fields like that. Left on my own I might have stopped every mile or two and probably have not gotten to Baraboo for a couple of days. Instead I drove without pause. I lunged into curves, rushed through the small towns I had hoped would charm my wife.

We came at last to a group of cabins near Baraboo. I stopped in front of the office. Anne had fallen asleep again but I nudged her awake. Motel rooms were her responsibility. I had the car worked on; she rented motel rooms. A few minutes later she stepped out of the office and waved a key. I started the engine and followed her at a creep to the cabin. The bottoms of her jeans were rolled in large jaunty cuffs. She looked like a pirate with a perky ass. I remembered then that Randy had warned me about that ass. "A snotty ass," he had said the first time he met her.

They were wood-frame cabins, looped around the top of a hill, each painted a different color. Ours was a pale green with a forest green trim. It had a small refrigerator and stove, a tiny side room for Kim. After we unloaded I stripped off my sweaty clothes and asked Kim if she wanted to swim.

Anne frowned but said nothing. I knew she was thinking about the ear problem and her concerns, even though unvoiced, annoyed me. It was hotter than hell out there. If Kim couldn't go in the water today she could never go. To avoid arguing I went into the bathroom. When I came out Anne had apparently decided it was all right. She was helping Kim put on the little swim suit with the lady bug on the front.

I wrapped a towel around my face and head and lumbered blindly across the floor growling ferociously.

"Daddy!"

Guided by my daughter's screams, I moved toward her. My bare feet slapped the floor; my noises were horrendous. I caught her, swirled the towel around her and rolled her across the bed.

"A present for the Monster Daddy," I growled, and pulling down her suit, sank my mouth into her quaking belly. My God how I loved that screaming laugh!

"Ah hah," Anne said dryly from a few feet away. "The Monster Daddy. Now I understand."

I couldn't help it. Her observation made me laugh.

Moments later we were hopping across the hot gravel to the pool. The sun was still shining but not so brightly. A thin haze had coated the sky and there was a pause in the air, as if the earth had caught its breath. I swam a few laps, played awhile with Kim while Anne swam and then got out. A couple of people in what looked to be their mid-sixties reclined on chaise longues. The old man had a mat of reddish-gray hair covering his chest and a spray of freckles flowing from one thick shoulder to the other.

"Looks like you got a new Esther Williams out there," the man said.

"Yeah, looks like it." Though at the moment, I could not decide why this man was reminded of Esther Williams. Hadn't she been an actress?

"I taught all my kids to swim before they were six," the man said. "They move like fish in the water, all four of them."

I spread my legs out on the warm cement. Anne was supporting our daughter belly-down on top of the water. Kim looked as though she were trying to beat the water to death with her arms and legs. The veil of clouds had thickened. The sky now gave the appearance of having been draped with a crocheted tablecloth. In the southwest I saw a gathering of angry clouds.

The old man reminded me a little of my father, what he might have looked like had he still been alive. My father had been smaller, but there was a similar red thickness, the same twang in the nose.

"Do you folks know if there's a drive-in around where we can get some food?"

The man leaned up and pointed. "There's a hamburger joint at the edge of town. And if I know anything about weather, I'd say you got just enough time to make it there and back before this thing hits."

By the time I had started back with the usual contingent of cheeseburgers, shakes and fries, the air had cooled and assumed a thick stillness that subtly exposed the undersides of the leaves along the wooded roadside. The sky had become a tormented artist, mixing shades of gray and yellow, thinning and thickening, turning the colors over and about. From a rise I could see a dark presence emerging from the southwest, a boiling up of charcoal and green. The sight freed in me a delicious sense of fear and anticipation.

Anne had turned on the lights and was busily flipping the channels on the TV. Moments later the invading darkness so engulfed the hill that the manager switched on the yard light. The last guest retired to his cabin, and the sharp and isolated slap of his closing screen door hung in the air for an instant before it disappeared.

Anne thought we should get in the car.

"We'll be all right." I was standing in the doorway watching the sky, holding Kim on one hip.

"I don't like being on this hill. You know this cabin was just thrown together."

"It'll be all right, Anne. Just turn off the TV and come over here."

"I was hoping to get a weather announcement."

"The weather's here now. We might as well enjoy it."

"I don't think I'm going to enjoy it," she said, turning off the television.

We were all in the doorway when it happened: a bright, intense flash over near the road coincident with an explosion of thunder. The cabin shuddered. The lights flashed once and then everything went dark. There followed a pause so intense it seemed to crouch above us. A few large drops of rain splashed on the gravel raising the smell of dust. "Jesus Christ," Anne whispered. I felt a shiver run through her body.

Enough light remained that we could see the clouds roiling overhead. There came a second flash, this farther away, followed by the answering thunder, a gust of wind and then a steady downpour. The doorway was suddenly too wet for comfort. I dashed to the car, grabbed the flashlight and returned to find Kim and Anne seated on the bed.

"I think we should leave, Jason."

I sat down on the bed and let them huddle against me.

For the next ten minutes the storm assaulted the hill with astonishing fury. Waves of rain slapped against the cabin walls; bolts of lightening sent eerie illumination through the windows; thunder shook the bed. Then gradually a wedge of time pushed itself between the light and the sound, ten seconds, twenty. From the back window we watched it rage over the far hills. Kim kept saying, "Daddy, look!"

By the time electricity was restored, we were seated on the bed eating cold sandwiches by flashlight. I got up and turned off the lights. I felt we had received a gift.

Morning came cool and clear. The air that moved in behind the storm carried the first touch of fall. The lake was blue but choppy, the day too cold for swimming. We toured the campgrounds. Leaves and twigs had been scattered across the roads. Here and there a large branch, its stub raw and white, lay at the base of a tree. Several families were packing sodden gear and preparing to leave.

"So, this is where you came with your parents?"

"We passed through here. Our destination was usually farther north. Better fishing up there. But this place was sort of special. We knew we were on vacation when we got this far."

"Did you have a trailer?"

"No, an old beat up tent. It would sleep four in a pinch but usually Dean and I slept outside. When I was a teenager I was embarrassed to be caught near the damn thing. It seemed like we were always surrounded by people in fancy aluminum rigs and strings of Japanese lanterns."

"I wish I could have known your parents."

"I know."

"And Kim too."

"Yeah, so do I."

We walked the beach, found skipping stones. The sand had been washed trackless, crusted and colored a fine brown by the rain. Bundled in corduroys and a jacket, Kim ran from stone to log, to mound of grass, She lifted what she could, peered into and around what she could not. A couple of boys were swirling a thick rope across the sand and shouting: "It's a snake! It's a snake!"

The lake had been created by glacial activity, a shoveling out, leaving to the east a great tossed up wall of boulders.

"Dean and I used to climb that every summer," I said.

"Would you like to climb it now?"

"Kim would never make it. It's more of a climb than it looks from here."

"She could stay with me while you go."

"And leave you with that snake? I wouldn't consider it."

Anne slapped at me playfully. She was terrified of snakes. After the incident with the copperhead, it was like pulling teeth to get her to walk on any grass that had not been mowed the day before.

We lunched on reubens and beer and then she lit a cigarette. Only her second of the day. If we had a week, I thought, to explore Wisconsin in the same haphazard manner that Kim had employed on the beach, she might quit completely. And she was eating better. Her breakfast had been respectable and she had finished her sandwich as quickly as I had. The hour on the beach had left a trace of color across her cheeks.

The afternoon we devoted to selling leather goods. We began in shops around Baraboo and then worked our way north toward Wisconsin Dells. Sales were difficult. Their season ending shortly after Labor Day, merchants were not anxious to take on additional inventory. But we had fun, making a game of the possibilities.

"Try this one," Anne said, referring to a solitary place set off the road. It's windows were crowded with doodads of every description.

"Looks too junky."

"Just try it."

So I lugged my trunk of samples inside and carried it back out again a moment later.

"I could have sworn that place sold leather," Anne said shaking her head.

"The guy wouldn't even look at the samples. His wife assembles cheap kits. The place is full of moccasins, gaudy wallets and belts. He didn't want the competition."

"So, I was right."

"What do you mean? You weren't right. I didn't sell anything."

"But I was right," she laughed. "You just didn't sell anything."

To save time Anne and Kim began going in first. She would look over the stock, chat with the owner. If they hadn't come back out in a few minutes, I would swing in with my trunk and my pitch. In the last place we tried, the owner had bluish hair, perfectly curled, and a pair of gold-framed eyeglasses hanging from a chain around her neck. She loved the caps and agreed to buy three. Then she picked out a couple of belts.

"Maybe I'll just get one of these little vests for my grandson." She dropped her glasses to her bosom and looked at Anne. "Not the one I was telling you about, dear. This is our daughter's child, the one who lives in Vermont. We only get to see the little angel once or twice a year." She returned the glasses to the bridge of her nose and held the vest up again. "Well, they seem to like it up there. John's a doctor and they have a lovely place."

"I'm sure they're very happy," Anne said, holding Kim away from the music boxes.

"Well, Ma'am, just let me say this. If I can interest you in one or two of these shoulder bags, I'd be willing to throw in a vest for your grandson at no charge."

"Well, that's nice." She lifted a bag and examined it. "The craftsmanship is lovely, I must say." She agreed to purchase three bags and then dropped her glasses and looked at Anne. "Do you help your husband in the shop, dear?"

"No, I'm an attorney."

"Not really," the woman suddenly exclaimed. "And you seem like such a nice person!"

"I am a nice person."

The woman was unfazed. "Oh, you know what I mean. You are so pretty, and in Chicago no less. Can you really stand up to those judges and lawyers?"

"I like to think I can." Anne's voice was very controlled.

It seemed a good time to total up the sale and move on. In a restaurant a few moments later, I pulled out the checks from the three sales.

"All right, 76, 114 and 140. That's 340 bucks, not much but something."

"Three-thirty," Anne said, looking up from the menu. "Do you think I should have said something to that woman? I can be a nice person and an attorney at the same time."

I was busy with a pencil and a napkin. "Yeah, you're right. Three-thirty. Well, its Labor Day weekend."

"She probably goes around saying insulting things to all kinds of people and doesn't even know it. I should have said something."

"Hey, you're nice, and I'm rich and we're all hungry. What they got?"

Anne handed over the menu. "I don't know why people have this stereotype of lawyers. I've known dozens of lawyers and hundreds of law students and they are at least as nice as other people."

It was a relief to see the waitress arrive. We had dinner and then afterward bought ice cream cones and browsed through some store windows. We had gone a couple of blocks when we came upon my fantasy: a store front divided down the middle with a bookstore on one side and a lawyer's office on the other. It took my breath away, that little office with its draped typewriter, its magazines neatly stacked in the waiting room.

We stopped and I watched as Anne stared in the window for a moment. She was licking her cone around the edges, just the way she had back in Carbondale the day I met her, and she appeared lost in thought.

In a liquor store I bought a bottle of champagne, a jar of herring in cream sauce and a box of crackers. Kim fell asleep on the way back to the cabin and we made love as soon as we had put her in bed. It was intense, this act of love, hurried, a release of desire that had been building through the day. Afterward I brought the champagne and food over to the bed.

"Remember the herring?"

"Of course. Your mouth was half full of it when you proposed."

"On Washington Street."

Anne nodded. "The first time you took me there, I thought the trains were going to crash right through the kitchen. It was a strange little place when you think about it, tiny, isolated, sort of sad."

It had been sad. I was living there when I learned about my parents. It had been about seven months later when I met Anne and I was far from recovered.

We sat now in near darkness. Night had risen up out of the valleys. The trees were no longer distinguishable on the hills. A narrow peach-colored band on the horizon represented the last of the sun. We watched it fade to a dark blue. Anne was heaping crackers with mounds of herring and transporting them to our mouths. I got up and switched on the bathroom light, then closed the door so that only a thin band of light stretched across the bed.

"You look different," I said.

"Really, how so?"

"Fleshier. Rounder. The muscles in your face and along your neck and shoulders have relaxed. Your eyes are quiet in a way I haven't seen in weeks." I kissed her. "And you taste like herring and not cigarettes. You've only smoked three all day. I've been counting."

Anne giggled, a little embarrassed. "My secret observer and guardian. Monitoring my health and timing my travels from office to home."

I refilled the plastic motel glasses, pouring slowly down the sides.

"We should drink a toast," Anne said, taking back her glass. "What do you want to drink to?"

"You name it."

"All right." She raised her glass. "To the great State of Wisconsin."

I grinned. "To Wisconsin."

The glasses clunked dully together. We drank and fell silent for a moment.

"Tell me something," I asked after a while. "What were

you thinking back there? When we were standing in front of that little office?"

"Where?"

"Outside the restaurant. You know, when we were poking around. You seemed struck by something. I was just curious."

"Oh, the law office."

"Yeah. That one." I waited.

"I don't know . . . well, I guess I was thinking about what it would be like to work in a place like that."

"Oh yeah?"

"The petty small town squabbles. 'He's building his fence six inches onto my back yard, that kind of thing. Evictions. The ugly little divorces. Custody fights over the kids. Drunken drivers. Jesus. You probably have to take everything that comes through the door just to make a living."

"I suppose."

"I guess I was thinking how lucky I was to have the chance I have. It's a real opportunity, you know."

"An investment." I had heard her use the term before.

"That's it," she said excitedly, "an investment in the future."

She raised her glass. "Another toast. I'm full of toasts."

"My turn."

"Not yet. Come on," she teased, "get it up." I raised my glass dutifully. "To my wonderful husband," she said, "who makes it all possible."

We drank.

"I love you," she said, her eyes misty above the glass. We made love a second time, slow and tender. Afterward she wanted to place her head on my shoulder. But I straightened myself and sat up.

"I think I'll take a short walk. Do you mind?"

"A short one?" She was teasing again.

"I think so." It was nearly two when I returned to the cabin. Anne was asleep in a tangle of rumpled covers and bits of cracker. The bathroom light was still on. From Kim's room I could hear coughing. I stood for a long time at the window where the night before we had watched the storm on the hills. In the light of a waning moon, the hills appeared illusive and far away. Far away in the State of Wisconsin.

By morning Kim's face was flushed. She was grouchy and her body felt hot. We put her in the backseat where she fell asleep sucking her thumb.

"Tomorrow, we are taking her to the doctor," Anne said on the way back.

"All right."

"We'll both go. Then we can talk about that operation, those little tubes."

"All right."

She groaned. "My desk is full of things I have to get done." She pulled the little book out of her bag and began making a list. "Maybe we can get an appointment for first thing in the morning."

Chicago's first signal was a gray haze hanging in the distance. It was an ugly, foreboding sight, and as we drew closer it seemed to flow around us and finally to seep into the car itself. I consciously took a deep breath of this permeating urbanity, gathered it into myself. Acclimation, you might call it. Breathed it in, breathed it out. Made it a part of me, and in the process washed out the last remnants of the silly Wisconsin dream.

At Nora's house, Anne called the doctor's office and got a recording.

"He's open at nine," she said when she hung up. "We'll

just have to be there and wait our turn. What a lousy time for this to happen."

Nora wanted us to stay for dinner but Anne pulled out her little book. "We have to get groceries yet this afternoon, Mom. Then we need to unpack, do a load of wash. And Kim has to get to bed as early as possible."

We bought the groceries and then were lucky enough to find a parking place only a couple of doors from the apartment. We were all dead tired. We got out, filled our arms with luggage and grocery bags and started down the walk.

Only then did I notice the two people in front of our building. A young girl was seated on a duffel bag. She looked to be a teenager, thin and washed out. Beside her stood an older man. He was thick chested, wearing dirty jeans, heavy boots and a bright turquoise-colored tank top that did not flatter his ample stomach. Streaks of gray ran through his long hair and his large upper arms were stained with old tattoos. He was watching us closely. Suddenly, I started to run.

"Randy?" I shouted. "Is that you, Randy?"

15

He was old standing there, heavy, smelling of sweat and tobacco, and it seemed to me that he was also wary, as though he had thought a long time before he decided to come, and then not finding us home, had decided to wait, and yet was not certain he should have done either. We greeted with the old handshake, fingers up, thumbs interlocked. Then we climbed the stairs behind Anne who was carrying Kim and not talking, and ahead of the girl and her heavy duffel bag.

The living room was gray and gloomy. Before we left I had lowered the shades again. I lifted them now, and because I was not ready yet to face the moment, went back to the shop and let in the afternoon light. I stood awhile looking out at the small and struggling grass.

When I hung up the telephone that afternoon when the call came from my uncle telling me my parents had been killed, Randy had been there. I never knew, and never bothered to ask, just how my uncle had come to call the ice cream parlor which was located next to our leather shop. We did not have a phone in the shop and maybe in an emergency the operator had given out the number she thought was closest. It had been very difficult for my uncle, a quiet, inarticulate man, to explain that there had been an accident, that the accident had been very bad, that my parents were dead. When I set down the phone and turned, I saw that Randy had followed me from the shop, as if he had known.

I left the back of the apartment and walked to Kim's room. I opened the curtains, revealing the narrow shaft between the buildings, and then did the same in our bedroom. Below the window the same man was again squeezing his Volvo out of a tiny parking space. A dark-haired boy of eight or nine sat on the passenger side lost in thought; he did not react as bumper rasped against bumper and the transmission lurched from first to reverse and back again.

When I returned to Carbondale from the funeral Randy was again waiting for me. For the next several weeks he was there when I needed him and never there when I preferred to be alone. In the fall of that year when the corn had dried and was being harvested—that same corn that in August had stood tall and green cutting off the view of the other driver—Randy and I went backpacking in the Shawnee National Forest, just as we had the other two years we had known each other. Sometimes on those outings Randy told stories about growing up along the Ohio River—stories Sam Clemens would have recognized and enjoyed. Other times we did not speak to each other for hours at a stretch. That fall and winter was the last time we camped regularly. In the spring I met Anne and most of my time from then on I spent with her. Around that time Randy began to transform a share-a-kilo-with-a-friend-for-a-free-lid operation into a big business, the actual size of which I did not fathom until it was smashed one night the following April.

I returned now to the living room. Randy and the girl were seated on the couch. Anne was in the rocker with the listless Kim in her lap. Everyone seemed interested in a different corner of the room. I stopped and leaned on the door frame.

"Anybody want a beer or something?"

"A beer, yeah," the girl said, coming to life. She possessed the soft, husky, too gentle voice of the dedicated doper. Her legs were twice folded and her arms skewed so as to hide her young breasts; she appeared oblique to the other shapes in the room as if she were trying to fit into a shadow.

"A beer'd be great." Randy's smile squinted his eyes and sent wrinkles shooting back toward his temples. It was the old smile and it slid with warm familiarity across the older, heavier, now beardless face, a face had I seen in a photograph, I might not have recognized.

Anne looked to be in a state of shock. I asked if she wanted some coffee. She muttered that she did.

I brought the drinks back to the living room with a bag of chips and settled myself on the floor with my head against the fireplace.

I asked Randy if he'd been in the city long.

"Since five this morning. We came in on a bus. Cheryl here got on in Lincoln. That's when I met her."

When I last saw Randy there had been a few gray flecks at his temples. Now it raced down his sideburns and raged in the hairs on his chest. But there was another difference, I decided, as I watched him roll a cigarette, something more elemental. Randy's movements used to have an exquisite, controlled purposefulness; he seemed never hurried or abrupt, yet always right, as though time waited, content to move at the pace he selected. It was clear now that his fingers had lost that easy assurance and his massive shoulders, while still conveying a sense of power, were held in a subtly different way. Long hours on the bus could have stiffened him, but I had the sense of a man at bay. Once the world had fallen away from Randy in all directions; now it leaned in.

"We've been waiting down there on the sidewalk since

six this morning," Cheryl said to Anne, filling her hand with chips. "Randy thought you'd be here but I guess you didn't know he was coming, huh?"

"I didn't know," Anne said pointedly, looking at me. "I haven't heard from Randy in some time."

"We haven't been in touch in several years," I found myself saying. "We would have been here. But we were up in Wisconsin, Devils Lake."

"Where you used to go with your parents," Randy said.

"Right." It pleased me that he should remember.

"You guys ever watch them making movies here?" Cheryl asked.

Cheryl, Randy explained, had read that a lot of movies were being made in Chicago.

"I don't hope to be a star or nothin' but I do hair pretty good," she said between mouthfuls. "I'd just like to work around them."

Hearing this, Anne gave me a strange look, one I couldn't, at that moment, read.

"There was something in the paper just the other day," I said. "Redford, Newman, somebody's here. They were set up over by the lake."

"I suspect they bring their own hair stylists with them," Anne said. The look on her face was obvious now: disgust, unambiguous disgust.

But Cheryl was cheered by this news. "I don't care what I do. I just want to work around them. Know what I mean?"

We all knew what she meant, but none of us had anything to add. The conversation wanted badly to unravel.

"I talked to Fletzer," Randy said after a while. "He said you were a lawyer now, Anne."

"That's right," I said, interrupting and speaking much

too soon. "She took the bar this summer and she's working for a big firm on La Salle Street."

It was almost deja vu. The moment was identical to a hundred others in which I had told one of them about a good quality in the other, and the listener had nodded and not believed it, or thought it was not a good quality, or saw devious motives behind it, or in some other way sought to devalue the currency. The two of them were staring at each other now like old poker players.

"That's really good," Randy said at last.

Anne nodded and thanked him in a voice little more than a whisper. Then she managed to stand up without releasing her grip on Kim. "There are a lot of things still in the car," she said on her way out the door.

Randy and I went back down the steps. Walking along beside him was like returning to an old haunt, a place that had long ridden pleasantly in the memory.

"Good to see you, man."

He snorted. It was an old habit, one that made him sound like a diver climbing out of a swimming pool.

"Business, Sydney. It's that simple. A guy lives up here owes me some money. Two days in this burg and I'm gone."

We arrived at the car. I opened the back and started setting things out on the curb.

"I hope to hell I never get caught in a courtroom with her on the other side."

"Who? Anne?"

"She's one tough bitch, that woman. I knew she set her mind to it she'd end up a lawyer or something."

"You two have always hated each other," I said, my voice betraying what I felt.

"I don't hate the woman. I admire the hell out of her. I'm just stating the fact. She is one tough bitch."

We filled our arms and walked back to the building. In the lobby Randy sat down on the solitary, fake-marble bench and motioned for me to join him.

"I'm still running, Sydney."

"I know."

"It's been the shits, man. Believe it." He stopped to roll a cigarette. There had always been a lot of silence between us. It was never uncomfortable, more a part of the pace. Only when Anne was there did the silences coil and tighten. Randy licked down the paper and looked at me. "Hard to believe you're married and got a little Sydney."

It was good to hear that worn old leathery name again, the one Randy called every man, woman and child.

"It's tearing me a new asshole." He went on. "I keep thinking all the cops got my picture in their pocket."

"You'll be all right here."

Randy was staring at the far wall. "I don't know. I'd forgotten how bad it was. She'd bust my ass if she thought she'd get away with it."

"Jesus, Randy." I started to laugh and then stopped when he clamped a heavy hand around my forearm.

"This isn't funny."

"I know. But I am Jason, remember? And that's Anne up there, not some spy or something. She doesn't love you, but, Jesus Christ, she's not going to get you busted." I pulled my arm away. It was red and burning.

Randy brought his elbows to his knees and buried his face in his hands. His hair was badly in need of washing and the skin at the joint of his elbow was dark and greasy.

"I'm sorry," he said, looking up. "I was fucking crazy to come here. But it's too late now. I just want to stay the night. Tomorrow I'll be out of here. Talk to her about it. See what she says. And send Cheryl down. We can finish with the car."

Anne was busy in the bathroom. The coffee cup rested on the back of the stool. She was washing out underwear in the lavatory and she had draped every protrusion in the shower with brightly colored panties. Work, it occurred to me, was always what Anne turned to when the tension climbed. Be working, she seemed to believe, and no one could scold or blame you. Be cleaning and the gods would protect you. Her mother's child.

I explained what Randy needed, and after I had finished, she stopped chewing on her lip.

"That's bullshit. I know what he's after." She pulled a brassiere from the gray water and rubbed the straps together with furious intensity. After four years, a half hour had cemented us back into the old roles.

"I don't know what you mean."

"Oh, come on. He didn't risk coming back to Illinois just to visit."

"He has business, that's what he said."

"Then why doesn't he stay with the person he has business with?" Her voice was streaked with sarcasm, as if it were inconceivable that Randy should be telling the truth.

It wearied me, that tone, the endless justifying of one to the other.

"I guess he wanted to see us. Is that so unreasonable? Besides, in Randy's line of work, I imagine you don't stay in the home of people who owe you money."

"Randy's line of work! You act like it's just another trade or profession. He's a creep, Jason! Did you catch the age of that child he's dragging along with him? The movies! I'll bet he fed her that horse shit. He probably met her on a school yard where he was slipping cocaine to kindergarten students. He's a crook, a punk, a common lowly pusher, a heel. There is no depth he wouldn't sink to. Why can't you. . . ."

Her hands were flailing the brassiere. I found I had to lean against the door frame to steady myself. She never did understand. She always hated the feelings I had for Randy. Hated and feared them.

"He's at the end of his rope, Anne," I said, in a voice as quiet as I could make it. "I have to help him. When I needed him, he was there."

"He has never helped you!" Anne said, furious. "He has used you! He has always used you and so long as you let him, he always will."

How old it all was, how very settled. In the beginning I had thought that Anne would just add to what Randy and I already had. More would be better. I used to have visions of the three of us—others too, why limit ourselves—buying a piece of land back in the hills. We'd build a large house, or several small ones. Anne would be an artist. Do a garden, plant an orchard. Bare footed kids running around in the dust, soup simmering, the smell of herbs. The usual hippie dream and it took a long and painful time for me to understand how empty it really was. I had not failed to properly explain one to the other. They truly disliked each other. They were emissaries from warring camps, pulling at my soul and it could never be the way I wanted it to be. When finally I understood, it baffled me. Why consent to doing death's work when death was so capable of doing it unaided?

Anne had slumped down on the stool.

"I have to let him stay, Anne. It's just something I have to do."

She pushed herself up and glared at me. Her face was tight, pinched. But she was not going to cry. She refused to cry.

"I want you to realize what you're doing. That girl is obviously a runaway. And who knows what all he's wanted for by now. It was bad enough when he ran away the last time. You are putting me in a terrible position, and, of course, he knows that. He knew I was an attorney before he came. Harboring a fugitive is no joke!"

She had been speaking with relative calm but the perceived injustice of it infuriated her and her voice began to rise. "And you say he's not using you. You're deceiving yourself. He's using you all right, and by letting him stay here, you're using me. You are forcing me to risk the whole thing. For him! For that creep!" Anne jumped back to her feet and began fishing around in the water for more underwear.

"It's just one night."

Though her hands continued to fumble in the gray water, they had lost their purpose. She squinted her eyes and gritted her teeth. She was absolutely not going to cry.

"Did you invite him here? Did you know he was coming?"

"Fletzer told me Randy had called him. That was weeks ago. I hadn't talked to Randy."

"I sometimes think he has a terrible power over you," she said now, quiet again. "He's perverse, a sorcerer or something. Even after all these years and as far away as he was, he could sense that you were unhappy and so he came."

This, I thought, was the great legal mind at work. The head of the pack.

"It's business, Anne. He stays the night and then he's gone."

"I don't think it's the business that he came for," she said now, her voice almost a whisper. "I think it's just like the last time, the night he ran away and left you holding the bag. I think he's come for you."

Beads of water gathered in drops at the bottom-most points of the hanging underwear, and when they were heavy enough they fell in random splats to the porcelain. That night in April had been fierce and storm-swept. The electricity was out and Anne and I were in bed when car lights flashed in the driveway. Moments later he was banging on our door. I had never seen Randy the way he was that night, an awesome creature pacing the kitchen in the flickering light of the candles. Anne left the room and stood behind the door. He was too alive for her; the storm had entered the kitchen. For a long time after that I continued to deny that Randy had wanted me to go away with him. He had come to say goodby, I would say, and to give me the shop. "It's clean," he told me. "They'll search but it's clean. I've always kept it clean. And now it's yours." But it was true, there had been an invitation, however subtle and unspoken. Randy had offered a vision, fierce as the storm roaring outside, timeless as the forces pulling at the trees: a vision of movement, of surviving by the quickness of your wits. A vision of the road. I had not gone of course. I was not the wayfaring man Anne feared I was. I might have wanted to be, but I was not. I was a holding-on man, a brooder man. I had seen how quickly the dying news comes, how broad and sure its scythe can sweep.

As it had been then, so it was now. Her fears were irrational, but I knew well that kind of fear, understood it at the core of my being. Knew too that nothing I could say would quell it. I touched her lightly on the temple. It felt warm and smooth. You can tell the blood edges up there as it slips past.

"There was a moment," she said after a few seconds, "when I almost called the police. I came within an eyelash and I probably would have if that child of his hadn't been stretched out on the couch watching TV."

"No. . . . You wouldn't."

"I might have." She nodded her head, realizing herself how close she had been. "He's a creep. He brings nothing but trouble and he wants to take you away from me."

I sat down on the tiled floor.

Anne gave a little laugh. "And it would have destroyed us. That's funny, isn't it?"

I hardly heard her. I was filled with it. I sat at its black center. After a while I felt her hand come to rest lightly on the top of my cap.

"Please don't let him catch you up in it, Jason. He destroys people. Think of everyone he left behind in Carbondale. And please get rid of him as fast as you can. He's an asshole."

She rose to her feet and pulled another brassiere from the water. It made me think of a song they used to sing at the revival meetings during the brief time my father had religion:

Work for the night is coming,
Work through the morning hours;
Work for the night is coming
When man's work is done.

On the stairs leading down to the lobby my legs were trembling so badly that I found it necessary to hold onto the banister.

The presence of Randy and the girl in our home that evening enraged Anne. She refused to cook dinner. She moved about tight-lipped, pale, corrosive. I thought of her mother. The nights I had to sit and listen to the two of them, the hours wandering malls. Didn't she owe me this? Did she really think the cops were going to suddenly burst in and nab us all? By bed time we were binary flames in careful orbits; between us a broad expanse of empty bed.

We beat the doctor to his office next morning. The three-day weekend had charged the waiting room with a frenzy of hacks, sniffles and snorts. Infants wailed; parents whispered pleas for silence. My hands became damp with sweat.

It was after eleven when the fat nurse, folder in hand, announced our moment. Then a long glum wait in the examining room.

"Do you have to pace?" Anne said. It was the first thing she had said to me since we left the apartment.

The doctor, when finally he arrived, was good with Kimberly. He lubricated his examination with quiet explanations and gentle manipulations. Then he took down his prescription pad and once again drew the diagram. He talked to Anne about fluid, canals and tubes, explaining the procedure as he had to me.

"Well, Doctor, we think it would be best to have the operation," Anne said.

Dr. Rubinsk set down his pad. "I think you've made the right decision. For your sakes as well as hers."

"Will you perform the surgery?" Anne asked.

"No, I'll refer you to Dr. Rosen. These are his specialty. He's a fine surgeon who has performed this procedure hundreds of times."

"I see. What time frame are we looking at, Doctor?"

The doctor rubbed his large hairy hands together. "First we have to clear up her ears, and, of course, Dr. Rosen has a tight schedule, but I would say with the antibiotics we should be able to arrange a date early in October. That will get it out of the way before the worst of the cold season sets in."

I stretched out my legs and in the uncompromising

light, studied the smudges on my toes.

"We haven't agreed on this, Anne. We've hardly discussed it."

For a moment Anne's face was a picture of horror.

"But it is so obvious!"

"Is it?"

"Can't you see she's miserable? Every sniffle ends up like this." She motioned toward Kim, woebegone on the examining table.

"I just think we should talk about it some."

"Of course," the doctor said, standing. He seemed anxious to be rid of this feuding couple. "You have time. I'll give you the usual prescription and you can call me when you've made a decision."

On the way to the El station Anne could barely control her voice. "I just can't believe you would do this to her."

"You put me in a terrible position back there."

"You know she has to have the operation."

"It's our decision, not yours alone."

"That's garbage. You just think something might go wrong and you can't face up to it. Yesterday you put that asshole in front of my needs and today you're putting your own hangups in front of Kim's. Well, I'm not going to let you do that!"

We reached the El station and I slammed on the brakes.

"Don't give me that righteous mother routine. I'm the one heading off to fill her prescription. I'm the one taking care of her all day. I don't need your goddamn nobility."

Anne got out of the car. She reached into the back seat, gave Kim a kiss and picked up her briefcase. I could see now that she was crying.

"I'm very pissed at you," she said through the window. "You are being cruel and mean. And it's because of him." The image of Randy passing through her mind dried the tears and rekindled her rage. "That bastard!"

"Be pissed!" I shouted as Kim began to wail. "Just be pissed. See if I care!"

She slammed the door and I pulled away from the curb with such reckless abandon that an elderly woman had to jump back for her own safety.

Beneath my anger, residing like a squatter, was an intense pain that had the texture of failure. I wanted to turn around. I wanted to roar back to the El-stop and jump from the car and take her into my arms and hold her and hold her until the trembling stopped.

Something had gone very wrong in the pattern we had been weaving. It needed to be unraveled, back to that night in June when we first drove into this massive grinder of a place, this place that reversed a river and then to tickle a few voters colored it green. I wanted to return to that moment when we first drove in. I wanted to wake her gently and tell her that a great power had passed its breath across my cheek, that we needed to be alert. Very very alert.

Were it possible.

I stopped at the bank to deposit the money I had made in Wisconsin. The three checks totaling $330.00. I put a hundred in my pocket—cold cash for the pharmacist, may his teeth rot out and his children defile him—and deposited the balance in checking, well less than a month's rent.

The apartment was empty when we got back, though Randy's back pack and sleeping bag were still in the shop. I gave Kim her medicine and had just put her down for a nap when the phone rang. It was Liz Trowbridge. She had followed my advice with the plant.

"Yeah, what happened?"

"It died. At least I think so. I was calling to see if you carry malpractice insurance."

"Maybe it's sleeping. A kind of rest cure."

"Don't think so. You sound funny. Not ha ha funny, the other kind."

"Kim's sick. And that guy Randy I told you about showed up here. He's wanted by the cops and he and Anne hate each other."

"Yuk."

"He's gotten old and sad, that's the worst part, old and heavy and sad."

There was a pause on the other end. "Would you like me to come over? I get off in a couple of hours."

Just who was speaking, I wondered. Was it a human or was it a professional counselor?

"No, that's all right," I said, having decided it sounded too much like the counselor. "So, how'd it go with Marty and Gretchen?"

"It didn't. Marty fell asleep on Gretchen's living room floor and she couldn't wake him. The next morning he was gone when she woke up. He has only a vague memory of the whole thing."

"Weird."

"Oh, well, it looks like Gretchen is going to get back with Eric."

"You're kidding."

"Wish I were. If you know anyone looking for an apartment hers will be available. She had to sign a year's lease." Liz excused herself and I could hear her talking with someone. "Jees," she said, a moment later, "I almost forgot the good news. There's a guy who works in the next office. He's the vice principal actually. Anyway, he was telling me today that he wants to buy some leather slacks. He was moaning about how they were priced above two hundred and not custom fit. So guess what I told him?"

"What?"

"Jason, you are having a bad day. I told him about a leather man I knew who has a little shop in the back of his apartment. I made you out to be quite exotic actually. He'd probably pay you two hundred for a pair that fit really well. He thinks he's quite the stud."

"Is he?"

"Actually, he's an idiot," she whispered, "but his cash is as good as anyones. Want to talk to him?"

The vice principal seemed to have learned his vocabulary and intonation from Henry Winkler's favorite character. He wanted very soft leather, camel colored, and he wanted the seam on the outside of the leg laced and not machine sewn. "Laced. Know what I mean?" I knew what he meant. "And just below the waist I want lacing both front and back. The same lacing like a triangle so I can pull them real snug. And no belt."

"Low on the hips?"

"Very low on the hips. And the lacing dark. Dark lacing."

The man had all his measurements memorized. He knew the circumference of his calves and thighs. "I work out," he said. He would pay one-fifty for a pair if they fit really well.

"And I got friends. If these are good, I'll make you the Pants Man."

"I'll need one-seventy-five."

"You should have held out for two hundred," Liz said, when she came back on. "Now he's going to be running around bragging about the great deal he got."

"That's all right."

"Yes," she said, after a pause, "I guess it is."

I was asleep on the couch when the doorbell rang. My state of mind was such that I had managed to fall asleep while watching the news. I released the lock and Randy came up the stairs. He was alone, carrying a six pack. At the doorway he stopped. He looked past me, first into the living room, and then down the hall.

"Is Anne here?"

"She's still at work, Randy."

"What's that noise?"

"It's the vaporizer. I have it on in Kim's room."

"Ah." He entered then, set the beers on the coffee table and took a seat on the couch. He had showered and changed shirts. This one was yellow. His belly emerged like a bright beach ball.

Some of the old magic was still there, I thought, as I watched his huge hand engulf a can of beer and toss it to me; the throw controlled, on target. The news was still on. They were showing footage of a warehouse fire. The captain, boots amid the hoses, back to the smoking hulk, suspected arson.

"New set? You must be doing all right, Anne being a lawyer and all."

"It's our second new one. The first was stolen. The cops figured some addicts broke in and grabbed it."

Randy popped the top of his can and squinted toward the TV.

I wondered if he saw any connection between his life and the behavior of addicts. Doubtful, but then you would hear no rationalizations from Randy either—nothing about how he had not gotten a fair break, or how the rich were ripping everyone off, or the laws were preposterous. For Randy dealing drugs was a way to get through life; the only philosophy was supply and demand and there was nothing absurd about the laws. The laws kept the price up.

A baby had drowned in a bathtub on the south side and the police had charged the boyfriend of the mother with murder. We watched them lead the bewildered looking fellow into the police station. He was handcuffed to prevent him from reaching out and grabbing another baby.

"Will Cheryl be along?" I asked, my mind on babies.

"Naw. I showed her the lake and she left to see if she could find Robert Redford." Randy pulled out his tobacco pouch and began to roll a cigarette. Even sixteen-year olds left him now. "I was hoping she could help me, but she was too young. I knew after a while I couldn't trust her." He glanced back down the hallway. "What time will Anne get here?"

"Usually about now, but then sometimes she works late. We're pissed at each other, so it's hard telling. Normally, she would call."

"Anne'd rather find a turd in her soup than me at her front door." He finished rolling the cigarette and pushed the pouch back in his pocket. He lit the cigarette and leaned forward. "I'm leaving tonight, Sydney, but I got myself a problem. Metcalf, the guy who owes me the money, he won't come to the city. He wants to meet at a truck stop out near Aurora."

"You need a ride."

Randy nodded his head. "It's a little more complicated than that."

I thought about that for a moment.

"When do we leave?"

"Meeting's at two."

"In the morning?"

Randy laughed. "You been married a long time,

Sydney."

When Kim woke we had soup and toasted cheese sandwiches. Then Randy went back to the shop, spread out his bag and lay down. Kim and I curled up on the couch.

It was after nine when Anne finally called. Her voice indicated a willingness to patch it up.

"I had to work late because I missed the morning. My desk was full. But I'm coming home now."

"You must be starved. I'll fix you something."

"I grabbed a sandwich. All I want to do is go to bed. How is she?"

"She's asleep on the couch. We were watching the tube. Must have been the re-runs that got her."

Anne didn't laugh. "Are they gone?" she asked.

"The girl is. Randy's leaving tonight. In a while."

"Do you know what it feels like to be coming home with him there?"

I took the question to be rhetorical. "He'll be leaving in a while."

She sighed. "Maybe tea would be nice, something herbal."

I met her on the landing, took her briefcase and handed her a cup of tea the way she liked it. Her briefcase was heavy. It was a mystery to me why she carried the damn thing home just to pick it up and carry it back again in the morning.

"Where is he?" she asked.

"In the shop, sleeping."

"Good."

I followed her into the bedroom where she took off her clothes and pulled on her nightgown and robe. Her body had a lean, hard sexless look, like that of a pre-

pubescent boy or a thin older woman who had done a life-
time of physical work. Eons had passed since we were in
Wisconsin and she was soft and tactile.

"There's a complication, Anne. He has to meet this
guy in Aurora at two. Two this morning."

Anne stopped brushing her hair. She turned and looked
at me.

"He has no way of getting there, so I'm going to take
him." Her arms and shoulders dropped, her back slumped.
She seemed instantly smaller.

"You let him talk you into that?"

"I offered. He had no other way."

"You're a fool." The hair brush twitched a few times
in her hand and then she threw it on the dresser. "Get
Kim up," she said, standing. "She and I are going to
Mother's."

"It's after ten. I'll only be gone a few hours."

"Get her up!" Anne screamed. "I am not going to sit
alone in this apartment with a sick child waiting for the
phone call that says you've been shot or arrested." She
removed her robe and nightgown and threw them on the
bed. She pulled on a T-shirt and jeans. "Just get Kim
ready."

I wrapped Kim in her blanket and lifted her out of her
crib. Anne was on the phone talking to her mother. When
she hung up, she looked toward the shop. The lights were
off. Randy had not moved. But then, almost as though he
could feel her gaze, the door opened and he appeared. He
was bare chested and huge, an old bear with faded tattoos.
He stepped up to the dining room table and placed his
hands on the back of a chair. For a moment the elegance
had returned, the calm purpose.

"Come morning, Sydney will be here, safe and alone.
And I'll be out of your life. I guarantee it."

Anne took Kim from my arms and stepped toward him. "Don't talk to me about guarantees, Randy. What kind of guarantees did you give the people you left hanging in Carbondale? Jason had to spend two days being grilled by narcotics agents. His shop was in shambles and he was left alone to explain himself as best he could. That's what you guarantee, Randy. Trouble."

"It was clean. I said it would be clean and it was. They could ask all the questions they wanted but there was nothing to hang on him. I made sure of that." He looked at me. "It was all right, wasn't it? They didn't find anything?"

Anne did not wait for me to speak. "Tell him how they came at four in the morning and dragged you down to the station. Tell him how they ripped up all the handbags and tore the paneling off the walls. Tell him how they even poured out the bottles of stain and how for months afterward strange men kept coming by trying to buy pills and dope. That's what you guarantee, Randy."

"Shit." Randy looked away. "I gave him that place. I set him up, taught him the trade and then ended up giving him the whole thing." We pointed a thumb over his shoulder. "Half the stuff back there I gave him. If it wasn't for me he wouldn't be a leather craftsman, and you probably wouldn't be a lawyer."

Anne laughed coldly. "Right, Randy. And if Cheryl becomes a movie star it will undoubtedly be because of you. You use people. You abandon them, and then you have the audacity to act like you helped them." She pointed to me and her anger mounted again. "He was your front! He did all the honest work and you got all the money. You never even gave him a fair share of the leather income, let alone the drug money."

Randy had had it. He turned toward me and shrugged.

It was an act of apparent disregard but the elegance had fled.

"Sydney," he said, "you'd better decide what you're going to do here."

"He already decided, Randy. He's fallen for your line once again. You've squeezed one more favor out of him. But let me tell you. . . ."

That was the last thing I heard. I walked into the kitchen, opened the back door and stepped outside. At first I thought I would just stand for a while on the dark landing and pull myself together. My chest felt very tight and my breath seemed to be stopping at the base of me throat. I decided I would run a little. It would feel wonderful to run.

I ran down the alley and then along the sidewalk beside the parked cars. I was going faster and faster. Several times I nearly tripped on the irregular sidewalk, heaved and fractured by roots and freezes. A man in a car watched warily as I crossed at the corner. I half realized now that I was jamming my legs down almost as if I were kicking the pavement rather than running across it. Then suddenly I came to the gate of the walled park.

I knew the path well by now. Even in the dark I could run its twists. It was not my intention to stop in the park. I did not feel entitled to sanctuary. I just wanted to pass through, from darkened gate across the dark lawn beneath the light and out the gate at the other end. A quick absolution, I thought, like a drive-through car wash.

As I left the bushes my pace quickened again. The rabbit was feeding in the circle of light. Its ears twitched as I approached; its body stiffened. It had grown heavy and comfortable this rabbit, bathed in safety. When I was but a few feet away it broke stolidly first in one direction then reversed itself and cut back across my path. It was past me, lumbering for the shadow when suddenly I veered and dove face forward, hands groping.

I caught the left rear foot in one hand and then the right in my other. My angled motion carried me into a roll, and as I rolled I could feel the rabbit's powerful legs thrusting against my hands and chest. I was on my knees when I stopped beneath the light, facing the old house with its long gray porch. My movements were automatic now. I bent the rabbit across my right knee and jerked sharply. The rabbit gave a short intense scream. I jerked again and this time I felt the snap. There followed a few violent spasms and the mound of warm soft fur lay limp across my lap.

I was desperate for air. The heat rising off my chest seemed to clog my nose. My body ran sweat.

Then from the direction of the porch I heard a sound. The back door opened and the silhouette of Michael entered the lighted, blue-walled room. The door closed behind him.

I had become what was chasing me, my own dark shadow, exact to the nanodegree.

16

When Randy and I reached the East-West Tollway Mo
Bandy was singing a song about a steel guitar and a dim-
lit bar.

"You still have the old twelve-string?"

"I didn't take a thing. I gave the guitar to Lu Ann on
the way out of town. Is she still around?"

"Saw her a couple times. I think she moved to
California."

There had been many women but Lu Ann was the one
he had cared about. The one who touched him, the one he
kept returning to. Toward the end they resembled weary
pit bulls more than lovers.

Randy made sure I had exact change and paid the toll.
"The irony of being an outlaw, Sydney, is that it makes
you one law abiding son of a bitch. I never drive. I never
open a beer in a car or on the street. I never cop a thing,
large or small, not even coffee."

"You got an ID?"

"Yeah, but I don't enjoy testing it. I get printed and
I've had it."

His solemn presence filled the passenger side. Boots,
jeans, dark jacket, his backpack between his legs. He
looked like he was about to bail out behind enemy lines.
And the smell was back, the mixture of tobacco and sweat
that was so much a part of him. I had forgotten about the
shoplifting. "Going on a coffee run," he would say. Only
it was more than coffee; he took what small things he

needed. For a time he had been addicted to a brand of spray decongestant and whenever he emptied one bottle he stole another. Then one day he kicked the habit and after that he just snorted. It all seemed distant now, not continuous with my experience, but separate and apart.

By twelve-thirty we were approaching the point of rendezvous. Randy did not want to arrive early so we stopped at a restaurant. He had a sandwich and beer, I settled for coffee.

"How am I supposed to know this guy?"

"You're not. He's supposed to know you. Just sit down and wait. He'll be along. He thinks you got what he wants, and he's prepared to pay for it. It's my money the bastard will be carrying."

The coffee was lousy and I added more sugar. "Be too simple, I suppose, to just ask him for the money."

Randy chuckled like a father. "That's why I always kept you out of it." He drank off half the schooner and wiped his mouth. "Get him out of the restaurant. I'll take over after that."

The waitress refilled my cup and Randy ordered a second beer.

"This thing is scaring the shit out of me. What if he's a cop?"

"He's no cop. I've known the bastard for years."

"What if he has a couple of friends with him? I can't see the guy being too happy you're taking his money."

"My money," Randy said, correcting me. "Metcalf has no friends. He's an asshole." He rotated his glass on the smooth wet table. "He does owe me the money, Sydney. Ten grand. I wouldn't do this even to Metcalf if he didn't owe me. But he knows the condition I'm in. There's nothing I can do for him, so there's no reason for him to pay me back. That's why I had to produce this little episode." He emptied the schooner. He seemed solid again; it was in his eyes. "This is Randy's last caper, Sydney. Believe it. And I'm going to take care of you."

We crossed the Fox River near Aurora and soon entered a stretch of farm country. There was no moon and now that we were away from the city, stars became visible and with the bright and solitary yard lights scattered across the landscape, we could have been traveling in space.

A glow appeared on the horizon and Randy looked at the map spread across his knees. "That's our baby. The place we're looking for is on the southwest corner, big truck stop." The glow became brighter and more defined. Signs appeared. "Yep, that's it." He slid the seat as far back at it would go and squeezed down on the floor beside his pack. "Remember now, park so I can see what's going on and with the passenger door away from the restaurant."

The restaurant and service station were surrounded by several acres of asphalt. Huge overhead lights cast a bluish tinge on the trucks parked along the darkened fringe. Quarter to two. About what Randy had wanted. I drove past the front of the building, then pulled away and parked near two semis opposite the restaurant windows.

"Can you see inside?" Randy was so cramped down his voice had become a grunt.

"Yeah. Looks pretty empty in there."

"He'll be there."

"What should I say?"

"Don't look at me, dammit. You're supposed to be alone." I looked toward the windows of the restaurant. "You don't have to say anything. He'll want to know where the stuff is and you say it's in the car. That's all there is to it."

"Okay." My stomach had started cramping, a rhythmic spasm like some dull alarm that keeps repeating itself.

Suddenly I farted.

"Christ."

"Sorry."

He snorted. "Anyway, you come outside and you're as surprised to see me as he is. You don't know me. Got that?"

I watched a waitress walking around inside with a pot of coffee. I decided to not have any more coffee.

"No, I don't get it. Why not?"

"Sydney, never commit a crime. It's not your game. Now, listen. I'm a stranger. I've just stolen your coke and now I'm going to steal his money."

Another fart. I couldn't help it.

"Jesus, you're killing me."

"Sorry."

"So, you jump in the car and you get the fuck out of here. Go back to that restaurant and wait for me. I'll show up or I'll call. If you haven't heard from me by dawn, just go home and forget any of this happened."

"And you?"

"Just forget it happened."

"Okay. I guess I'll go in now."

Randy snorted. "Sydney. . . ."

I stopped, my hand on the door handle.

"I'll never forget this."

The night air was damp and smelled more strongly of fields than of the highway. My legs were wobbly. I wanted to run again.

It was a large restaurant with pale yellow walls and booths, most of which had been cordoned off for the night. Mo Bandy must have been following me. First he was on the radio and now he was on the jukebox singing about an unhappy woman.

I sat down in a booth facing the windows. The waitress

was an old, tired (someone's unhappy) woman wearing a uniform of the same ghastly yellow. I ordered a vanilla milkshake and thought about Anne tossing in her childhood bed. I imagined that high performance mind popping up pictures of her father slipping out and her husband running off, popping them up like targets in a shooting gallery. She and Kim had not been at the apartment when I got back. Nora had come and taken them away.

A state trooper sat at the counter; four truckers occupied a reserved booth. The milkshake was made from soft icemilk, the kind I detested. Still, I could not resist gulping it down and soon I experienced the familiar sharp pain in the temples. Two o'clock came and went. I had to piss badly but I could not go to the john now. The guy might show up and leave again thinking I was not there.

At two-fifteen the waitress came over and asked if I wanted something else. Still no appetite. I ordered another shake.

"You really like them things, don't you, honey."

By two-thirty, the second shake was almost finished. Something had obviously gone wrong. Or maybe it was all a joke and Randy was out in the car laughing. I was smiling at the possibility when a shadow crossed the yellow table.

"Where's the stuff?"

I had no idea where the man had come from, but he had the coldest blue eyes I had ever seen.

"It's in the car."

"Let's go."

It was just another human being, I thought. The eyes were cold but he looked civil enough. Clean cut, nice slacks, gray loafers. Could have been taking the family out to a Friday night fish fry.

"Would you mind if I went to the john first? I have to piss like crazy."

"No way." He picked up my check. On the way to the door he wrapped a bill around it and dropped it beside the cash register. I could hardly keep up.

Metcalf seemed to know which car was mine. He was walking straight toward it. Then suddenly he stopped.

"What the shit!" He turned, bumping against me and began to run toward the corner of the building.

Across the gloomy apron of asphalt I could see Randy's screw up. It was too dark and the car too far away for Metcalf to have noticed the passenger door opening on the far side, but the flash of the interior light was unmistakable. Randy's backpack flew through the air and landed on the pavement. He ran toward me.

"Get the fuck out of here!" he said hoarsely. That was my last sight of him, a large square figure in dark charging past and then disappearing around the same corner as Metcalf. He could have been an old fullback under full steam except that where the ball should have been was a pistol dark and mean. I did as I was told, full bladder and all.

Dawn came slowly to the prairie that September morning. The darkness leached out and the light spread in across the long flat landscape. I had an excellent view from the corner booth in the restaurant near Warrenville and lots of time. Time to eat an omelet I could not taste, time to drink three glasses of milk, time to try and read the morning paper when it came. The phone rang only once; a waitress told someone to give someone else an aspirin.

I left when the first rays of the sun began to color the corn tassels. A half hour later I was back at the truck stop.

The lights in the parking area were off. Many of the rigs were now gone. I parked near where I had before. There was no backpack lying around. The restaurant was crowded but I was not interested in the restaurant; I knew Randy would not be in there. I followed the path he had taken around the corner to the back. A large area had been asphalted, fifty yards to a side, and beyond that a field of alfalfa newly mowed—the smell I had noticed the night before. It's stalks lay in windrows waiting first the drying sun and then the baler.

For the next half hour I paced back and forth across the pavement. I studied each stain. I peered beneath the cars and behind the tandem wheels of the parked trucks. I walked through the first rows of alfalfa and my sandals raised clouds of noisy grasshoppers. Nothing appeared amiss, no sign of violence. Just the rattle of refrigeration units, the deep throated diesels. I wanted to lie down in the stubble, lie face down with my nostrils buried in the sweet vegetation.

I walked back to the car and then drove toward Chicago with the sun intense and too low for the visor.

Emmy's litter box reeked and she was out of food. She followed me to the kitchen meowing and writhing around my feet, as if to make certain I did not forget or change my mind. I fed her and then emptied her litter box and washed it out in the basement. I watered the plants and took a shower.

I knew I should call Anne. It was terribly cruel not to call her. I went to the telephone and turned down the bells. Then I toasted two slices of bread and covered them thickly with the very last of the strawberry jam. I took the toast to the living room and turned on the TV. The phone gurgled five or six times but I did not pick it up. Mr. Rogers sat on the floor of his porch building with blocks and listening to a symphony. It seemed a ridiculous thing to do. I turned off the TV and turned the radio on to a news station. The bodies of two high school girls had been found in a suburban woods. The station kept finding them every half hour until they were tattered and worn and then it discovered the body of a man in an apartment building. He had been tied up with wire and had a dagger between his shoulder blades.

Around noon the doorbell rang. I allowed it go on for a long time before releasing the lock. I stepped out on the landing, suddenly hopeful. But it was Liz Trowbridge, a suburban girl who had stayed out of the woods. It was too late to close the door so I watched her climb the stairs, eyes down, her hair bouncing with each step. She smiled the instant she saw me, making her announcement.

"I have something for you," she said, as the first wave of perfume reached my nose. I was sure of one thing: what Liz Trowbridge had was not what I wanted or needed.

"You're looking professional," I said, leading her inside. Does she, I wondered, consider this a professional call?

Liz wrinkled her nose. "I came from a job interview. I hope the superintendent had the same impression you did."

I directed her to the rocking chair, the one chair in the house I always tried to keep Kim out of to insure its relative freedom from yogurt, jam and Silly Putty. Suddenly I remembered Kim. Where was Kim? Nora must have stayed home to watch her. I had to go over there.

"Job interview?"

"Yes, for a possible promotion." She was standing in front of the rocker surveying the room. "Everything looks so cheery with the shades up. Everything but you. You do not look cheery."

There it was, I thought, the counselor's first probe. I sat down on the couch.

"I thought you liked your job."

"Oh, I do, but this is an administrative position." Liz sat down and with her long fingers adjusted the hem of her skirt. "My boss's job. She handed in her resignation the first week of school, can you believe it?"

I did not believe it or disbelieve it; I didn't care. My attention had been drawn to a hay baler chugging through a field and sweeping up a coil of alfalfa. I watched as it hit something solid. The wooden paddles came down and jammed. I could feel the jolt pass through the baler and up the tractor to the hands of the driver. There would be a heavy dull thud at the point of contact. I looked up. Liz was watching me.

"You are not wearing your cap," she said, after a moment. "I had always assumed it grew there."

"One time when Kim was about a year old she started crying when she saw me without it."

Liz giggled. "I'll try to control myself. How are you feeling?"

"I'm fine." Actually, I felt the way I did in doctors' offices; I wanted to pace. They had identified the body of the man bound with wire and a dagger between his shoulder blades. Some guy named Francis who was suspected of having been a fence. I turned off the radio and asked Liz if she wanted some Postum.

"Isn't that for children?"

"We're not checking ID's today. It's not bad if you're not into caffeine." The last thing I needed was more caffeine. It had been a big mistake, I now realized, to indicate to this woman that I had troubles.

"I'll try it," she agreed, her smile condescending to Postum. I got up and then turned toward the mantel.

"On second thought, maybe a joint would be better."

Liz, who had just reached in her purse, looked up surprised. "Isn't it kind of early?"

"Just a hit," I said bringing the cigar box back to the couch. "Then we can have the Postum." I rolled a fat joint, ran my tongue along the seam and smoothed it firm.

"This is from Barbeer," she said, handing me a check. "The vice principal. I realized after we hung up that you had not asked for anything up front."

"I thought you knew him."

"I do. That's why I asked for a check."

I took a deep drag and offered her the joint. She hesitated, squinting her eyes, then took it and placed it cautiously between her lips. The check, I was thinking, had been a ruse; her acceptance of the joint, an act of ingratiation. Liz Trowbridge had come to counsel. She was a do-gooder needing a fix.

"Bill says the only way to make money in education is to get into administration."

I nodded, took back the joint. I realized suddenly that I had never learned Randy's alias. Well, it would not have been Francis.

"I have mixed feelings about it," Liz went on. "I really enjoy working with the kids and I'll miss that, but there are advantages in addition to the money."

Perhaps, I thought now, she had come *to be* counseled. I filled my lungs with smoke and stared up at the ceiling.

"The baby thing," I said.

"That's part of it. He'll think its a big deal if I get this. There are several applicants."

"Can't you just tell him?"

"I do tell him. I tell him and tell him. Bill is a very powerful person. He does not take no easily."

"Ahh." I saw no reason to go into it. The man was a

grown-up bully. She did not need to hear that and I had nothing else to say about it. So the joint went back and forth and Liz rattled on about Gretchen and Eric, about Marty's play. I had only to pay a vague attention, a nod now and then to keep her going. I now recognized that the dope had been another mistake. There were more shadows in the room all of a sudden, and physically I did not feel comfortable. I should have stayed in that alfalfa field. I wished I was there now, lying in the hay with the sun baking down and the grasshoppers buzzing.

A gun! I drew up my legs and sat with my chin resting on my knees. I thought I had lost all my illusions about Randy. The moment I saw him standing outside our apartment, I realized that he had crossed edges I didn't even know existed. But a gun! That had stunned me, it really had.

". . . and I'll have my own secretary. That's nice. And of course it will look great on my resume." Liz paused. "Jason, is that your phone ringing?"

"I don't think so."

"It sounds like it's trying to. Do you want me to answer it?"

Emmy was running around. I hugged my knees and focused on her. She pounced on one of Kim's blocks and rolled over on her back. For a couple of seconds she batted it back and forth between her front paws. Then it flew loose and she was after it again.

"Jason?"

"Naw, that's all right. I turned it down so I wouldn't have to answer it." Liz put out the joint and studied me, eyebrows arched. "It's always some asshole," I added, "trying to sell me something."

"What if Anne wants to reach you?"

"We have a signal," I said, lying. "She rings once, then

hangs up and dials again." I was finding that it took a lot of effort to talk. I wished she would just go back to the gossip.

"You guys are very clever," Liz said, her smile wide and dope induced.

The phone finally stopped ringing. It could very well have been Anne, I realized. She had to be going crazy. I knew I had to get up and call her. Then it struck me that I had never made the Postum. I tried to focus myself. I had to get up. I would put some water on and then call Anne. Just a quick call to tell her I was all right and that Randy was gone. He was gone. Randy was gone.

"Has your friend Randy gone?"

"Yes, he's gone."

I was aware of a definite tension in the room. I perceived it as shadows at the periphery of my vision. Bad idea, the dope. But I was all right. It was not as though anything was going to hurt me. I just didn't want to deal with the whole room. I wanted to shrink it down.

"Did you have a nice time together?"

"It was short," I said. Liz was all right. She was not the source of the tension. Still, I did not want to look at her. By now I was sitting sideways on the couch, hugging my knees and listing against the back. I was okay, I told myself. It was just like being a little too drunk. Only not exactly.

"How long had it been since you last saw him?"

"Five years." For a moment I was not sure that it was I who had answered. The voice seemed strange and a long way off. Off. I had run off and left Randy. Anne too. I had left Anne.

"Jason? Are you all right?"

This was ridiculous, I thought. Just one joint. I had been smoking this stash for months. It was clean mellow dope. But there was no problem, I kept telling myself. It can't last too long. I would take a few deep breaths and then put on the water and call Anne.

"Jason?"

"I'll put on the water in a minute." She was sitting beside me now. I could smell her perfume.

"I don't want any Postum. I have to go back to work, but you look very pale. Are you sure you're all right?"

I nodded. My God, I thought, she had me now. I was going to be counseled whether I wanted it or not. My body felt all tingly. I said to myself as firmly as I could: You are not going to scream. Her hand when it touched the back of my neck felt very warm.

"I was awake all night and I guess it's getting to me."

Her touch was awkward, tentative. But at least she was not saying anything.

"Would you hold me?" I asked. "For a few seconds?"

With one arm around my shoulders and the other around my folded legs, she must have felt as though she were carrying a huge basket of laundry. On her wrist was a narrow gold bracelet with a delicate woven pattern. I decided to focus on that pattern at the point where it peeked out from behind my folded legs. Jesus, I thought, this was absurd.

"I feel ridiculous."

"There's no reason to. I know how you feel. I feel that way lots of times. You don't have to talk. We can just keep rocking like this if you like."

So this was counseling. Liz allowed her head to rest on my shoulder and we fell into a slow rhythm that gradually subsided like a tremor. Then for a long time neither of us moved until from somewhere down near my diaphragm a deep and wonderful breath rose. Another came, then another. This new rhythm altered the mood, changed the angles. Deep down near my core, something inside slowly uncurled as if stretching itself. It was new, luxuriant, proud as a prince.

I turned and faced her. In her eyes I saw a delicious fear. She looked the way a child might look staring up at a Ferris wheel. I reached out and placed my fingers on the uppermost button of her blouse.

"Jason?"

"Shhh." It was a beige blouse with a pronounced synthetic component that I had to avoid with the rough edges of my fingers. But the buttons, the thick little pearl-colored plastic buttons, slipped easily free. She was trembling, eyes wide.

"Jason, are you sure. . . ?"

"It's all right," I replied, cutting her off. My voice was dead, drained of inflection, the features of my face immobile. I had a sense of myself turned cunning. A certain distance was required, a gap for the energy to arc. Slowly I folded the blouse back over her shoulders. Then one cuff at a time I pulled the sleeves free of her arms, motions I had made with Kim a thousand times. The bra, also beige, was more cumbersome, but in a moment it too lay across an arm of the couch.

I stopped then and stared at her. She had pressed her hands together into her lap as if steadying herself or perhaps she was simply trying to flatter the shape of her breasts with her upper arms. She was visibly shaking, and yet on her lips there rose now a small hesitant smile.

Afterward, clothing herself, Liz said, "I only wanted to help you. You seemed to need something very badly."

I was silent, naked. On the fake mantel my dead parents' clock continued to tick. The smell of marijuana still lingered in the room.

"I just don't want you to misunderstand," she continued, standing and hurrying now with the zipper on her skirt. "I want you to know what I was doing."

"I know what you were doing, Liz," I said after a long pause. "I know what we both were doing. We were hating them for being strong. That's what we were doing."

At the doorway, we embraced.

"We're friends?" she asked, eyes red.

"I want us to be."

I watched as she descended the stairs, her hair bouncing above the squared shoulders of her suit. When I turned, the phone had once again started to gurgle.

"Sydney, my man."

"Randy?" I could hear music at the other end, people laughing.

"The same, and considerably more prosperous than this time yesterday."

"You got it?"

"Plus interest, Sydney. Plus interest." Randy continued to talk but the phone was filled with a burst of laughter. "You hear it, Sydney?"

"No, what?"

"The music, listen."

Randy must have moved the receiver because I could hear the music in the background more clearly now. It was Willie Nelson singing about a home where no storm clouds rise.

Randy was laughing. "That's where I'm headed, Sydney."

"You know, Randy. If you used that money to get a good lawyer. . . . Anne's always said someone could cut you a deal."

Randy's voice was loud and clear now. "Not my kind of gamble, Sydney. Maybe some day, but not now. I want to turn this over one time, one last time. Then I'm going to settle down and build myself a good record, know what I mean? Maybe I'll marry myself a lawyer and have a kid, who knows." He chuckled again, a happy man. "I'll give you a call when I'm settled."

I hung up and began to push buttons. As the phone started to ring at Anne's firm, my lips formed confessions. I wanted to fall at my wife's feet and pour it all out. "I'm sorry," I wanted to say. "Please forgive me." My sins were multiple and complex and I wanted her to know each one in gristly detail from betrayal to mayhem to aiding and abetting. "I'm sorry. Please forgive me."

17

Fortunately, as it turned out, Anne was in a meeting when I called.

"When will she be out?" I asked the nasal voice.

"I can't say."

I was desperate to talk to her. "Do you know her schedule? When will she be free?"

"Sir, I'm not privy to that information."

Privy? Was this woman from the back woods, or just spending too much time around lawyers?

"Tell her to please call. I am all right."

"I am all right?" The receptionist repeated my strange words, sought a conformation.

"Yes, that's the message. 'I am all right. Please call.'"

"The number?"

"Home," I said. "Have her call home."

I got off the phone and took a deep breath. Cold sweat suddenly appeared on my forehead. Holy shit, that was close! And what a disaster it would have been! Confession? Thank God she hadn't been there.

And yet, it's true, life without confession is cold. When gaps appear I would need to fill them with crudely shaped stories, with explanations, and if necessary, with lies. I would become circumspect, distant, vague. Alone with my secrets.

Since I was no longer interested in a bare soul, I decided not to wait for Anne's call. The reasonable thing was to pick up Kim, buy something for dinner, straighten up around the place. Be of some use.

I showered again and drove to Nora's house. Nora was at the door when I arrived. She must have been watching for me to drive up. She was dressed for the office, purse in hand.

"Kim is asleep," she said, her eyes avoiding mine. "I am very late. Please lock up when you leave." She opened the door and stepped outside. Her demeanor was all rush, as if the very survival of the bank depended on Nora Dycheck arriving there in the next moment. But then as she started across the porch she could not resist glancing in my direction. I caught and held her gaze.

"Nora, I'm sorry I put you through this. I'll try to make sure it doesn't happen again."

She nodded. "I really do have to go." She turned and half-ran down the steps. Not to work, but away from me.

If Anne returned my call it was before I got back. I tried two other times but neither time was she available. I was obviously being screened.

Five came, then six and seven. Kim and I read *Goodnight Moon* three times, a book she had not been interested in for eight months, and we both fell asleep on the couch.

It was dark in the living room when I awoke. I could hear noises coming from the kitchen. When I opened the door on the bright yellowish light the first thing I saw was Anne's briefcase on the counter beside the refrigerator, that useless briefcase brought home for no purpose. Brought even to the kitchen, like a security blanket dragged along behind a two-year old.

My wife stood before the stove wearing a dress that belonged to her mother. She was chewing on the salad I had left out for her and she was reheating the soup. She held a breadstick in her free hand. I wanted to put my arms around her and lift her up. I wanted our energy to flow together. I wanted to cry and kiss and have wet faces and runny noses and make love crying and kissing and laughing.

"Hi," I said.

"He's gone?"

"Yes, he's gone."

She busied herself with the soup, stirring it down, bringing the hot bottom to the cool surface.

"Kim and I fell asleep on the couch. I carried her in to the crib."

She nodded.

I waited a while leaning on the door frame, then I said: "You didn't return my call." She didn't respond to that. "Are you thirsty?" I asked after another long pause. "I can get you a beer, glass of wine?"

She shook her head. The soup was ready. She poured it into a bowl and settled herself at the table. I sat down across from her. She dipped her breadstick into the soup and took a mouthful—the woman was a confirmed dunker.

"Anne, I'm very sorry I put you through this. Your mother too."

She returned the breadstick to the soup, let it soak a moment, started to pull it out, changed her mind and let it stay. Then for the first time she looked at me.

"I know you think you were being loyal. But I think your loyalty is misplaced." Her voice possessed an unusual stillness. It wasn't flat exactly, or dead, more resigned.

"I came back," I said.

"After you finished, you came back. Everyone comes back, after they're finished."

Surprising how quickly you can go from contrite guilt to righteous anger. Which is what I was beginning to now feel. Her easy facility with words always annoyed me when we were at odds.

I got up and put some water on for tea.

"We were so close in Wisconsin," she went on, almost musing. "I thought we'd turned the corner. We'd come back, set up some child care, get on with our life here."

"A bump in the road," I suggested, standing at the stove. "We are back now." I was still hoping for a quick fix.

"Right!" She laughed without pleasure. "A bump in the road!"

With that laugh I felt the stock value of the whole enterprise drop sharply. A fight between people who love one another is a curious kind of puzzle. At some level both of us wanted to put all the pieces together and get on with the fun stuff. But it's intricate and a certain order has to be maintained. My mistake, I now realized, had been to apologize at the beginning. I had thrown away the most important piece on the table.

"Randy's still got the string, buddy," my dear wife now announced. "He pulls and you hop. Why does he have so much power over you? How could he pull you away from your family, from everything you believe in, just by showing up?"

It was a good question. One I might choose to ponder in more tranquil times. But this was not one of them.

"You want my soul," I now claimed. "You want me here in Chicago. You want me caring for Kim so you can get on with your career. And you got all that. But is it enough? Hell no it's not enough. You want my hair styled, you want me in a suit. You want my undivided, twenty-four hour a day devotion. You want my fucking soul, that's what you want." I was furious suddenly. "I came back, goddammit! I apologized to you and your mother. I'm just a human being, that's the best I can do."

Time for another run, and out the back door I went just as the water pot began to whistle.

So. A bit of a chill in the old apartment. We'd both had enough of the fireworks, and we both regretted the whole thing, but neither of us was ready to act yet like it hadn't happened. Time for a few days of injured decorum, minimal talk, exaggerated politeness, the turned back and quick to sleep.

Kim talked about our private park while we were eating dinner the next evening. She wanted to go there. She loved the slide, the whole place.

"The gate's been closed," I had to tell her. "There's a chain and a padlock."

"Maybe the caretaker is just there during the summer," Anne suggested. "He may be a monk and after Labor Day he returns to his monastery."

"Maybe," I said.

My dreams that night were populated by men with tanned skins, their white shirts open at the throat. They wore wide slacks and snap-brim hats and they gathered in small clusters at the edges of my awareness, their hands deep in their pockets. They watched me from the corners of their eyes. Con men, I decided.

I turned to leather the way others might turn to booze or prayer. The vice principal's leather pants. The next morning Kim and I scouted out the competition. Then in the afternoon while she napped, I drew a precise pattern and began to cut the leather. The pants I made for the vice principal were not simply leather pants. They were cocaine-snorting, disco-dandy, ass-hugging, thigh-kissing, ball-snugging leather pants with dark lacing fore and aft and running down the sides.

When they were finished, and before I delivered them to the vice principal, I wrapped them in paper and carried them back to the same boutiques and malls that Kim and I had visited earlier. Most of the stores bought nationally, often from foreign markets, but I did receive some orders. A couple of places were also interested in my cap.

Then I delivered the pants to the school. I couldn't remember the vice principal's name. The circumference of his calves, I remembered, his name I had forgotten.

I asked for Liz. She came out and led me back to her office. She looked professional and . . . well, beautiful. She closed the door and had me sit in a chair at the corner of her desk. She pulled her chair up so our knees were nearly touching. I held the leather pants on my lap.

"I got the job," she said. "This is my new office."

"Liz, that's great."

"There were twelve applicants. They picked me."

"That's wonderful."

"Yes, it's quite an accomplishment, I guess."

"Sure it is. Twelve applicants? That's a tough field."

"Bill's real impressed." She looked at me, and I knew then that it wasn't at all what she wanted.

"Gotta be a pile of benefits, right, Liz? This new office."

"I'm responsible for a lot of paperwork. And meetings. A lot of meetings."

"It's something though that they chose you. Twelve applicants."

She winced. "Jason, I feel terrible about what happened."

"What happened?"

"Us. What happened."

"Oh, yeah. What happened. Well. . . ."

"I made is sound like . . . like I was doing you a favor,

or something."

She had leaned forward and was looking at me very intently. I could see her contact lenses floating on her hazel eyes as if in defiance of gravity and I realized suddenly that I was holding the leather pants in front of me like a shield, like one of those lead aprons dental technicians drape over you before administering the zap.

"I was having a bad day, Liz. I took advantage of your kindness. I'm sorry. Really."

"No, that's my point. You didn't take advantage."

"I did. It wouldn't have happened any other way."

I touched the back of her hand on the desk. Just rested my hand there for a moment on top of hers. I felt like crying suddenly and so it seemed did she.

"So, what's this bastard's name again?" I said after a long sigh. "I forget."

Liz lifted her wet eyes toward me, surprised. "You mean Bill?"

The vice principal's name was Barbeer. Liz introduced us and Barbeer took me to his office. He closed the door and told me to guard it while he tried on the pants.

"No locks on the doors," he grumbled. "They say that's for our protection."

He tightened up all the laces and did a few gyrations around the room, humming a tune.

"Goddamn, these are great! I'm on the show!"

He took them off again and then he insisted on giving me a tour of the school. Barbeer wore Italian shoes and tight slacks. Muscles bulged from his short-sleeved shirt. As we walked down the hall he had a ready quip for every kid he met. Barbeer was obviously the biggest kid, the coolest kid, the strongest kid in the school. Barbeer had arrived.

He led me into the cafeteria, deserted at this hour, and poured me a cup of coffee. He appeared anxious suddenly, babbling on about the great things Liz had said about me. Mainly that I could be trusted. Barbeer said he needed a man he could trust. In his position he had to be careful. Then he came out with it. He was looking for a safe, steady supply of weed.

I must have looked shocked because after a pause Barbeer's expression became perplexed. Then worried.

"You know what I'm talking about don't you? Weed? Dope?"

"I understand," I said. "But that's not my line of work."

Barbeer looked relieved. "Hey, you're not making a career decision here. You're just helping a guy out."

"It's not what I do," I said.

The appointment with Dr. Rosen was Thursday afternoon. It was a matter worthy of the whole family and Anne took off work. While we sat in the waiting room I read an article about the creation of disco music. The article said that the music was layered like a cake, thirty, forty, fifty layers of sound each recorded independently of the others. The musicians on one track did not see or hear the musicians on the others, and no one but the technician who stirred and mixed the various ingredients knew what the end result would be—except that it would have 120 beats per minute and would sound a lot like every other disco record.

Dr. Rosen wore blue canvas deck shoes and no socks. He had a high tan forehead and a trophy on his desk with a golden man completing a golf swing. He examined Kim and then brought out a plastic model of the human ear. No simple diagrams for Dr. Rosen. His model had the front section cut away and he indicated the various parts of the inner ear and explained what he proposed to do. After he was finished with the plastic ear he let Kim play with it.

Anne asked how many operations of this kind he had performed. He replied that the figure was in excess of a hundred. The operation was very simple, he explained. None of his patients had ever lost their lives or had their hearing impaired as a result of it.

"On occasion the tubes can slip back out." With his check list of consequences the doctor appeared very efficient. "There are steps we can take to minimize that happening, and after the operation I will give you a list of instructions." He smoothed back his thin, sun-lightened hair and folded his hands on his lap.

Finally, Anne turned to me and said, "How do you feel, Jason? Is this what we want to do?"

We set the 14th of October as the day. Then the doctor stood. Others were waiting: ears, noses and throats seeking the knife. He reclaimed his plastic ear and showed us to the door.

In the lobby Anne returned to the operation. "Are you sure it's all right? I want you to feel comfortable."

The thought of my daughter going under the knife terrified me. That was the truth of it.

"It's best," I said. "I think it's best."

Anne sighed with relief. "I like him. He's a pro."

The office was in an old ornate building. The door of the elevator was cream colored and set in marble. Kim wanted to push the button and I lifted her up so she could reach it.

I became very busy filling orders for the pants and by the middle of September I needed to arrange child-care. We chose a woman named Arlene who lived within walking distance of our apartment. Kim wrapped her arms around my leg that first morning and pleaded with me, viscous tears caught in her lashes. Arlene was saying, "Kim, don't you want to stay and hear the story we're reading?" No, I thought, she does not. She wants to hold tight, just as I do. Still, I did leave, and quickly, making the pattern sharp and clear.

Touching the sidewalk I started to run. I jogged all the way home and this became a routine, first just back to the apartment, then as the days passed and my legs and heart adapted, outward, down previously unexplored streets.

We made arrangements to attend Marty's play with Liz and Bill Trowbridge on the last day of summer, that strange restless day with its slanting sun. It was a Saturday, clear, cool and windy. I took time in the afternoon to install a new windshield wiper motor. The old one had died with a foul scream a few days earlier. I remembered my dad as I worked, the way he would ponder and muse before a machine, appear to be tinkering, stand back and wipe his hands thoughtfully with a shop towel. It occurred to me that I had not thought about him or Mom in several days.

There were signs of autumn on the street. A few yellow maple leaves lay in the curb; a cluster of pre-teen Hispanic girls cruised the sidewalks on roller skates, their ribs snug beneath down vests, their faces serious, their arms swinging in deft arches.

When I returned through the back yard gate Anne was coming out the basement door with a basket of laundry. She was wearing old tennis shoes, jeans, a faded yellow sweatshirt with "Kellogg Hall" just visible across the floppy front. The old sweatshirt, the mussed hair, the same perky bottom as I followed her up the stairs. I opened the door and she edged in sideways, protecting her knuckles.

"Mom called to bemoan her fate," she said, setting the

basket on the table. "She had a physical yesterday and the doctor said her blood pressure was up markedly from the year before. It may have been a fluke, the anxiety of the appointment or something, but it has her worried." Anne began to separate and fold the clothing. "She suggested I bring Kim over early. She thought you and I might like to have dinner out before the play."

"Sounds fine to me."

"Would you take Kim? I know what she's thinking I'll come over and we can talk for a while, but I'm not up to it."

"Sure, I'll do it. Let me wash first."

I was rinsing the last of the soap from my hands when Anne came into the bathroom.

"Maybe I should do it," she said.

"Whatever you want, Anne. The car's together."

"You don't feel burdened? Like I was putting it all on you?"

"No. I'll enjoy it."

Anne took the sponge from the rim of the bathtub and began to wipe the outside of the toilet bowl.

"Well, I'd appreciate it. Maybe it's just me. I just think I should do it. Mom could draw guilt out of the Virgin Mary."

Nora was cleaning house when Kim and I arrived. I was tempted to open the vacuum bag to see if there was anything inside. I suspected it was empty, that all she was doing was sucking up stale air and blowing it out again refurbished to languish until the next time. Even dust refused to settle in that house. I could sense that Charlie had been so cut by the clean sharp lines, so sliced by the harsh divisions (magazines in the rack, never on the floor) that he finally ran back to the mess that was his family. I could imagine Norman finding the surfaces so slick and smooth that they sent him spinning beyond control. And along her veins and arteries were the same dauntless urgings to hold firm and true, to keep the forms aligned against the vitality she perceived as foreign. The pressure built inexorably.

But it was also true, I realized as I watched her lift Kim for a shy kiss, that I had developed an affection for Nora, almost in spite of myself. I had come to recognize the effort she made, the needs she hid beneath the fine veneer.

"Mother," I could call her that now, "Anne got behind on the laundry. She said she'd be over in the morning to pick Kim up."

"Of course." She was disappointed but the resistance was all inside, holding her plumb, keeping her clean, crossing her legs when they should be crossed.

She led us back to the kitchen where on the table was a cardboard box half full of apples.

"They've been falling," she said, pleased.

"I'll bring you a pie," I promised.

"No, no. You keep them."

"I want you to share the risk. There's plenty for two pies."

Nora laughed, a genuine laugh. Kim, standing on a chair and peering into the box, looked up at her grandmother, surprised by the laugh.

At the restaurant that night Anne wanted to talk about her mother.

"I should have gone over there. What would it have taken, a half hour or so?"

"You can't do everything. You were busy."

"Busy? Putting away the damn laundry. Big deal. Did the laundry have to get put away right then? Couldn't you've put away the laundry? And I would have had a few minutes alone with Kim on the drive over. Mom'll be dead some day, and I'll think how all I did was put away the laundry."

"You're beating yourself up. And you don't give yourself credit for all you do. Beside's she's very proud of you. She knows how busy you are."

"Sometimes I think I keep busy just to avoid the real stuff. Like with Kim or Mom. I leave that to you. I put away the laundry. Make lists. Play lawyer." She dug into her enchilada. Her appetite was considerably improved. "I'm afraid of them."

"Afraid?"

"Mom and Kim. I'm afraid to be alone with them over long periods. Kim's energy frazzles my mind. The constant interruptions, the blather. I'd go crazy in your shoes. And Mom. With Mom there's this sense of sadness. Know what I mean?" She was talking with her mouth full.

"I'm not sure."

"She's stuffed with it. Regrets, recriminations. Believe me, I've been there. Those nights waiting for Norman? Long nights. Say the wrong thing and it comes pouring out. It's like lancing a boil."

"Now that's appetizing."

Anne smiled. "Are they any good?"

"The rellanos? Not as good as yours."

"What a line." She leaned back in her chair and sighed. "Let's don't go to the damn play. Let's just eat and drink and molest each other."

"The real stuff."

"That's right. The real stuff."

It was a fine moment, and I savored it. We went anyway of course, arriving at the theatre out of breath just as the lights were blinking in the lobby. But Bill Trowbridge was in no hurry. He stood feet apart in the middle of the sidewalk discussing treasury notes, the prime rate and money market funds with a man who either had need of a toilet or was also concerned about missing the beginning of the performance.

Liz begged her husband to end the conversation and come inside. We all leaned toward the door but he talked on. Still, we need not have worried. It was in the nature of Bill Trowbridge to recognize that the play would not dare begin before he was ready, and sure enough, the houselights fell the moment we reached our seats.

The play was *Hot L Baltimore* and though Marty had but a series of bit parts—drunk, cab driver, delivery boy— his energy and presence commanded as much audience support as the principal actors. After the performance he joined us in a bar where we ordered a round of Benedictine and brandy.

The drinks came and Bill Trowbridge leaned forward over the table. "That kind of thing is good practice," he said. "All good trial lawyers are good actors. There are acting courses now just for lawyers. I was thinking of taking one myself."

"Yeah, those courses are great," Marty said, sardonically. "They specialize in the sleight-of-hand school of acting. How to address the court while at the same time picking your client's pocket."

Anne and Bill looked at each other and moaned. "With lawyers like you," Anne said, "the profession has no need of enemies."

Trowbridge jabbed a finger at Marty. "You can bitch all you want, Flanagan, but just try and pull down the bucks you're getting at the firm by jumping around on the boards of a neighborhood stage."

I had been thinking that afternoon while working on the car that maybe I had been wrong about Bill Trowbridge. Maybe I was jealous of him, jealous of his money, his energy, his wife. I had decided I would try to see him more objectively, but now as his finger thrust its bold way across the table, I realized that I could be watching Bill Trowbridge from the moon and I would still think he was an ass. Marty raised his glass as if to offer a toast.

"Ah yes, bucks!" he announced. "Here's to the Buck, the beginning and the end, Buckaroos." He took a long swallow and motioned toward Liz. "Now you, Madam, will you be so kind as to tell the audience just what Bucks mean to you?"

Liz frowned. "I know, Marty, you don't think I should have taken the job. But money is important. It isn't everything but it certainly is important."

"You sold it girl," Marty said softly. "You sold it for bucks."

Liz winced.

"That's bullshit," Trowbridge said brusquely. "What do you expect her to do, stay in the same lousy job all her life?"

Marty told me that Liz had sold Ariel. He saw it as another example of her copping out.

"I'm sure she had her reasons, Marty."

"I did," Liz said. "I only got up there five times all summer, and now with this job being a twelve month position, it just wouldn't be fair to Ariel. I sold her to a thirteen-year old girl. They adore each other."

Marty refused to quit. "The last time I was over at your place, do you remember what you were talking about? Report deadlines, forms that had to be filled out." He emptied his glass and shook his head. "You used to talk about kids, Liz. Kids. Now you talk about Report Deadlines. Are you going to tear down all the pictures of Ariel and put up Report Deadlines?"

Liz put her face in her hands.

"That's enough, Marty," I said. "There's no point. . . ."

Bill stalked over to the jukebox. Anne touched Marty's arm.

"Marty, let's change the subject."

"Really," Trowbridge said from a few feet away.

Marty pulled his arm free. "Goddammit!" he shouted, slamming down his fist. "Can't you see what you're doing to yourself?" He turned his face away. "Oh, what the fuck." He got up and went to the men's room.

On the way home Anne wanted to talk about Marty. "He's going to blow it if he's not careful," she said. "This whole thing with the play was supposed to help, but, God, he just seems to get worse. Sometimes he comes in after ten and then the other afternoon he walked out at three o'clock and didn't tell anyone where he was going. Lawrence was calling around looking for him. Marty had a memorandum he was supposed to have turned in. Bill and I tried to cover for him but we can't go on putting ourselves in jeopardy just to keep him out of trouble."

She groaned and told me to turn right at the next light. The next light was Ashland. I had planned on turning right on Ashland. There were parts of the city that I now knew better than she did.

"Frankly," Anne continued, "it's beginning to annoy the hell out of me. If he would just come in and do his job like everyone else, there wouldn't be a problem." She lit a cigarette. "The results should be out in a couple of weeks. Maybe that will help."

We drove around the neighborhood for ten minutes

looking for a place to park. No luck. I let Anne out, waited until a light came on in the apartment and then resumed the search. I got back to the building a half hour later. Anne was in bed but still awake. She was wearing the filmy pale blue nightgown I bought her after Kim was born. Her mind was still firing on all cylinders.

"You know, Marty really blew it back there. Liz is getting on with her life. She's seizing the opportunity. Bill's very proud that she took a chance and applied for that job. He thinks administration is the only way to get ahead in education. And now she's on her way. But Jesus, I don't think Marty understands the investment he has. What do you think?"

I turned out the light and crawled into bed. I could picture her at the office, stratagems sprouting at the coffee pot, points of law honed over a hurried sandwich. No one dare mention the kids or a newly discovered restaurant. Her octane was too high for that kind of dribble.

"Well?"

"I think Marty's in a lot of pain."

"He was being an ass."

"That's my point. Marty's not an ass."

"That's true." She was slowed momentarily. "But why? The bar? We're all living with that."

"The bar, the work. The commitment that's required, I suppose. It's hard for you and you love it."

"Maybe when the results are out," she said, rolling over on her stomach and wriggling the way she did when she wanted her back rubbed. I began at her neck and swept downward moving the energy out of her mind and into her body. "If he passes he'll be okay."

"Pass or fail, he'll never be a lawyer. Not like you or Bill." My fingers slid from the warmth at the base of her neck down over the cool of her back, then lower into the warmth again, drawing her attention along beneath my touch. "Some part of Marty is burned by it," I added "There is some part he wants to save and keep pure and that part is threatened."

"Jason, that's ridiculous." She started to lift her head and shoulders off the pillow. "Ouch!"

"Never," I whispered into her ear, "never disagree with a masseur."

During the first week in October while walking to Arlene's, Kim and I met an old woman and her basset. Having less time with Kim I had grown to enjoy it more. Our walks were often extended dawdles, explorations of curbs and weeds and tree bark. We squatted now in the dog's path and watched it amble slowly toward us. It appeared as ancient as the woman at the other end of the leash. Its stomach dragged on the ground, its ears drooped, its lower lids had become empty pouches waiting to catch the bloodshot eyes. The dog stopped when it reached us. The long, sad, sagging form had appealed to so many passersby over the years that the dog had become as comfortable with admiration as the police horses on State Street.

Kim stroked his head and neck. She had gained confidence from her experience with Emmy. The woman, too, was familiar with the ritual; her expression as she waited was patient if condescending.

"Hales," she said in response to my question, and then correctly anticipating my next, added, "He's thirteen." I started to calculate. "That's ninety-one in our years," she concluded, jutting her jaw slightly, drawing the tendons in her neck.

She had survived to an old age, and she still walked her dog along the city's streets. She had earned her arrogance, it seemed to me. The same could not be said for the young man who now stopped his car to wait the light, tape deck blasting.

"Do you realize," I fumed to the woman, when once again we could hear each other, "that most of the musicians who made that tape never heard each other play?"

"Then they are more fortunate than we." She tugged at the leash and Hales resumed his pace.

Fortunate, I thought. Unfortunate. Good fortune, bad fortune. The Great Wheel of Fortune. I turned and watched my daughter running down the sidewalk. She was exuberant, in perfect health. The three rainy days that stilled the wiper motor had given Brian, Arlene's son, a cold, but Kim had not caught a sniffle. Dr. Brown had said she might outgrow it, and maybe she had. I wanted to think that but I knew it wasn't true. Besides, it was a greased track. The doctor was scheduled, the nurses were standing by, the anesthesiologist waited to clamp the mask over her face.

Not far from Arlene's was a low retaining wall at the edge of the sidewalk. Every day Kim wanted to climb up and try to walk along the edge. On this day she covered the distance on all fours, barking. She was an old basset in blue corduroys. We arrived late at Arlene's and then I did a long run before returning to the leather pants waiting in their several piles corresponding to their varied states of completion, size and color. With each completed pair I seemed to touch again a fountain of desire. Stores called wanting more. Without effort I was selling as many as I could make.

The caps were also in demand, but I did not have the time to make them. Through Liz I got in touch with Gretchen. She had a strong sewing machine and knew how to use it. She began to make hats for me on a contract basis. I provided the materials and she put them together. One day she asked if I could lay some dope on her. Her supplier had moved to Vermont. I stood beside her sewing machine listening as she spoke. She had a nice view through the window to the street below.

"Gretchen, I don't sell dope."

"You'd be doing me a favor," she said.

"It's not what I do."

That night Nora came over for dinner. We had begun to share a meal one night a week. Anne and I had decided to make it a formal thing. One night every week. And whatever else came up we tried to work around it.

Nora aged but had not grown arrogant. She just tried to stay even and when I greeted her at the door, I could smell the Great Evener seeping through her mouthwash. She thanked me again for the pie and I told her once again that the crust was too thick. That simple, doughy pie had meant so much to her.

Anne served Polish sausage, cabbage and baked potatoes. We all drank beer. It was a dinner, she said, in honor of the coming visit of the Pope, an event that had so filled the media that I for one was sick of it.

"Are you going to Grant Park for the Mass?" Nora asked. At the dinners Nora always pressed the conversation. She prepared for them, I imagined, making mental lists of possible subjects, reminding herself of ongoing sagas—Anne's projects at work, the little crippled boy at Arlene's, my sales.

Anne smiled, hearing Nora's question. "No," she said. "I understand that wherever you sit there will be a Pole in front of you."

"Oh, not at Grant Park. . . ." Nora began, then catching herself began to laugh.

Later that evening while we were watching a show on albatrosses, the Trowbridges showed up with Marty.

"He's quitting," Bill Trowbridge announced, stepping into the room.

"Marty, not really," said Anne.

"Yep," Bill said. "He's going to walk in there tomorrow and quit."

Marty stood in the doorway looking embarrassed.

"We've spent the entire evening trying to talk him out of it," Liz said, "but his mind's made up."

Anne hugged Marty and then stepped back. "But what if you pass?"

"Doesn't matter. A friend in Tucson has a job for me. I'm going there."

"His friend has a dinner theatre," Trowbridge said by way of dismissal. "He's paying all of eight hundred a month and on slow nights you wait tables."

Anne's eyes had the expression she usually reserved for viewing dead animals. "The results will be out in a few days, Marty. Just hang in there. We'll help."

"Exactly what I told him." Trowbridge had wandered over to the mantel and was examining my parents' old clock.

Marty turned to me. "You know what I'm afraid of, don't you."

"I think so."

"What?" Anne and Liz spoke in unison, turning to me in mutual frustration. But just then Bill Trowbridge picked up the clock to examine the back and in the process knocked my cigar box to the floor where the baggy, papers and roach clip all rushed off in their own directions.

"Hello, I'm Anne's mother." Nora, who had been standing awkwardly beside her chair as if astounded that all this activity could go on in the absence of proper introductions, spoke to Liz.

"I'm pleased to meet you," Liz said, extending her hand. Pleased, yes, but also horrified as over Nora's shoulder she watched her husband scrambling around on the floor.

"Get out some glasses, Anne," I said. "I'll open a bottle of wine."

"You're glad Marty's quitting, aren't you?" Anne said when we were in bed. She was curled up in the fetal position, her back to me.

"I'm glad he finally made a decision. He was miserable at the firm" I began to run my hand along her arm, then stopped. Her skin was covered with goose bumps. She was shivering. "What's the matter? Are you sick?"

"You just lit up, telling jokes, running around filling glasses." I reached for her hand; her fingers were cold.

"Anne, what's the problem?"

"The fact is, you wish you were going with him, isn't that true?"

"No, I. . . ."

"Isn't that what all your heroes do when things get complicated? They run off. Isn't that what Randy did?

"Yes, that's what Randy did."

"Isn't that what you did that night he was here? Ran out the back door. Isn't that the same thing you did the other night? Ran out?"

My hand now was moving along her leg pressing down the thousands of tiny mounds.

"I ran, yes. But I didn't leave. I came back. And Marty may have just stopped running. Going to law school because his senator father wanted him to, that was running."

"So, what's the answer?" she said belligerently.

"What's he afraid of?"

"Of passing, I suppose."

"The bar?"

"Yeah, then it would be even harder to quit." It was amazing the way her body was shaking. "Anne, I'm not leaving." I folded myself around her. "You're my family. This is my home."

"You can't say that for sure. You can say it but you can't know it. I'll bet Dad never thought he was going to leave either. He didn't plan it out for months in advance. It was just that he wasn't happy with Mom. Oh, he was happy in some ways, but in other ways he was unhappy, and when the chance came he ran off. He just ran off and left her, left both of us really."

"It's okay, Anne."

"I'm sorry about the suit," she said, her teeth chattering. "I was incredibly stupid to buy you that suit. I don't want to change you, Jason, honest."

"I know."

"But it seemed that way, didn't it?"

"It's all right. I needed a suit."

"I can't believe this is happening," she said. "This is totally irrational."

I made a delivery to the Loop the next day and afterward had a quick lunch with Anne. She was solid again. She gobbled down a decent meal.

I said goodby and was leaving the elevator when I ran into Bill Trowbridge coming back from lunch. He directed me to a marble wall and got close to my face. It was the only time I ever heard him stammer around. His supplier had moved to Vermont, and he was wondering, you know, after that little incident with the cigar box. . . ."

"Absolutely not," I told him. "I won't even share a

joint. It's for Anne's protection. You should know that."

One morning a couple of weeks later I sat on the toilet seat sipping coffee and watched Anne dry her hair. When she turned off the drier I said, "I keep remembering the article about that little girl—I think it was in Philadelphia—perfectly normal little girl except they decided she needed her tonsils out. They put her under and she never came out of it. A vegetable without tonsils."

Anne picked up the curling iron. She had been letting her hair grow out a little and was adding a sweep to the ends.

"It's because of what happened to your parents," she said, curling the strands around the rod. "You have this fear that people around you are going to die. It was the same way about my having to call every day before I left the office. It was irrational but I love you so I did it."

"People do die. My parents did die."

"Of course. But your fear is irrational, just like my fear that you are going to leave. Irrational."

Rational fears, I thought, irrational fears. Rats-on-all-fears. "You're right, it's irrational, but I'm still afraid she's going to die."

"That's all right," Anne said, turning the right side of her head toward the mirror. "She isn't. I'll be home by three. Would you see if you can find the flight bag? I'll have to pack a few things for myself."

"I'll have her ready," I promised. "She probably won't even know she's had an operation."

"It's going to be fine."

"I know that. Except I have this feeling that if I let myself really know it, then it won't be fine. Does that make any sense?"

"Don't think so." She kissed my cheek, and then rushed

into the bedroom.

We were all ready when Anne returned from the office. Kim was wearing her pale blue dress with red trim, another dress that Nora had bought her when we first moved to Chicago. Her hair was neatly combed and she had filled a bag with toys to take along. She was only going to be in the hospital for twenty-four hours, but I had packed a week's supply of clothing.

Her room was on the fifth floor and it was painted the same sickeningly pale yellow as the restaurant walls where I last saw Randy. There were two beds, two chairs, a TV hanging from the wall and a smell of sterile cleanliness that made me shudder.

"I maked better here, Mommy?" Kim asked, spouting her version of the official line.

"That's right, kiddo." Anne was looking out the window. "You can see the lake from here."

"When, Mommy?"

"Tomorrow," I said. "That's when they'll make you better." I joined Anne at the window. There were sailboats in the distance.

"How?" Kim's voice had assumed a whine.

"We're ignoring her," I said to Anne. "We're afraid and we're ignoring her."

"You're right," Anne said. She turned and scooped Kim up and brought her to the window. "Well, first they will put you to sleep, and then when you wake up, you'll be all better."

"That's silly!" It was a word she had picked up at Arlene's and the way she used it always implied great disdain.

"Yep, silly," I said. "They put you to sleep and then you are all better."

A few moments later Dr. Rosen entered the room with

a, "Hello, how are you folks?" The coming of autumn had done nothing to fade the tan on his high forehead. He examined Kim's ears and looked inside her mouth and up her nose. His movements had a brisk certainty about them. He was, I thought, the kind of man who seldom erred; he was also the kind who when he did, shrugged it off quickly. "The operation," he added, "is scheduled for nine." Then with a pat on Kim's head he was gone, his deck shoes squeaking slightly on the spotless tile floor.

Nora arrived at 5:30 and we went down to the cafeteria for dinner. I had meatloaf, mashed potatoes and green beans. In our garden in Carbondale green beans had been one of my favorite plants. I grew them near the fence on tripods. They would grow to the top of the poles and then their long tendrils would wave in the air seeking additional support. Some would drop down to the fence and weave themselves through the wire.

Nora was reminded that her mother had died in this same hospital. "I ate in this cafeteria for two weeks," she said.

"What did grandmother die from?" Anne asked. "I can't remember."

"A stroke. A series of them actually. She had one before we brought her in. Another the next morning. Then the last one two weeks later. She was a vegetable after the first one, so it was just as well."

I saw the green beans reaching, green and leafy, their white flowers peeking out from the green leaves. As autumn came on the bean pods would become splotched and brittle. Then one frosty morning all the leaves would be hanging, dark and lifeless.

"We should take you out to the cemetery some day," Anne said to me. "Grandmother has a beautiful spot."

I nodded and then stood up. "I'm going to get some

coffee. Either of you want some?"

When I got back to the table, they were discussing the noodles that Nora's mother used to make. My mother used to make egg noodles. I remembered how she would press the dough out very thin, then roll it up like a crepe and slice the noodles off the end. When they fell to the board they would open into coils.

"My mother would have been a vegetable if she had lived," I said, interrupting them. "My uncle told me the doctors had told him that. Her head went through the windshield."

Anne and Nora looked at me. Nora said, "Then it was just as well."

"She made egg noodles."

Nora smiled. "Yes, that's the kind my mother used to make."

We finished the coffee and returned to Kim's room and watched TV. At seven thirty I pushed myself off the bed and stretched.

"I'm going to get going," I said.

"Already?" Anne was surprised. "I thought you would stay until ten or so. You wanted to stay all night."

"I know, but I'm feeling antsy. I think I'll just go home and come back in the morning."

"Well get here early." Anne hugged me. "I want you with me."

"I will," I said.

It was not until I was on the elevator, falling through the floors with an old man in pajamas slumped in a wheelchair and his heavy wife in a navy blue raincoat and thick black shoes, her swollen pink ankles reminding me of a sow's feet, that I realized I had not said goodbye to my daughter.

In the lobby I had the thought that maybe I would call

my aunt and uncle or maybe even my brother, but I didn't; there was nothing they could tell me. At the same time I could not bring myself to return to the apartment. I followed the lake shore downtown and turned off in the vicinity of where Anne had taken the bar. Night had come. Street lights were gleaming off the cabs and busses. Most of the shops along Michigan Avenue were closed but a parade of consumers continued peering in the windows. I snaked slowly through the Loop, waiting the lights, watching the pedestrians and motorists. I saw thousands of people, but none I recognized.

Eventually I found myself on the Dan Ryan Expressway heading south. The route was familiar from the days when we used to travel between Carbondale and Chicago to visit Nora. In my memory it was always dark when we reached the city, and the road was black with dirty snow and the windows of the car steamed. Surely we came at times other than Christmas but that is what I remembered. And I remembered leaving Chicago in daylight with the radio on and Anne opening the wax paper to get me a slice of the turkey Nora had so carefully packed away. It had always been daylight when we left and now it was night. Night and the traffic light and no snow and the streets slipping quickly by: 47th, Garfield, 63rd, Interstate 90 breaking off, 79th, 87th, 95th, Interstate 94 up and away.

The names of the south suburbs were also familiar: Blue Island, Riverdale, Markham, a million lights each turned on by a stranger. Just ahead fields waited in the dark.

18

It's a long and boring drive from Chicago to Carbondale. At night the scenery consists of scattered lights in a sea of dark, the rush and rumble of trucks. I had more than enough time to think and more than enough to think about.

It was almost one when I walked into the Pyramid Lounge. Fletzer was announcing his last call. The place was more dingy than I had remembered, dark and dirty with its ragtag assemblage of chairs and tables, its row of pinball machines, its smell of stale cigarettes and watery beer. A couple of diehards circled the pool table. Two others fussed over the dice at the bar. Fletzer sat on his stool and leaned against the cash register. He looked mean, half asleep and balding. I slid to the end of the bar and ordered a beer.

"Jesus H. Christ, what you doin' here?"

"Trying to get some Pyramid piss."

He drew two lights and dragged over his stool. "If you came to see Randy, you're early. They're still holding him in Texas."

I took a long slow swallow of beer. "They got him."

"San Antonio, according to tonight's paper. I tried to call you. Cocaine. 'Big Drug Bust,' but then they always say that."

"Well, he's alive."

Fletzer shrugged. "If you can call being in a Texas jail with a drug felony hanging over your head and a State's Attorney in Illinois already drooling at the mouth—if you can call that being alive, then, yeah, he's alive."

The beer tasted terrible. "Texas. Bad place to get busted. I heard about a guy who got twenty years in Texas for possessing a joint."

Jim Fletzer chuckled. "Remember how we used to sit around and try and guess just where he was hiding? You figured he was in Mexico and I always said he was digging ditches somewhere, working his ass off." Fletzer chuckled again, a brittle, cheerless sort of laugh. "Well, we're going to know where he's at for the next few years. The poor bastard."

I managed to get down another swallow of beer. "Are the geese back yet?"

"Is that why you're here? To see the goddamn geese?"

"You could say that. I felt like a ride."

"You felt like a ride?"

"A long ride in the dark."

Over at the pool table one of the players began to pound on the floor with the butt of his cue stick; the other laughed. Fletzer pulled out the cash drawer, set it on the bar and began to count the evening's take. When the till was empty he chased out his four faithful customers. I washed the glassware while he swiped off the bar and tables and turned out the lights. Then we stepped out onto the street. I wanted to take a look at the old shop.

"Some chicks rented it," Fletzer said as we walked along."They're selling candles."

"Candles?"

"Some doodads, but mostly candles. I was in there the other day. The place has a funny smell, incense, or something, but they do got a shit-pot full of candles."

"They really changed it around," I said when we were outside the window.

"They painted it all white inside."

"The counter's gone too, and they tore out the old barn siding. Randy and I got that siding down by Makanda. Looks like they redid the floor, and installed new light fixtures." I stepped back and slid my hands into my pants pockets. I felt tired all of a sudden.

The night was cool and very still. We started walking slowly down the street. At this hour the sidewalks were nearly empty; only an occasional car passed along the road. We walked south toward the campus and Fletzer described how Illinois Avenue had looked when he came to Carbondale as a freshman.

"None of this was here," he kept saying. "All this was just houses, old houses filled with students. You were so goddamn smart to leave, Winter. This place is going to hell and I'm riding on the front bumper."

Jim Fletzer kicked a beer can and sent it rattling over the curb. "I came here to spend four years and I've stayed for twenty-one. You are looking at the last of the hippies, Winter."

Fletzer had caught me in his game and I was trying to isolate the changes that had happened during the ten years I spent in Carbondale. I had bought my first lid in one of the houses along this street. But it was all over, behind me now. The place no longer seemed like home.

"Hippies, shit!" Fletzer was still reminiscing. "We were beatniks, man!" He cackled. "God, how they hated us in our dirty goddamn sweatshirts, our stinky thongs and scraggly beards. Every fall we came down during Orientation Week and walked around campus grossing out the goddamn freshmen and their parents. Ha!Ha! Round assed little chicks with their clean, smooth skin staring at us from beneath those fucking green beanies the freshmen used to wear. Staring at us with a mixture of horror and lust while their goddamn sour-pussed daddies hung onto their arms as if they were in the middle of a zoo and all the animals had just been let out."

Fletzer released a long haunting moan. "Oh, God, Winter! We were missionaries, don't you see? Secreting the sons away from their deodorant, parting the thighs of the daughters." The lusting cackle again. "God, I loved every minute of it."

We entered the campus where here and there a lonely light shone in otherwise darkened buildings. The walks were sprinkled with dry fallen leaves that crunched beneath our feet. We walked past the fountain near where Old Main had been then over past the library. We came out on Poplar and started back past darkened houses and lawns long ruined by student feet. It was after two and I felt weary to the marrow. I suggested we return to the car, find a cup of coffee. But Fletzer wanted to walk. The night and the talk seemed to give him energy.

"Randy was one of the first kids I corrupted," he explained gleefully. "He was a dumb southern Illinois kid who thought the far side of the Ohio was the end of the world. I was in my third year and living in an apartment on Jackson Street with two other guys from the design department. What a pad! Bare mattresses on the floor, candles sticking out of chianti bottles, black shades on the windows and red shades on the lights. We sat around drinking wine, listening to jazz, reading Corso and Ginsberg and thinking we were cool. When I first met Randy he was a freshman living in a goddamn dorm. Can you believe that? Randy in a dorm? I brought him over to the apartment and couldn't get rid of him. He loved that place. Later he moved in. The bastard had an unbelievable ability to lure chicks to that apartment. He was always a master of that, even when he was a punk freshman."

We arrived in the middle of a block and Fletzer stepped

off the walk and dropped down to the lawn before a sleeping house. I stretched out beside him, looking up into the dark trees. The night was perfectly still, damp. It smelled faintly of burnt leaves.

"We studied design under Bucky Fuller," Fletzer said softly. "We were going to change the world."

I didn't know where it had gone wrong for Jim Fletzer but it had gone badly wrong and he knew it. He had become a ruin, a relic from a culture whose memory evoked as much embarrassment as nostalgia. After a long time he pushed up on one elbow and pointed with his hand.

"The apartment was right there."

"In the parking lot?"

"Yeah. They tore the house down to make room for the goddamn hospital parking lot. It's all gone to hell, Winter. All those guys are gone and I've lost track of them. Even Bucky left. They built the Arena out there—a round domed structure—and they didn't even make it geodesic. I don't know if that's why he left, but Jesus H. Christ. A prophet in his own country."

"I parked there a few times," I said, sitting up. "Kim was born in that hospital."

Fletzer held up his hands as if to frame the air above the parking lot. "Randy and I had some damn good times in that chunk of space. There should be a marker or something, you know? Moments like that. And now it's just a goddamn hospital parking lot." He dropped his arms and allowed his head to fall back onto the leaves. "God, I loved that old bastard. You just knew about Randy. If you really needed someone, I mean really, really needed someone, Randy was your man. He would get it done. Didn't matter what it was, Randy would get it done."

"That's true," I said, "Randy would get it done."

Fletzer suddenly jumped to his feet and began to dance around on the leaves. "Of course, Winter! Of course! And now it's our turn." He was shouting, swinging first one booted foot in the air and then the other.

"What are you talking about?" I had to roll out of his way.

"I'm talkin' about obligation, man! I'm talkin' about livin' again. You and I are goin' to Texas!" He let out a loud piercing yell. "We can be in good ol' San Antone in less than twenty-four hours. Jesus H. Christ! Why didn't I think of that before? Ha! Haa! Goddamn! Can you see the expression on his face when we walk in there?"

But the expression I saw so clearly at that moment was not Randy's but Anne's. Labor had begun in the early evening and through the long night I had sat beside her, timing her contractions and wiping her face whenever the wrenching pain would set it free. It was a very long night for both of us, haunted for her by pain and for me by fear—dreaded fear and dark imaginings. At the same time, the night had about it a kind of loony hope, an inexpressible closeness, as if some mad spirit were whispering in my ear that every birth was Christmas. Finally, the doctor allowed me into the recovery room. Anne was alone. She lay still and pale and small on the white bedding. She was so exhausted and drugged that she did not yet know, and so I had the honor of telling her. It was that expression, rising from a weak and tender smile, and so pleased with itself that it refused to fade as she passed into sleep, that I saw now as Jim Fletzer danced around me.

"I can't do it, Jim."

Fletzer stopped, feet apart, hands on his knees, his heavy lower lip protruding like the edge of a bagel.

"But why not?"

"I have to leave now." I stood up and began to brush myself off.

"Oh shit, man. We owe it to him, don't you see? We owe it."

"I don't," I said. "Randy and I are even."

I put my arm around Jim Fletzer and we started walking. I knew the town well. The shortest distance to the car was through the parking lot, and that was the way we went.

On a drizzly afternoon in late October I drove to Nora's bank. Two storms earlier that week had stripped the deciduous trees of their remaining leaves and darkened the stone and brick. Only the cartons, cups and discarded wrappings that littered the sidewalks and curb sides retained a brightness, and these too were soon splashed with the grays and browns that seemed destined to permeate everything from the stolid old buildings to the clothing of their inhabitants. When she saw me Nora left her desk and hurried over.

"The suit looks wonderful," she said, stopping a few steps away and smiling.

"Would you like me to model it? I could jump up on your desk and do a couple of turns."

"Jason." She frowned, hands pressing her thighs. "I'll get my things and be right with you. Is Kim alone in the car?"

"Yes, but it's all right. There's a dog protecting her."

"A dog . . . " Nora caught herself. She studied me from the corners of her eyes, proud that she had not believed a word of it.

A moment later she returned from the back room. She looked trim in a tan raincoat and carrying an umbrella. Snug at her neck was a red scarf. That scarf, it seemed to me, represented an act of courage. It challenged the gray cold of winter (both hers and nature's) and was a small gift to everyone she met.

Kim was anxious to display her new possession. "See, Grandma? Hales."

Nora did not respond immediately. She wanted to get into the car before any drops fell on her raincoat. It was only when she had seated herself and set down her umbrella that she turned awkwardly and peered between the backs of the seats.

"Oh, I see, dear. A new toy."

"That is not a toy, Mother," I said. "That is a leather sculpture designed and constructed by a master craftsman. Do you think anyone would buy such a thing?"

"Well. . . ."

"For a rich, spoiled child maybe? Or the boyfriend who has everything? I'm also thinking of doing a pig, a big fat pig, and maybe a koala. I could fix its feet so you could hang it from a lamp pole or bedpost. What do you think?"

"Well, someone. . . ." Nora paused, her eyes focused on the road. She was never able to quite relax when I was driving. "How much will they sell for?"

"Probably around two-fifty retail."

"Two *hundred* and fifty?"

"Impractical. That's what you're thinking." I wheeled onto the expressway with a certain elan. I had come to enjoy driving in Chicago where every driver was fast, precise and expert. The bad ones were killed off within days of their arrival.

"Well. . . ." Nora did not want to commit herself.

"Now, here's my theory, Mom. Practicality has nothing to do with anything anymore. In this country there is no fantasy so bizarre you can't find someone to share it, and no product so useless that a million people won't rush to buy it, providing they believe that in some kinky way it's diverting. Disgusting, isn't it."

"I thought you were making money from the pants and caps."

"Oh, I am. These animals are my new line. Skirts too, short skirts. And Gretchen and I are thinking about opening a retail outlet. Want to invest? We're looking for startup capital." Nora did not bite. "Not just our stuff," I went on, "but imports as well. Sort of snooty, you know. Uptown. Over priced. 'All Things Leather,' we might call it. Trade or be trampled, Mom. That's Chicago. The clay beneath this pavement was beaten smooth by traders' feet. Running among other things alcohol to the Indians. That part was illegal, of course."

Nora opened her purse and pulled out her cigarettes. "Well, I'm certain you know more about it than I do," she said and she filled the car with smoke.

We parked in a covered lot and walked to the Civic Center. The streets were crowded with people banging their umbrellas into one another. On the way we passed a tall hawk-nosed man who was walking along slowly beside his bicycle. On the bars and fenders were nylon bags that seemed to be stuffed with everything he owned. There was one who had chosen the road.

Kim began to complain about the distance and the pace so I picked her up and carried her. It was a decision I made too late. Her white shoes had become filthy. They promptly smudged my trousers and the tails of my suit coat.

"I'm so naturally grubby," I lamented to Nora when we had stopped inside the lobby. "Filth just leaps out and grabs me."

"It's all right." She bent over and rubbed at my slacks with a spit-dampened tissue.

"That's why I've always hated these things. You can't sit down, you can't lean against anything, you can't take them off and throw them on a chair. Really, Mother, they're a perfect example of the useless things people buy. And this goddamn tie." I tugged at the knot.

"There. It's all off. You look wonderful."

"You have to stay in pairs so you can preen each other like kittens." I grabbed Kim's arm before she could run off. "God, just look at them. Grays and browns and blues. Hundreds of them, each with his briefcase, his determined stride, his feeling of importance."

There was a crowd of them in front of the elevators, pressing for the doors. I picked Kim up again, afraid she might be crushed. Then we saw Liz Trowbridge laughing and waving on the other side of the herd. After a few grueling moments we were all mashed together in the same compartment.

"Jason, you look marvelous."

"Are my face and neck all red? When my father got religion he started wearing suits. He always looked like a boiled lobster in a suit."

"You look very sophisticated. Doesn't he, Nora?"

"I think so," Nora said, wiping at Kim's shoes.

The elevator rose, becoming less crowded at each floor as we moved toward the top.

"This is very special, you know," Liz was saying. "Most people will not be admitted until mid-November, but the firm is exercising its influence. One of the Supreme Court Judges is a former partner."

"Is he going to swear them in personally?" Nora asked.

"That's what Bill says. It's become a tradition since he was appointed to the court. We might even get to meet him afterward."

With its seal, its flags, its long raised bench and seven

empty chairs, the room was intimidating even though the court was not in session. I stopped at the doorway and again lifted Kim to my arms. God, I wondered, what if she should start screaming?

Then I saw Anne inside. She was standing with Bill Trowbridge and Marshall Wollan waving at us. The room was divided by a low wall with a gate at its center. On one side were some seats for the public; on the other were tables for the lawyers, a lectern and the long imposing bench. After a few moments of conversation, Wollan opened the gate and Bill and Anne passed through taking seats at a dark, solid looking table. Everyone sat in silence until a side door opened to admit a man who ordered us to rise.

Then a short fat fellow, wearing a robe over a shimmering blue suit, his paunchy red jowls spread in a very prosperous, very political grin, stepped behind the bench and with a wave of his flowing arms authorized us to sit down. Only Marshall Wollan remained standing now. He approached the lectern and I leaned toward Liz.

"My God, the Judge is a hack. I put on a suit for this?"

"Jason, that's not very nice."

In his rolling accent, Marshall Wollan told the court of the pleasure he had in introducing these two fine young attorneys. Anne and Bill were standing now. She was wearing her new brown-tweed suit. To my eyes she looked incredibly lovely, calm, confident, and even here somewhat apart and aloof, as if she could, without doubt or hesitation, step forward and seat herself at one of those seven chairs.

And yet as I looked at her now, I also saw in the new lawyer something of the stranger. This long march had changed us both. Each grimy little secret I had felt I could not share had nudged me a notch or two from our common center. And was it not reasonable to assume that she too had her secrets, her preoccupations? What a relief it must be for her at times to escape the spongy morass of family for the clean analytical world of the law, where winners are declared, decisions rendered, precedents preserved.

The clerk asked Anne and Bill to raise their right hands. Then the Judge, no longer grinning, but with his eyes still appraising the women one after another, began to recite the oath. I nudged Nora's arm and she glanced at me quizzically. Seeing my eyes, she reached into her purse and pulled out the packet of tissues.

Afterward we went for a drink and dinner. Nora could not stop beaming whenever she looked over at her daughter. I taught Kim how to play tic tac toe with some wrinkled copies of the bar exam questions that Anne still had in her purse. Then Bill Trowbridge started talking about an administrator at the school where Liz worked who had been caught down in the boiler room giving students drugs in exchange for sex.

"Boys or girls?" Wollan asked.

"Didn't seem to matter," Trowbridge said. "Liberal kind of guy."

Liz was wrinkling up her nose.

"Our friend?" I asked.

She nodded.

The waitress appeared. Her large oval tray was heaped with steaming dishes. Her cheeks glowed in anticipation of a Bill Trowbridge tip. The smells were pungent and alive and I found that I was very hungry.

Later, when we were back on the street, Marshall Wollan pulled me aside. He wondered if I knew where he could get some decent dope.

"Just a lid every few months," he said. "I need a person I can trust."

I had thought it was the leather, this type casting. But here I was in a suit.

I studied Marshall Wollan's face in the artificial glow of the Chicago night. It was arrogant of course, hard. But underneath I saw a man who worked too many hours and spent too little time with the family growing up and old around him. On a Saturday night he might share a toke with his wife and watch a little soft porn to help get it up. Your average kind of guy, busting his balls and never quite sure why.

I liked him. I felt a kinship toward him, and there was something tempting in his request, quite frankly. In Carbondale I had made leather products for the people who would use them personally or who would give them to people they loved. (The sandals Anne had bought that first day for Frank.) Now I sold to buyers and delivered to receiving clerks and I missed the pleasure of an intimate exchange.

I looked down the sidewalk. Anne and Nora were walking along with Kim between them. They each held one of her hands. Long arms going down, short arms going up: the matriarch, the new lawyer, and where the arms met, my urban daughter, her white shoes running along so bright and quick.

"I'm sorry," I said to Marshall Wollan. "I can't help you. I hardly touch the stuff myself anymore."

It had been Marty, I suddenly realized as I pulled down my leather cap. He must have gone around with a megaphone.